Stories of the Golden West: Book Seven

Other Five Star Titles
edited by Jon Tuska:

Stories of the Golden West: Book Seven

A Western Trio

Edited by Jon Tuska

Five Star • Waterville, Maine

First Edition
First Printing: May 2006

Published in 2006 in conjunction with Golden West Literary Agency.

Set in 11 pt. Plantin by Al Chase.

Printed in the United States on permanent paper.

Library of Congress Cataloging-in-Publication Data

Stories of the Golden West. Book seven : a western trio / edited by
   Jon Tuska.—1st ed.
       p. cm.
     ISBN 1-59414-344-7 (hc : alk. paper)
     1. Western stories.   I. Tuska, Jon.   II. Grey, Zane, 1872–1939. From Missouri.   III. Brand, Max, 1892–1944. Over the northern border.   IV. L'Amour, Louis, 1908– Riders of the dawn.
   PS648.W4S7519 2006
     813′.087408—dc22   2005033735

Stories of the Golden West: Book Seven

TABLE OF CONTENTS

Foreword

A short novel is a story too short to be a novel—40,000 words or less—and too long to be a short story. It was a literary form that once was encouraged and flourished when there were numerous fiction magazines published weekly, monthly, or quarterly in the United States, and it is a form at which numerous American writers excelled. Although a great many authors have written excellent Western fiction, beginning with Mark Twain and Bret Harte, only three managed as a result of their Western stories to attract a sufficient readership to become wealthy. Zane Grey, Max Brand, and Louis L'Amour were the three, and their work has endured with generations of readers throughout the world. For this collection I have selected a short novel by each of these authors, consisting of stories I regard as among their best work. This is the third, and last, time I shall do so. Earlier collections of short novels by these three authors have been titled *The Golden West* and *The Untamed West* respectively for first publication in paperback.

The greatest lesson the pioneers learned from the Indians is with us still: that it is each man's and each woman's *inalienable* right to find his own path in life, to follow his own vision, to achieve his own destiny—even should one fail in the process. There is no principle so singularly revolutionary as this one in human intellectual history before the American frontier experience, and it grew from the very soil of this land and the peoples who came to live on it. It is this principle that has always been the very cornerstone of the Western story. Perhaps for this reason critics have been wont to dismiss it as subversive and inconsequential because this principle reduces their voices to only a few among many. Surely it is why the Western story has been consistently banned by totalitarian governments and is sneered at by the purveyors of political correctness. Such a principle undermines the very foundations of totalitarianism and collectivism because it cannot be accommodated by the political correctness of those who would seek to exert power over others and replace all options with a single, all-encompassing, monolithic pattern for living.

There is no other kind of American literary endeavor that has so repeatedly posed the eternal questions—how do I wish to live?, in what do I believe?, what do I want from life?, what have I to give to life?—as has the Western story. There is no other kind of literary enterprise since Greek drama that has so invariably posed ethical and moral questions about life as a fundamental of its narrative structure, that has taken a stand and said: this is wrong; this is right. Individual authors, as individual filmmakers, may present us with notions with which we do not agree, but in so doing they have made us think again about things that the herd has always been only too anxious to view as settled and outside the realm of questioning.

The West of the Western story is a region where generations of people from every continent on earth and for ages immeasurable have sought a second chance for a better life. The people forged by the clash of cultures in the American West produced a kind of human being very different from any the world had ever known before. How else could it be for a nation emerging from so many nations? And so stories set in the American West have never lost that sense of hope. It wasn't the graves at Shiloh, the white crosses at Verdun, the vacant beaches at Normandy, or the lines on the faces of their great men and women that made the Americans a great people. It was something more intangible than that. It was their great willingness of the heart.

What alone brings you back to a piece of music, a song, a painting, a poem, or a story is the mood that it creates in you when you have experienced it. The mood you experience in reading a Western story is that a better life *is* possible if we have the grit to endure the ordeal of attaining it, that it requires courage to hope, the very greatest courage any human being can ever have. And it is hope that distinguishes the Western story from every other kind of fiction. Only when courage and hope are gone will these stories cease to be relevant to all of us.

Jon Tuska
Portland, Oregon

From Missouri

Zane Grey®

Zane Grey (1872-1939) was born Pearl Zane Gray in
Zanesville, Ohio. He was graduated from the University of
Pennsylvania in 1896 with a degree in dentistry. He conducted a
practice in New York City from 1898 to 1904, meanwhile
striving to make a living by writing. He met Lina Elise Roth in
1900 and always called her Dolly. In 1905 they were married.
With Dolly's help, Grey published his first novel himself, *Betty
Zane* (Charles Francis Press, 1903), a story based on certain of
his frontier ancestors. Eventually closing his dental office, Grey
moved with Dolly into a cottage on the Delaware River, near
Lackawaxen, Pennsylvania. It is now a national landmark.

Although it took most of her savings, it was Dolly Grey
who insisted that her husband take his first trip to Arizona in
1907 with C. J. "Buffalo" Jones, a retired buffalo hunter
who had come up with a scheme for crossing the remaining
bison population with cattle. Actually Grey could not have
been more fortunate in his choice of a mate. Dolly Grey as-
sisted him in every way he desired and yet left him alone
when he demanded solitude; trained in English at Hunter
College, she proof-read every manuscript he wrote and polished his prose; she managed all financial affairs and per-
mitted Grey, once he began earning a good income, to

indulge himself at will in his favorite occupations, hunting, fishing, sailing, and exploring the Western regions.

After his return from that first trip to the West, Grey wrote a memoir of his experiences titled *The Last of the Plainsmen* (Outing, 1908) and followed it with his first Western romance, *The Heritage of the Desert* (Harper, 1910). It remains one of his finest novels. The profound effect that the desert had had on him was vibrantly captured so that, after all of these years, it still comes alive for a reader. In a way, too, it established the basic pattern Grey would use in much of his subsequent Western fiction. The hero, Jack Hare, is an Easterner who comes West because he is suffering from tuberculosis. He is rejuvenated by the arid land. The heroine is Mescal, desired by all men but pledged by the Mormon church to a man unworthy of her. Mescal and Jack fall in love, and this causes her to flee from Snap Naab, for whom she would be a second wife. Snap turns to drink, as will many another man rejected by heroines in other Grey romances, and finally kidnaps Mescal. The most memorable characters in this novel, however, are August Naab, the Mormon patriarch who takes Hare in at his ranch, and Eschtah, Mescal's grandfather, a Navajo chieftain of great dignity and no less admirable than Naab. The principal villain—a type not too frequently encountered in Grey's Western stories—is Holderness, a Gentile and the embodiment of the Yankee business spirit that will stop at nothing to exploit the land and its inhabitants for his own profit. Almost a century later, he is still a familiar figure in the American West, with numerous bureaucratic counterparts in various federal agencies. In the end Holderness is killed by Hare, but then Hare is also capable of pardoning a man who has done wrong if there is a chance for his reclamation, a theme Grey shared with Max Brand.

Grey had trouble finding a publisher for his early work, and it came as a considerable shock to him when his next novel, *Riders of the Purple Sage*, arguably the greatest Western story ever published, was rejected by the same editor who had bought *The Heritage of the Desert*. Grey asked the vice president at Harper & Bros. to read the new novel. Once he did, and his wife did, it was accepted for publication. However, the version that ultimately appeared was extensively bowdlerized. Finally, after more than ninety years, this novel as *Riders of the Purple Sage: The Restored Edition* (Five Star, 2005) has been published as Zane Grey wrote it.

The same censorship process that had plagued *Riders of the Purple Sage* was also much in evidence when Grey wrote his sequel to it, *The Desert Crucible* (Five Star, 2003). Significant parts of this story were suppressed at the time the book, titled *The Rainbow Trail*, was published by Harper & Bros. in 1915. Among the most significant of these parts of the story is that Fay Larkin, the heroine, is forced into a marriage with one of her Mormon captors, a man with five wives and fifty-five children, forced for two years to live as a sealed wife, during which time she gives birth to a child. A confession concerning all of this is brought into evidence at her trial before a Supreme Court judge following her arrest by the Department of Justice on a charge of polygamy. Actually, due to editorial interventions at the time Zane Grey wrote his finest fiction, what he really wrote in his best books has not been published until now in the Five Star Westerns, making worthless much of the literary criticism of Grey as an author since it has been based on bogus editions. These restorations follow other equally notable Zane Grey titles published for the first time in book form, based on his holographic manuscripts: *Last of the Duanes* (Five Star, 1996), *Rangers of the Lone Star* (Five Star, 1997), *Woman of the Frontier* (Five Star, 1998), *The Great*

Trek (Five Star, 1999), *Open Range* (Five Star, 2002), and *Tonto Basin* (Five Star, 2004). Similarly it was necessary to go back to Zane Grey's handwritten manuscripts to publish his short stories, contained so far in two collections: *The Westerners* (Five Star, 2000) and *Rangle River* (Five Star, 2001). In *Stories of the Golden West: Book Three* (Five Star, 2002), retitled *The Golden West* in paperback and large print, "Tappan's Burro" appeared for the first time as Zane Grey intended, and the same is true for "Cañon Walls" that appeared in its restored version in *Stories of the Golden West: Book Five*, retitled for paperback and large print as *The Untamed West*.

Yet, despite the difficulties Grey encountered in getting his stories published as he wrote them, what did appear led to a degree of success that exceeded even his wildest dreams. The magazine serials, the books, the motion picture versions—and Grey at 108 films still holds the world's record for cinematic derivations based on the works of a single author—brought in a fortune. He had homes on Catalina Island, in Altadena, California, a hunting lodge in Arizona, a fishing lodge in the Rogue River area in Oregon.

Whatever his material prosperity, Grey continued to believe in the strenuous life. His greatest personal fear was that of growing old and dying. It was while fishing the North Umpqua River in Oregon in the summer of 1937 that Grey collapsed from an apparent stroke. It took him a long time to recover use of his faculties and his speech. Cardiovascular disease was congenital on Grey's side of the family. Despite medical advice to the contrary, Grey refused to live a sedentary life. He was convinced that the heart was a muscle and the only way to keep it strong was to exercise it vigorously. Early in the morning on October 23, 1939, Dolly was awakened by a call from her husband. Rushing to his room, she found Grey clutching his chest. "Don't ever leave me, Dolly!" he pleaded. He lived until the next morning when, after rising and dressing, he sat down on his bed, cried out suddenly, and fell over dead.

Even more than with Bret Harte, there has always been a tendency among literary critics to dismiss Zane Grey, although, unlike Harte, Grey at no point enjoyed any great favor with them. Part of this attitude may have come about because he was never considered a realistic writer—and yet that is in so many ways precisely what he was! "There was so much unexpressed feeling that could not be entirely portrayed," Loren Grey once commented about his father, "that, in later years, he would weep when re-reading one of his own books." The ultimate reason for the tears, I suppose, was the author's keen awareness that his editors had effectively prevented him from telling his Western stories as he wanted to tell them and felt they must be told. Readers of the present generation now have the opportunity to do precisely that, something Zane Grey surely never imagined possible. "From Missouri" was filmed as *Life in the Raw* (Fox, 1933), starring George O'Brien and Claire Trevor, and directed by Louis King.

I

With jingling spurs a tall cowboy stalked out of the post office to confront his three comrades crossing the wide street from the saloon opposite.

"Look heah," he said, shoving a letter under their noses. "Which one of you longhorns has wrote her again?"

From a gay careless trio his listeners suddenly grew blank, then intensely curious. They stared at the handwriting on the letter.

"Tex, I'm a son-of-a-gun if it ain't from Missouri!" ejaculated Andy Smith, his lean red face bursting into a smile.

"It shore is," declared Nevada.

"From Missouri!" echoed Panhandle Ames.

"Wal?" queried Tex, almost with a snort.

The three cowboys jerked up to look from Tex to one another, and then back at Tex.

"It's from *her*," went on Tex, his voice hushing on the pronoun. "You-all know thet handwritin'. Now how aboot this deal? We swore none of us would write ag'in to this heah schoolmarm. Some one of you has double-crossed the outfit."

Loud and unified protestations of innocence emanated from his comrades. But it was evident Tex did not trust them, and that they did not trust him or each other.

"Say, boys," said Panhandle suddenly. "I see Beady in there lookin' darn' sharp at us. Let's get off in the woods somehow."

19

"Back to the bar," replied Nevada. "I reckon us'll all need stimulants."

"Beady!" ejaculated Tex, as they turned across the street. "He could be to blame as much as any of us."

"Shore. It'd be more like Beady," replied Nevada. "But, Tex, your mind ain't workin'. Our lady friend from Missouri has wrote before without gettin' any letter from us."

"How do we know thet?" demanded Tex suspiciously. "Shore the boss's typewriter is a puzzle, but it could hide tracks. Savvy, pards?"

"Gee, Tex, you need a drink," returned Panhandle peevishly.

They entered the saloon and strode to the bar, where from all appearances Tex was not the only one to seek artificial stimulus strength. Then they repaired to a corner, where they took seats and stared at the letter Tex threw down before them.

"From Missouri, all right," said Panhandle wearily, studying the postmark. "Kansas City, Missouri."

"It's her writin'," added Nevada in awe. "Shore I'd know thet out of a million letters."

"Ain't you goin' to read it to us?" queried Andy Smith.

"Mister Frank Owens," replied Tex, reading from the address on the letter. "Springer's Ranch. Beacon, Arizona. . . . Boys, this heah Frank Owens is all of us."

"Huh! Mebbe he's a darn' sight more," added Andy.

"Looks like a low-down trick we're to blame for," resumed Tex, seriously shaking his hawk-like head. "Heah he reads in a Kansas City paper aboot a schoolteacher wantin' a job out in dry Arizonie. And he ups an' writes her an' gets her a-rarin' to come. Then, when she writes an' tells us she's *not over forty,* then us quits like yellow coyotes. An' we four anyhow shook hands on never writin' her again. Wal, somebody did,

20

an' I reckon you-all think me as big a liar as I think you. But thet ain't the point. Heah's another letter to Mister Owens an' I'll bet my saddle it means trouble. Shore, I'm plumb afraid to read it."

"Say, give it to me," demanded Andy. "I ain't afraid of any woman."

Tex snatched the letter out of Andy's hand.

"Cowboy, you're too poor educated to read letters from ladies," observed Tex. "Gimme a knife, somebody. . . . Say, it's all perfumed."

Tex impressively spread out the letter and read laboriously:

Kansas City, Mo.
June 15
Dear Mr. Owens:

Your last letter has explained away much that was vague and perplexing in your other letters.

It has inspired me with hope and anticipation. I shall not take time now to express my thanks, but hasten to get ready to go West. I shall leave to-morrow and arrive at Beacon on June 19 at 4:30 p.m. You see I have studied the timetable.

Yours very truly,
Jane Stacey

Profound silence followed Tex's perusal of the letter. The cowboys were struck dumb. But suddenly Nevada exploded.

"My Gawd, fellers, today's the Nineteenth!"

"Wal, Springer needs a schoolmarm at the ranch," finally spoke up the practical Andy. "There's half a dozen kids growin' up without any schoolin', not to talk about other ranches. I heard the boss say this hisself."

"Who the hell did it?" demanded Tex in a rage with himself and his accomplices.

"What's the sense in hollerin' aboot thet now?" returned Nevada. "It's done. She's comin'. She'll be on the Limited. Reckon us're got five hours. It ain't enough. What'll we *do?*"

"I can get awful drunk in thet time," contributed Panhandle nonchalantly.

"Ahuh! An' leave it all to us," retorted Tex scornfully. "But we got to stand pat on this heah deal. Don't you know this is Saturday an' thet Springer will be in town?"

"Aw, Lord! We're all goin' to get fired," declared Panhandle. "Serves us right for listenin' to you, Tex. Us can all gamble this trick hatched in your head."

"Not my haid more'n yours or anybody," returned Tex hotly.

"Say, you locoed cowpunchers," interposed Nevada. "What'll we do?"

"Shore is bad," sighed Andy. "What'll we do?"

"We'll have to tell Springer."

"But, Tex, the boss'd never believe us about not followin' the letters up. He'd fire the whole outfit."

"But he'll have to be told somethin'," returned Panhandle stoutly.

"Shore he will," went on Tex. "I've an idea. It's too late now to turn this poor schoolmarm back. An' somebody'll have to meet her. Somebody's got to borrow a buckboard an' drive her out to the ranch."

"Excuse me!" replied Andy. And Panhandle and Nevada echoed him. "I'll ride over on my hoss, an' see you-all meet the lady," Andy added.

Tex had lost his scowl, but he did not look as if he favorably regarded Andy's idea. "Hang it all!" he burst out hotly. "Can't some of you gents look at it from her side of the fence?

Nice fix for any woman, I say. Somebody ought to get it good for this mess. If I ever find out. . . ."

"Go on with your grand idea," interposed Nevada.

"You-all come with me. I'll get a buckboard. I'll meet the lady an' do the talkin'. I'll let her down easy. An' if I cain't head her back, we'll fetch her out to the ranch an' then leave it up to Springer. Only we won't tell her or him or anybody who's the real Frank Owens."

"Tex, that ain't so plumb bad," declared Andy admiringly.

"What *I* want to know is who's goin' go do the talkin' to the boss?" queried Panhandle. "It mightn't be so hard to explain now. But after drivin' up to the ranch with a woman! You-all know Springer's shy. Young an' rich, like he is, an' a bachelor . . . he's been fussed over so he's plumb afraid of girls. An' here you're fetchin' a middle-aged schoolmarm who's romantic an' mushy! My Gawd, I say send her home on the next train."

"Pan, you're wise on hosses an' cattle, but you don't know human nature, an' you're daid wrong about the boss," rejoined Tex. "We're in a bad fix, I'll admit. But I lean more to fetchin' the lady up than sendin' her back. Somebody down Beacon way would get wise. Mebbe the schoolmarm might talk. She'd shore have cause. An' suppose Springer hears about it . . . that some of us or all of us played a low-down trick on a woman. He'd be madder at that than if we fetched her up. Likely he'll try to make amends. The boss may be shy on girls but he's the squarest man in Arizona. My idea is we'll deny any of us is Frank Owens, an' we'll meet Miss . . . Miss . . . what was that there name? . . . Miss Jane Stacey and fetch her up to the ranch, an' let her do the talkin' to Springer."

During the next several hours, while Tex searched the

town for a buckboard and team he could borrow, the other cowboys wandered from the saloon to the post office and back again, and then to the store, the restaurant, and all around. The town had gradually filled up with Saturday visitors.

"Boys, there's the boss," suddenly broke out Andy, pointing, and he ducked into the nearest doorway, which happened to be that of another saloon. It was half full of cowboys, ranchers, Mexicans, tobacco smoke, and noise.

Andy's companions had rushed pell-mell after him, and not until they all got inside did they realize that this saloon was a rendezvous for cowboys decidedly not on friendly terms with Springer's outfit. Nevada was the only one of the trio who took the situation nonchalantly.

"Wal, we're in, an' what the hell do we care for Beady Jones an' his outfit," he remarked, quite loud enough to be heard by others besides his friends.

Naturally they lined up at the bar, and this was not a good thing for young men who had an important engagement and who must preserve sobriety. After several rounds of drinks had appeared, they began to whisper and snicker over the possibility of Tex meeting the boss.

"If only it doesn't come off until Tex gets our forty-year-old schoolmarm from Missouri with him in the buckboard!" exclaimed Panhandle in huge glee.

"Shore. Tex, the handsome galoot, is most too blame for this mess," added Nevada. "Thet cowboy won't be above makin' love to Jane, if he thinks we're not around. But, fellows, we want to be there."

"Wouldn't miss seein' the boss meet Tex for a million," said Andy.

Presently a tall striking-looking cowboy, with dark face and small bright eyes like black beads, detached himself from a group of noisy companions, and confronted the trio, more particularly Nevada.

"Howdy, men," he greeted them, "what you-all doin' in here?"

He was coolly impertinent, and his action and query noticeably stilled the room. Andy and Panhandle leaned back against the bar. They had been in such situations before and knew who would do the talking for them.

"Howdy, Jones," replied Nevada coolly and carefully. "We happened to bust in here by accident. Reckon we're usually more particular what kind of company we mix with."

"Ahuh! Springer's outfit is shore a stuck-up one," sneered Beady Jones in a *quite* loud tone. "So stuck up they won't even ride around drift fences."

Nevada slightly changed his position.

"Beady, I've had a couple of drinks an' ain't very clear-headed," drawled Nevada. "Would you mind talkin' so I can understand you?"

"Bah! You savvy all right," declared Jones sarcastically. "I'm tellin' you straight what I've been layin' to tell your yaller-headed Texas pard."

"Now you're speakin' English, Beady. Tex an' me are pards, shore. An' I'll take it kind of you to get this talk out of your system. You seem to be chock full."

"You bet I'm full an' I'm a-goin' to bust!" shouted Jones, whose temper evidently could not abide the slow cool speech with which he had been answered.

"Wal, before you bust, explain what you mean by Springer's outfit not ridin' around drift fences."

"Easy. You just cut through wire fences," retorted Jones.

"Beady, I hate to call you a low-down liar, but that's what you are."

25

"You're another!" yelled Jones. "I seen your Texas Jack cut our drift fence."

Nevada struck out with remarkable swiftness and force. He knocked Jones over upon a card table, with which he crashed to the floor. Jones was so stunned that he did not recover before some of his comrades rushed to him, and helped him up. Then, black in the face and cursing savagely, he jerked for his gun. He got it out, but, before he could level it, two of his friends seized him, and wrestled with him, talking in earnest alarm. But Jones fought them.

"Ya damn' fool!" finally yelled one of them. "He's not packin' a gun. It'd be murder."

That brought Jones to his senses, although certainly not to calmness.

"Mister Nevada . . . next time you hit town you'd better come heeled," he hissed between his teeth.

"Shore. An' thet'll be bad for you, Beady," replied Nevada curtly.

Panhandle and Andy drew Nevada out to the street, where they burst into mingled excitement and anger. Their swift strides gravitated toward the saloon across from the post office.

When they emerged sometime later, they were arm in arm, and far from steady on their feet. They paraded up the one main street of Beacon, not in the least conspicuous on a Saturday afternoon. As they were neither hilarious nor dangerous, nobody paid any attention to them. Springer, their boss, met them, gazed at them casually, and passed without sign of recognition. If he had studied the boys closely, he might have received an impression that they were hugging a secret, as well as each other.

In due time the trio presented themselves at the railroad station. Tex was there, nervously striding up and down the

26

platform, now and then looking at his watch. The afternoon train was nearly due. At the hitching rail below the platform stood a new buckboard and a rather spirited team of horses.

The boys, coming across the wide square, encountered this evidence of Tex's extremity, and struck a posture before it.

"Livery stable outfit, by gosh," said Andy.

"Son-of-a-gun if it ain't," added Panhandle with a huge grin.

"Thish here Tex spendin' his money royal," agreed Nevada.

Then Tex espied them. He stared. Suddenly he jumped straight up. After striding to the edge of the platform, with face as red as a beet, he began to curse them.

"Whash mashes, ole pard?" asked Andy, who appeared a little less stable than his comrades.

Tex's reply was another volley of expressive profanity. And he ended with: " . . . you-all yellow quitters to get drunk an' leave me in the lurch. But you gotta get away from heah. I shore won't have you aboot when thet train comes."

"Tex, your boss is in town lookin' for you," said Nevada.

"I don't care a damn," replied Tex with fire in his eye.

"Wait till he shees you," gurgled Andy.

"Tex, he jest ambled past us like we wasn't gennelmen," added Panhandle. "Never sheen us a-tall."

"No wonder, you drunken cowpunchers," declared Tex in disgust. "Now I tell you to clear out of heah."

"But, pard, we just want to shee you meet our Jane from Missouri," replied Andy.

"If you-all ain't a lot of four-flushes, I'll eat my chaps!" burst out Tex hotly.

Just then a shrill whistle announced the train.

"You can sneak off now," he went on, "an' leave me to

face the music. I always knew I was the only gentleman in Springer's outfit."

The three cowboys did not act upon Tex's sarcastic suggestion, but they hung back, looking at once excited and sheepish and hugely delighted.

The long gray dusty train pulled into the station, and stopped. There was only one passenger for Springer—a woman—and she alighted from the coach near where the cowboys stood waiting. She was not tall and she was much too slight for the heavy valise the porter handed to her.

Tex strode grandly toward her.

"Miss . . . Miss Stacey, ma'am?" he asked, removing his sombrero.

"Yes," she replied. "Are you Mister Owens?"

Evidently the voice was not what Tex had expected and it disconcerted him.

"No, ma'am, I . . . I'm not Mister Owens," he said. "Please let me take your bag. . . . I'm Tex Dillon, one of Springer's cowboys. An' I've come to meet you . . . an' fetch you out to the ranch."

"Thank you, but I . . . I expected to be met by Mister Owens," she replied.

"Ma'am, there's been a mistake . . . I've got to tell you . . . there ain't any Mister Owens," blurted out Tex manfully.

"Oh!" she said with a little start.

"You see, it was this way," went on the confused cowboy. "One of Springer's cowboys . . . not *me* . . . wrote them letters to you, signin' his name Owens. There ain't no such named cowboy in this county. Your last letter . . . an' here it is . . . fell into my hands . . . all by accident, ma'am, it sure was. I took my three friends heah . . . I took them into my confidence. An' we all came down to meet you."

She moved her head and evidently looked at the strange

trio of cowboys Tex had pointed out as his friends. They came forward then, but not eagerly, and they still held to each other. Their condition, not to consider their immense excitement, could not have been lost even upon a tenderfoot from Missouri.

"Please . . . return my . . . my letter," she said, turning again to Tex, and she put out a small gloved hand to take it from him. "Then . . . there is no Mister Frank Owens?"

"No, ma'am, there ain't," replied Tex miserably.

"Is there . . . no . . . no truth in his . . . is there no school-teacher wanted here?" she faltered.

"I think so, ma'am," he replied. "Springer said he needed one. That's what started the advertisement an' the letters to you. You can see the boss an' . . . an' explain. I'm sure it will be all right. He's the grandest fellow. He won't stand for no joke on a poor old schoolmarm."

In his bewilderment he had spoken his thoughts, and that last slip made him look more miserable than ever, and made the boys appear ready to burst.

"Poor old schoolmarm," echoed Miss Stacey. "Perhaps the deceit has not been wholly on one side."

Whereupon she swept aside the enveloping veil to reveal a pale and pretty face. She was young. She had clear gray eyes and a sweet sensitive mouth. Little curls of chestnut hair straggled from under her veil. And she had tiny freckles.

Tex stared at this apparition.

"But you . . . you . . . the letter says she wasn't over forty!" he ejaculated.

"She's not," rejoined Miss Stacey curtly.

Then there were visible and remarkable indications of a transformation in the attitude of the cowboy. But the approach of a stranger suddenly seemed to paralyze him. This fellow was very tall. He strolled up to them. He was booted and spurred. He halted before the group and looked expectantly from the boys to the young woman and back again. But at the moment the four cowboys appeared dumb.

"Are you Mister Springer?" asked Miss Stacey.

"Yes," he replied, and he took off his sombrero. He had a dark frank face and keen eyes.

"I am Jane Stacey," she explained hurriedly. "I'm a schoolteacher. I answered an advertisement. And I've come from Missouri because of letters I received from a Mister Frank Owens of Springer's Ranch. This young man met me. He has not been very . . . explicit. I gather that there is no Mister Owens . . . that I'm the victim of a cowboy joke. But he said that Mister Springer won't stand for a joke on a poor old schoolmarm."

"I sure am glad to meet you, Miss Stacey," responded the rancher with the easy Western courtesy that must have been comforting to her. "Please let me see the letters."

She opened a handbag and, searching in it, presently held out several letters. Springer never even glanced at his stricken cowboys. He took the letters.

"No, not that one," said Miss Stacey, blushing scarlet. "That's one I wrote to Mister Owens, but didn't mail. It's . . . hardly necessary to read that."

While Springer read the others, she looked at him. Presently he asked for the letter she had taken back. Miss Stacey hesitated, then refused. He looked cool, curious, businesslike. Then his keen eyes swept over the four cowboys.

"Tex, are you Mister Frank Owens?" he queried sharply.

"I . . . shore . . . ain't," gasped Tex.

Springer asked each of the other boys the same question and received the same maudlin but negative answers. Then he turned again to the girl.

"Miss Stacey, I regret to say that you are indeed the victim of a low-down cowboy trick," he said. "I'd apologize for such heathen if I knew how. All I can say is I'm sorry."

"Then . . . then there isn't any school to teach . . . any place for me . . . out here?" she asked, and there were tears in her eyes.

"That's another matter," he replied with a winning smile. "Of course there's a place for you. I've wanted a school-teacher for a long time. Some of the men out at the ranch have kids an' they sure need a teacher."

"Oh, I'm . . . so glad," she murmured in great relief. "I was afraid I'd have to go . . . all the way back. You see, I'm not so strong as I used to be . . . and my doctor advised a change of climate . . . dry Western air."

"You don't look sick," he said with his keen eyes on her. "You look very well to me."

"Oh, indeed, I'm not very strong," she returned quickly. "But I must confess I wasn't altogether truthful about my age."

"I was wondering about that," he said gravely. There seemed just a glint of a twinkle in his eye. "Not over forty!"

Again she blushed and this time with confusion.

"It wasn't altogether a lie. I was afraid to mention I was only . . . so young. And I wanted to get the position so much . . . I'm a good . . . a competent teacher, unless the scholars are too grown-up."

"The scholars you'll have at my ranch are children," he replied. "Well, we'd better be starting if we are to get there before dark. It's a long ride. Is this all your baggage?"

Springer led her over to the buckboard and helped her in, then stowed the valise under the back seat.

"Here, let me put this robe over you," he said. "It'll be dusty. And when we get up on the ridge, it's cold."

At this juncture Tex came to life and he started forward.

But Andy and Nevada and Panhandle stood motionlessly, staring at the fresh and now flushed face of the young school-teacher. Tex untied the halter of the spirited team and they began to prance. He gathered up the reins as if about to mount the buckboard.

"I've got all the supplies an' the mail, Mister Springer," he said cheerfully. "An' I can be startin' at once."

"I'll drive Miss Stacey," replied Springer dryly.

Tex looked blank for a moment. Then Miss Stacey's clear gray eyes seemed to embarrass him. A tinge of red came into his tanned cheek.

"Tex, you can ride my horse home," said the rancher.

"That wild stallion of yours!" expostulated the cowboy. "Now, Mister Springer, I shore am afraid of him."

This from the best horseman on the whole range!

Apparently the rancher took Tex seriously. "He sure is wild, Tex, and I know you're a poor hand with a horse. If he throws you, why, you'll have your own horse."

Miss Stacey turned away her eyes. There was a hint of a smile on her lips. Springer got in beside her, and, taking the reins without another glance at his discomfited cowboys, he drove away.

II

A few weeks altered many things at Springer's Ranch. There was a marvelous change in the dress and deportment of cowboys off duty. There were some clean and happy and interested children. There was a rather taciturn and lonely young rancher who was given to thoughtful dreams and whose keen eyes watched the little adobe schoolhouse under the cottonwoods. And in Jane Stacey's face a rich bloom and tan had begun to warm out the paleness.

It was not often that Jane left the schoolhouse without meeting one of Springer's cowboys. She met Tex most frequently, and according to Andy that fact was because Tex was foreman and could send the boys off to the ends of the range.

And this afternoon Jane encountered the foreman. He was clean-shaven, bright, and eager, a superb figure. Tex had been lucky enough to have a gun with him one day when a rattlesnake frightened the schoolteacher and he had shot the reptile. Miss Stacey had leaned against him in her fright; she had been grateful; she had admired his wonderful skill with a gun and had murmured that a woman always could be sure with such a man. Thereafter Tex packed his gun unmindful of the ridicule of his rivals.

"Miss Stacey, come for a little ride, won't you?" he asked eagerly.

The cowboys had already taught her how to handle a horse and to ride, and, if all they said of her appearance and accomplishment were true, she was indeed worth watching.

"I'm sorry," replied Jane. "I promised Nevada I'd ride with him today."

"I reckon Nevada is miles an' miles up the valley by now," replied Tex. "He won't be back till long after dark."

"But he made an agreement with me," protested the schoolmistress.

"An' shore he has to work. He's ridin' for Springer, an' I'm foreman of this ranch," said Tex.

"You sent him off on some long chase," averred Jane severely. "Now, didn't you?"

"I shore did. He comes crowin' down to the bunkhouse . . . about how he's goin' to ride with you an' how we-all are not in the runnin'."

"Oh, he did. And what did you say?"

"I says . . . 'Nevada, I reckon there's a steer mired in the sand up in Cedar Wash. You ride up there an' pull him out.'"

"And then what did he say?" inquired Jane curiously.

"Why, Miss Stacey, I shore hate to tell you. I didn't think he was so . . . so bad. He just used the most awful language as was ever heard on this heah ranch. Then he rode off."

"But *was* there a steer mired up in the wash?"

"I reckon so," replied Tex, rather shame-facedly. "'Most always is one."

Jane let scornful eyes rest upon the foreman.

"That was a mean trick," she said.

"There's been worse done to me by him, an' all of them. An' all's fair in love an' war. . . . Will you ride with me?"

"No."

"Why not?"

"Because I think I'll ride off alone up Cedar Wash and help Nevada find that mired steer."

"Miss Stacey, you're shore not goin' to ride off alone. Savvy that?"

"Who'll keep me from it?" demanded Jane with spirit.

"I will. Or any of the boys, for that matter. Springer's orders."

Jane started with surprise, and then blushed rosy red. Tex, also, appeared confused at his disclosure.

"Miss Stacey, I oughtn't have said that. It slipped out. The boss said we needn't tell you, but you were to be watched an' taken care of. It's a wild range. You could get lost or thrown from a horse."

"Mister Springer is very kind and thoughtful," murmured Jane.

"The fact is, this heah ranch is a different place since you came," went on Tex as if emboldened. "An' this beatin' around the bush doesn't suit me. All the boys have lost their haids over you."

"Indeed? How flattering," replied Jane with just a hint of mockery. She was fond of all her admirers, but there were four of them she had not yet forgiven.

The tall foreman was not without spirit.

"It's true all right, as you'll find out pretty quick," he replied. "If you had any eyes, you'd see that cattle raisin' on this heah ranch is about to halt till somethin' is decided. Why, even Springer himself is sweet on you."

"How dare you!" flashed Jane, suddenly aghast.

"I ain't afraid to tell the truth," declared Tex stoutly. "He is. The boys all say so. He's grouchier than ever. He's jealous. Lord, he's jealous! He watches you. . . ."

"Suppose I told him that you dared to say such things?" interrupted Jane, trembling on the verge of strange emotion.

"Why, he'd be tickled to death. He hasn't got nerve enough to tell you himself."

This cowboy, like all his comrades, was hopeless. She was about to attempt to change the conversation when Tex took her into his arms. She struggled—fought with all her might. But he succeeded in kissing her cheek and the tip of her ear. Finally she broke away from him.

"Now . . . ," she panted. "You've done it . . . you've insulted me. Now I'll never ride with you again . . . even speak to you."

"I shore didn't insult you," replied Tex. "Jane . . . won't you marry me?"

"No."

"Won't you be my sweetheart . . . till you care enough to . . . to . . . ?"

"No."

"But, Jane, you'll forgive me, an' be good friends again?"

"Never!"

Jane did not mean all she said. She had come to understand these men of the ranges—their loneliness—their hunger for love. But in spite of her sympathy she needed sometimes to be cold and severe.

"Jane, you owe me a good deal . . . more than you've any idea," said Tex seriously.

"How so?"

"Didn't you ever guess about me?"

"My wildest flight at guessing would never make anything of you, Texas Jack."

"You'd never have been here but for me," he said solemnly.

Jane could only stare at him.

"I meant to tell you long ago. But I shore didn't have nerve. Jane . . . I . . . I was that there letter-writin' feller. I wrote them letters you got. I am Frank Owens."

"No!" exclaimed Jane. She was startled. That matter of

Frank Owens had never been cleared up. It had ceased to rankle within her breast, but it had never been forgotten. She looked up earnestly into the big fellow's face. It was like a mask. But she saw through it. He was lying. Almost, she thought, she saw a laugh deep in his eyes.

"I shore am the lucky man who found you a job when you was sick an' needed a change. . . . An' you've grown so pretty an' so well you owe all thet to me."

"Tex, if you really were Frank Owens, *that* would make a great difference. I owe him everything. I would . . . but I don't believe you are he."

"It's a sure honest Gospel fact," declared Tex. "I hope to die if it ain't!"

Jane shook her head sadly at his monstrous prevarication.

"I don't believe you," she said, and left him standing there.

It might have been mere coincidence that during the next few days both Nevada and Panhandle waylaid and conveyed to her intelligence by diverse and pathetic arguments the astounding fact that each was Mr. Frank Owens. More likely, however, was it the unerring instinct of lovers who had sensed the importance and significance of this mysterious correspondent's part in bringing health and happiness into Jane Stacey's life. She listened to them with anger and sadness and amusement at their deceit, and she had the same answer for both: "I don't believe you."

And through these machinations of the cowboys Jane had begun to have vague and sweet and disturbing suspicions of her own as to the real identity of that mysterious cowboy, Frank Owens. Andy had originality as well as daring. He would have completely deceived Jane if she had not happened, by the merest accident, to discover the relation between him and certain love letters she had begun to find in her desk. She was deceived at first, for the typewriting of these was precisely like that in the letters like that of Frank Owens. She had been suddenly aware of a wild start of rapture. That had given place to a shameful open-eyed realization of the serious condition of her own heart. But she happened to discover in Andy the writer of these missives, and her dream was shattered, if not forgotten. Andy certainly would not carry love letters to her that he did not write. He had merely learned to use the same typewriter and at opportune times he had slipped the letters into her desk. Jane now began to have her own little aching haunting secret that was so hard to put out of her mind. Every letter and every hint of Frank Owens made her remember. Therefore she decided to put a check to Andy's sly double-dealing. She addressed a note to him and wrote:

> **Dear Andy,**
>
> **That day at the train when you thought I was a poor old schoolmarm you swore you were not Frank Owens. Now you swear you are! If you were a man who knew what truth is, you'd have a chance. But now . . . No! You are a monster of iniquity. I don't believe you.**

She left the note in plain sight where she always found his letters in her desk. The next morning the note was gone. And so was Andy. She did not see him for three days.

It came about that a dance to be held at Beacon during the late summer was something Jane could not very well avoid. She had not attended either of the cowboy dances that had been given since her arrival. This next one, however, appeared to be an annual affair, at which all the ranching fraternity for miles around would be in attendance. Jane was wild to go. But it developed that she could not escape the escort of any one of her cowboy admirers without alienating the others. And she began to see the visions of this wonderful dance fade away when Springer accosted her.

"Who's the lucky cowboy to take you to our dance?" he asked.

"He's as mysterious and doubtful as Mister Frank Owens," replied Jane.

"Oh, you still remember him," said the rancher, his keen dark eyes quizzically on her.

"Indeed, I do," sighed Jane.

"Too bad! He was a villain. . . . But you don't mean you haven't been asked to go?"

"They've all asked me . . . that's the trouble."

"I see. But you mustn't miss it. It'd be pleasant for you to meet some of the ranchers and their wives. Suppose you go with me?"

"Oh, Mister Springer, I . . . I'd be delighted," replied Jane.

"Thank you. Then it's settled. I must be in town all that day on cattle business . . . next Friday. I'll ask the Hartwells to stop here for you, an' drive you in."

He seemed gravely, kindly interested as always, yet there was something in his eyes that interfered with the regular beating of Jane's heart. She could not forget what the cowboys had told her, even if she dared not believe it.

Jane spent much of the remaining leisure hours on a gown to wear at this dance that promised so much. And because of the labor, she saw little of the cowboys. Tex was highly offended with her and would not deign to notice her anyhow. She wondered what would happen at the dance. She was a little fearful, too, because she had already learned of what fire and brimstone these cowboys were made. So dreaming and conjecturing, now amused and again gravely pensive, Jane awaited the eventful night.

The Hartwells turned out to be nice people whose little girl was one of Jane's pupils. That, and their evident delight in Jane's appearance, gave the adventure a last thrilling anticipation. Jane had been afraid to trust her own judgment as to how she looked. On the drive townward, through the crisp fall gloaming, while listening to the chatter of the children, and the talk of the elder Hartwells, she could not help wondering what Springer would think of her in the beautiful new gown.

They arrived late, according to her escorts. The drive to town was sixteen miles, but it had seemed short to Jane. "Reckon it's just as well for you an' the children," said Mrs. Hartwell to Jane. "These dances last from seven to seven."

"No!" exclaimed Jane.

"They sure do."

"Well, I'm a tenderfoot from Missouri. But that's not going to keep me from having a wonderful time."

"You will, dear, unless the cowboys fight over you, which is likely. But at least there won't be any shootin'. My husband an' Springer are both on the committee an' they won't admit any gun-totin' cowpunchers."

Here Jane had concrete evidence of something she had begun to suspect. These careless love-making cowboys might be dangerous. It thrilled while it repelled her.

Jane's first sight of that dance hall astonished her. It was a big barn-like room, roughly raftered and sided, decorated enough with colored bunting to take away the bareness. The lamps were not bright, but there were enough of them to give collectively a good light. The volume of sound amazed her. Music and trample of boots, gay laughter, deep voices of men all seemed to merge into a loud hum. A swaying wheeling

horde of dancers circled past her. No more time then was ac-
corded her to clarify the spectacle, for Springer suddenly confronted her. He seemed different somehow. Perhaps it was an
absence of ranchers' corduroys and boots, if Jane needed assurance of what she had dreamed of and hoped for. She had it
in his frank admiration.

"Sure it's somethin' fine for Bill Springer to have the pret-
tiest girl here," he said.

"Thank you . . . but, Mister Springer . . . I sadly fear you
were a cowboy before you became a rancher," she replied
archly.

"Sure I was. An' that you may find out." He laughed. "Of
course, I could never come up to . . . say . . . Frank Owens. But
let's dance. I shall have little enough of you in this outfit."

So he swung her into the circle of dancers. Jane found him
easy to dance with, although he was far from expert. It was a
jostling mob, and she soon acquired a conviction that, if her
gown did outlast the whole dance, her feet never would.
Springer took his dancing seriously and had little to say. Jane
felt strange and uncertain with him. Then soon she became
aware of the cessation of hum and movement.

"Sure that was the best dance I ever had," said Springer
with something of radiance in his dark face. "An' now I must
lose you to this outfit comin'."

Manifestly he meant his cowboys Tex, Nevada, Panhandle, and Andy who presented themselves four abreast,
shiny of hair and face.

"Good luck," he whispered. "If you get into trouble, let
me know."

What he meant quickly dawned upon Jane. Right there it
began. She saw there was absolutely no use in trying to avoid
or refuse these young men. The wisest and safest course was
to surrender, which she did.

41

"Boys, don't all talk at once. I can dance with only one of you at a time. So I'll take you in alphabetical order. I'm a poor old schoolmarm from Missouri. It'll be Andy, Nevada, Panhandle, and Tex."

Despite their protests she held rigidly to this rule. Each one of the cowboys took shameless advantage of his opportunity. Outrageously as they all hugged her, Tex was the worst offender. She tried to stop dancing, but he carried her along as if she had been a child. He was rapt, and yet there seemed a devil in him.

"Tex . . . how dare you," panted Jane, when at last the dance ended.

"Wal, I reckon I'd aboot dare anythin' for you, Jane," he replied, towering over her.

"You ought to be . . . ashamed," went on Jane. "I'll not dance with you again."

"Aw, now," he pleaded.

"I won't, Tex . . . so there. You're no gentleman."

"Ahuh!" he ejaculated, drawing himself up stiffly. "All right, I'll go out an' get drunk, an', when I come back, I'll clean out this heah hall."

"Tex! Don't go," she called hurriedly as he started to stride away. "I'll take that back. I will give you another dance . . . if you promise to . . . to behave."

Then she got rid of him, and was carried off by Mrs. Hartwell to be introduced to ranchers and their wives, to girls and their escorts. She found herself a center of admiring eyes. She promised more dances than she could remember or keep.

Her new partner was a tall handsome cowboy named Jones. She did not know quite what to make of him. But he was an unusually good dancer, and he did not hold her so that she had difficulty in breathing. He talked all the time. He was witty and engaging, and he had a most subtly flattering

42

tongue. Jane could not fail to grasp that he might even be worse than Tex, but at least he did not make love to her with physical violence. She enjoyed that dance and admitted the singular forceful charm about this Mr. Jones. If he was a little too bold of glance and somehow primitively assured and debonair, she passed it by in the excitement and joy of the hour, and in the certainty that she was now a long way from Missouri. Jones demanded rather than begged for another dance, and, although she laughingly explained her predicament in regard to partners, he said he would come after her anyhow.

Then followed several dances with new partners, between which Jane became more than ever the center of attraction. It all went to her head like wine. She was having a perfectly wonderful time. Jones claimed her again, in fact whirled her out on the floor, and it seemed then that the irresistible rush of the dancers was similar to her sensations. Twice again before the supper hour at midnight she found herself dancing with Jones. How he managed it she did not know. He just took her, carried her off by storm. Jane did not awaken to this unpardonable conduct of hers until she discovered that a little while before she had promised Tex his second dance, and then she had given it to Jones, or at least had danced it with him. What could she do when he walked right off with her? It was a glimpse of Tex's face, as she was being whirled round in Jones's arms, that filled Jane with remorse.

Then came the supper hour. It was a gala occasion, for which evidently the children had heroically kept awake. Jane enjoyed the children immensely. She sat with the numerous Hartwells, all of whom were most kindly attentive to her. Jane wondered why Mr. Springer did not put in an appearance, but considered his absence due to numerous duties.

When the supper hour ended and the people were stirring about the hall, and the men were tuning up, Jane caught sight of Andy. He looked rather pale and sick. Jane tried to catch his eye, but failing that she went to him.

"Andy, please find Tex for me. I owe him a dance, and I'll give him the very first, unless Mister Springer comes for it."

Andy regarded her with an aloofness totally new to her.

"Wal, I'll tell him. But I reckon Tex ain't presentable just now. All of us are through dancin' tonight."

"What's happened?" queried Jane, swift to divine trouble.

"There's been a little fight."

"Oh, no!" cried Jane. "Who? What? . . . Andy, tell me."

"Wal, when you cut Tex's dance for Beady Jones, you sure put our outfit in bad," replied Andy coldly. "At thet there wouldn't have been anythin' come of it here if Beady Jones hadn't got to shootin' off his chin. Tex slapped his face an' thet sure started a fight. Beady licked Tex, too, I'm sorry to say. He's a pretty bad customer, Beady is, an' he's bigger'n Tex. Wal, we had a hell of a time keepin' Nevada out of it. Thet would have been a uneven fight. I'd like to have seen it. But we kept them apart till Springer come out. An' what the boss said to thet outfit was sure aplenty. Beady Jones kept talkin' back, nasty like . . . you know he was once foreman for us . . . till Springer got good an' mad. An' he said . . . 'Jones, I fired you once because you was a little too slick for our outfit, an' I'll tell you this, if it comes to a pinch, I'll give you the damnedest thrashin' any smart-aleck cowboy ever got!' Gee, the boss was riled. It sort of surprised me, an' tickled me pink. You can bet that shut Beady Jones's loud mouth."

After that rather lengthy speech Andy left her unceremoniously standing there alone. She was not alone long, but it was long enough for her to feel bitter dissatisfaction with herself.

Jane looked for Springer, hoping yet fearing he would come to her. But he did not. She had another uninterrupted dizzy round of dancing until her strength failed. At four o'clock she was scarcely able to walk. Her pretty dress was torn and mussed; her white stockings were no longer white; her slippers were worn ragged. And her feet were dead. From that time she sat with Mrs. Hartwell looking on, and trying to keep awake. The wonderful dance, that had begun so promisingly, had ended sadly for her.

At length the exodus began, although Jane did not see any dancers leaving. She went out with the Hartwells, to be received by Springer, who had evidently made arrangements for their leaving. He was decidedly cool to Jane.

All through the long ride out to the ranch he never addressed her or looked toward her. Daylight came, cold and gray to Jane. She felt crushed.

Springer's sister and the matronly housekeeper were waiting for them, with cheery welcome, and invitation to a hot breakfast.

Presently Jane found herself momentarily alone with the rancher.

"Miss Stacey," he said, in a voice she had never heard, "your flirtin' with Beady Jones made trouble for the Springer outfit."

"Mister Springer!" she exclaimed, her head going up.

"Excuse me," he returned, in cutting dry tone that recalled Tex. Indeed, this Westerner was a cowboy, the same as those who rode for him, only a little older, and therefore more reserved and careful of speech. "If it wasn't that . . . then you were much taken with Mister Beady Jones."

"If that was anybody's business, it might have appeared so," she retorted, tingling all over with some feeling she could not control.

"Sure. But are you denyin' it?" he queried soberly, eying her with grave wonder and disapproval. It was this more than his question that roused hot anger and contrariness in Jane.

"I admired Mister Jones very much," replied Jane. "He was a splendid dancer. He did not maul me like a bear. I really had a chance to breathe during my dances with him. Then, too, he could talk."

Springer bowed with dignity. His dark face paled. It began to dawn upon Jane that there was something intense in the moment. She began to repent of her hasty pride.

"Thanks," he said. "Please excuse my impertinence. I see you have found your Mister Frank Owens in this cowboy Jones, an' it sure is not my place to say any more."

"But . . . but . . . Mister Springer . . . ," faltered Jane, quite unstrung by that amazing speech. The rancher, however, bowed again, and left her. Jane felt too miserable and weary for anything but rest. She went to her room, and, flinging off her hateful finery, she crawled into bed, a very perplexed and distraught young woman.

About mid-afternoon Jane awakened greatly refreshed and relieved and strangely repentant. She dressed prettily and went out, not quite sure of or satisfied with herself. She walked up and down the long porch of the ranch house, gazing out over the purple range, on to the black belt of forest up the mountains. How beautiful this Arizona! She loved it. Could she ever go away? The thought reposed, to stay before her consciousness. She invaded the kitchen, where the matronly housekeeper, who was fond of her, gave her wild-turkey sandwiches and cookies and sweet rich milk. While Jane mitigated her hunger, the woman gossiped about the cowboys and Springer; and the information she imparted renewed Jane's concern.

From the kitchen Jane went out into the courtyard, and naturally, as always, gravitated toward the corrals and barns. Springer appeared, in company with a rancher Jane did not

46

know. She expected Springer to stop her for a few pleasant words as he always did. This time, however, he merely touched his sombrero and passed on. Jane felt the incident almost as a slight. It hurt her.

Then she went on down the lane, very thoughtful. A cloud had appeared above the horizon of her happy life there at the Springer Ranch. The lane opened out into the wide square, around which were the gates to corrals, entrances to barns, the forge, granaries, and the commodious bunkhouse of the cowboys.

Jane's sharp eyes caught sight of the boys before they espied her. And when she looked up again, every lithe back was turned. They allowed her to pass without any apparent knowledge of her existence. This was unprecedented. It offended Jane bitterly. She knew she was unreasonable, but could not or would not help it. She strolled on down to the pasture gate, and watched the colts and calves. Upon her return, she passed closer to the cowboys. But again they apparently did not see her. Jane added resentment to her wounded vanity and pride. Yet even then a still small voice tormented. She went back to her room, meaning to read or sew, or do schoolwork. But instead she cried.

Springer did not put in an appearance at the dinner table, and that was the last straw for Jane. She realized she had made a mess of her wonderful opportunity there. But those stupid fiery cowboys! This sensitive Westerner! How could she know how to take them? The worst of it was that she was genuinely fond of the cowboys. And as for the rancher—her mind seemed vague and unreliable about him, but she said she hated him.

Next day was Sunday. Heretofore every Sunday had been a full day for Jane. This one bade fair to be empty. Company came as usual, neighbors from nearby ranches. The cowboys were off duty and other cowboys visited them.

Jane's attention was attracted by sight of a superb horseman riding up the lane to the ranch house. He seemed familiar, but she could not place him. What a picture he made as he dismounted, slick and shiny, booted and spurred, to doff his huge sombrero. Jane heard him ask for Miss Stacey. Then she recognized him. Beady Jones! She was a once horrified, and something else she could not name. She remembered now he had asked if he might call Sunday and she had certainly not refused. But for him to come after the fight with Tex and the bitter scene with Springer! It seemed an unparalleled affront. What manner of man was this cowboy Jones? He certainly did not lack courage. But more to the point— what idea had he of her? Jane rose to the occasion. She had let herself in for this, and she would see it through, come what might. Looming disaster stimulated her. She would show these indifferent, deceitful, fire-spirited, incomprehensible cowboys. She would let Springer see she, indeed, had taken Beady Jones for Mr. Frank Owens.

To that end Jane made her way down the porch to greet her cowboy visitor. She made herself charming and gracious, and carried off the embarrassing situation—for Springer was present—as if it were perfectly natural. And she led Jones to one of the rustic benches down the porch.

Jane meant to gauge him speedily, if that were possible. While she made conversation, she brought to bear all that she possessed of intuition and discernment, now especially excited. The situation here was easy for her.

Naturally Jones resembled the cowboys she knew. The same range and life had developed him. But he lacked certain things she liked so much in Tex and Nevada. He was a superb animal. She had reluctantly to admire his cool easy boldness in a situation certainly perilous for him. But then he had reasoned, of course, that she would be his protection. She did not fail to note that he carried a gun, inside his embroidered vest.

Manifest, indeed, was it that young Jones felt he had made a conquest. He was the most forceful and bold person Jane had ever met, quite incapable of appreciating her as a lady. Soon he waxed ardent. Jane was accustomed to the sentimental talk of cowboys, but this fellow was neither amusing nor interesting. He was dangerous. When Jane pulled her hand, by main force, free from his, and said she was not accustomed to allow men such privileges, he grinned at her like a handsome devil.

"Sure, sweetheart, you have missed a heap of fun," he said. "An' I reckon I'll have to break you in."

Jane could not feel insulted at this brazen lout, but she certainly raged at herself. Her instant impulse was to excuse herself and abruptly leave him. But Springer was close by. She had caught his dark wandering covert glances. And the cowboys were at the other end of the long porch. Jane feared another fight. She had brought this upon herself, and she must stick it out. The ensuing hour was an increasing torment. At last it seemed she could not bear the false situation any longer, and, when Jones again importuned her to meet him out on horseback she stooped to deception to end the interview. She really did not concentrate her attention on his plan or take stock of what she'd agreed to, but she got rid of him with lax dignity before Springer and the others. After that, she did not have the courage to stay out and face them. How bitterly she had disappointed the rancher! Jane stole off to the darkness and loneliness of her room. There, however, she was not above peeping out from behind her window-blind at the cowboys. They had grown immeasurably in her estimation. Alas! No doubt they were through with the little tenderfoot schoolmarm from Missouri.

III

The school teaching went on just the same, and the cowboys thawed out and Springer returned somewhat to his kindliness, but Jane missed something from her work and in them. At heart she grieved. Would it ever be the same again? What had happened? She had only been an emotional little tenderfoot unused to Western ways. Indeed, she had not failed, at least in gratitude and affection, although now it seemed they would never know.

There came a day, when Jane rode off alone toward the hills. She forgot the risk and the admonitions of the cowboys. She wanted to be alone to think. Her happiness had sustained a subtle change. Her work, the children, the friends she had made, even the horse she loved were no longer all-sufficient. Something had come over her. She tried to persuade herself that she was homesick or morbid. But she was not honest with herself and knew it.

It was late fall, but the sun was warm that afternoon, and it was the season when little wind prevailed. Before her lay the valley range, a green-gray expanse dotted with cattle, and beyond it the cedared foothills rose, and above them loomed the dark beckoning mountains. Her horse was fast and liked to run with her. She loved him and the open range, with the rushing breeze on her face, and all that clear lonely vast and silent world before her. Never would she return to live in the crowded cities again, with their horde of complaining people. She had found health and life—and something that wrung her heart and stung her cheek.

She rode fast till her horse was hot and she was out of breath. Then she slowed down. The foothills seemed so close now. But they were not really close. Still she could smell the fragrant dry cedar aroma on the air.

Then for the first time she looked back toward the ranch. It was a long way off—ten miles—a mere green spot in the gray. And there was a horseman coming. As usual some one of the cowboys had observed her, let her think she had slipped away, and was now following her. Today it angered Jane. She wanted to be alone. She could take care of herself. And as was usual with her she used her quirt on the horse. He broke into a gallop. She did not look back again for a long time. When she did, it was to discover that the horseman had not only gained, but was now quite close to her. Jane looked hard, but she could not recognize the rider. Once she imagined it was Tex, and again Andy. It did not make any difference which one of the cowboys it was. She was angry, and, if he caught up with her, he would be sorry.

Jane rode the longest and fastest race she had ever ridden. She reached the low foothills, and, without heeding the fact that she would at once become lost, she entered the cedars and began to climb. She ascended a hill, went down the slope, up a ravine, to climb again. At times her horse had to walk, and then she heard her pursuer breaking through the cedars. He had to trail her by her horse's tracks, and so she was able to keep in the lead. It was not long until Jane realized she was lost, but she did not care. She rode up and down and around for an hour until she was thoroughly tired out, and then up on top of a foothill she reined in her horse and waited to give this pursuer a piece of her mind.

What was her amaze, when she heard a thud of hoofs and cracking of branches in the opposite direction from which she expected her pursuer, to see a rider emerge from the cedars and trot his horse toward her. Jane needed only a second glance to recognize Beady Jones. Surely she had met him by chance. Suddenly she knew that he was not the pursuer she had been so angrily aware of. Jones's horse was white. That checked her mounting anger.

Jones rode straight at her, and, as he came close, Jane saw his bold dark face and gleaming eyes. Instantly she realized she had been mad to ride so far into the wild country, to expose herself to something from which the cowboys had always tried to save her.

"Howdy, sweetheart," said Jones in his cool, devil-may-care way. "Reckon it took you a long time to meet me as you promised."

"I didn't ride out to meet you, Mister Jones," replied Jane spiritedly. "I know I agreed to something or other, but even then I didn't mean it."

"Yes, I had a hunch you was playin' with me," he returned darkly, riding right up against her horse.

He reached out a long gloved hand and grasped her arm.

"What do you mean, sir?" demanded Jane, trying to wrench free.

"Sure I mean a lot," he said grimly. "You stood for the love-makin' of that Springer outfit. Now you're goin' to get a taste of somethin' not so mushy."

"Let go of me . . . you . . . you ruffian!" cried Jane, struggling fiercely. She was both furious and terrified. But she seemed to be a child in the grasp of a giant.

"Hell! Your fightin' will only make it interestin'. Come here, you deceitful little cat."

And he lifted her out of her saddle over in front of him. Jane's horse, that had been frightened and plunging, ran away into the cedars. Then gently the cowboy proceeded to embrace Jane. She managed to keep her mouth from contact with his, but he kissed her face and neck, kisses that seemed to pollute her.

"Jane, I'm ridin' out of this country for good," he said. "An' I've just been waitin' for this chance. You bet you'll remember Beady Jones."

Jane realized that this Jones would stop at nothing. Frantically she fought to get away from him and to pitch herself to the ground. She screamed. She beat and tore at him. She scratched his face till the blood flowed. And as her struggles increased with her fright, she gradually slipped down between him and the pommel of his saddle with head hanging down on one side and her feet on the other. This was awkward and painful, but infinitely preferable to being crushed in his arms. He was riding off with her as if she had been an empty sack. Suddenly Jane's hands, while trying to hold onto something to lessen the severe jolt of her position, came in contact with Jones's gun. Dare she draw it and shoot him? Then all at once her ears filled with the tearing gallop of another horse. Inverted as she was, she was able to see and recognize Springer ride right at Jones and yell piercingly.

Next she felt Jones's hard jerk at his gun. But Jane had hold of it, and suddenly she made her little hands like steel. The fierce energy with which Jones wrestled to draw his gun threw Jane from the saddle. And when she dropped clear of the horse, the gun came with her.

"Hands up, Beady!" she heard Springer call out, as she lay momentarily face down in the dust. Then she struggled to her knees, and crawled to get away from proximity to the horses. She still clung to the heavy gun. And when breathless and almost collapsing she fell back on the ground, she saw Jones with his hands above his head and Springer on foot with leveled gun.

"Sit tight, cowboy," ordered the rancher in hard tone.

"It'll take damn' little to make me bore you." Then, while still covering Jones, evidently ready for any sudden move, Springer spoke again. "Jane, did you come out to meet this cowboy?"

"Oh, no! How can you ask that?" cried Jane, almost sobbing.

"She's a liar, boss," spoke up Jones coolly. "She let me make love to her. An' she agreed to ride out an' meet me. Wal, it sure took her a spell, an', when she did come, she was shy on the love-makin's. I was packin' her off to scare some sense into her when you rode in."

"Beady, I know your way with women. You can save your breath, for I've a hunch you're goin' to need it."

"Mister Springer," faltered Jane, getting to her knees, "I . . . I was foolishly taken with this cowboy . . . at first. Then . . . that Sunday after the dance when he called on me at the ranch . . . I saw through him then. I heartily despised him. To get rid of him I did say I'd meet him. But I never meant to. Then I forgot it. Today I rode for the first time. I saw someone following me and thought it must be Tex or one of the boys. Finally I waited and presently Jones rode up to me. . . . And Mister Springer he . . . he grabbed me off my horse . . . and handled me most brutally . . . shamefully. I fought him with all my might, but what could I do?"

Springer's face changed markedly during Jane's long explanation. Then he threw his gun on the ground in front of Jane.

"Jones, I'm goin' to beat you half to death," he said grimly, and, leaping at the cowboy, he jerked him out of the saddle until he was sprawling on the ground. Next Springer threw aside his sombrero, his vest, his spurs. But he kept on his gloves. The cowboy rose to one knee, and he measured the distance between him and Springer, and then the gun that lay on the ground. Suddenly he sprang toward it. But

Springer intercepted him with a powerful kick that tripped Jones and laid him flat.

"Jones, you're sure about as low-down as they come," he said in dark scorn. "I've got to be satisfied with beatin' you when I ought to kill you."

"Ahuh! Wal, boss, it ain't any safe bet thet you can beat me," returned Jones sullenly while he got up.

As they rushed together, Jane had wit enough to pick up the gun, and then with it and Jones's, to get back to a safe distance. She wanted to run away out of sight. But she could neither do that nor keep her fascinated gaze from the combatants. Even in her distraught condition she could see that the cowboy, fierce and active and strong as he was, could not hold his own with Springer. They fought over all the open space, and crashed into the cedars, and out again. The time came when Jones was on the ground about as much as he was erect. Bloody, disheveled, beaten, he kept on trying to stem the onslaught of blows.

Suddenly he broke off a dead branch of cedar and, brandishing it, rushed at the rancher. Jane uttered a cry, closed her eyes, and sank down. She heard fierce imprecations and sodden blows. When at length she opened her eyes in terror, fearing something dreadful, she saw Springer erect, wiping his face, and Jones lying prone on the ground.

Then Jane saw him go to his horse, untie a canteen from the saddle, remove his bloody gloves, and wash his face with a wet scarf. Next he poured some water on Jones's face.

"Come on, Jane!" he called. "Reckon it's all over."

Then he tied the bridle of Jones's horse to a cedar and, leading his own animal, turned to meet Jane.

"I want to compliment you on gettin' that cowboy's gun," he said warmly. "But for that, there'd sure have been somethin' bad. I'd have had to kill him, Jane. Here, give me the guns. . . . You poor little tenderfoot from Missouri. No, not tenderfoot any longer, you became a Westerner today."

His face was bruised and cut, his dress dirty and bloody, but he did not appear the worse for that fight. Jane found her legs scarcely able to support her, and she had apparently lost her voice.

"Let us put you on my saddle till we find your horse," he said, and lifted her lightly as a feather to a seat crosswise. Then he walked with a hand on the bridle.

Jane saw him examining the ground, evidently searching for horse tracks. "Ha! Here we are." And he led off in another direction through the cedars. Soon Jane espied her horse, calmly nibbling at the bleached grass. In a few moments she was back in her own saddle, beginning to recover somewhat from her distress. But she divined that as fast as she recovered from one set of emotions she was going to be tormented by another.

"There's a good cold spring down here in the rocks," remarked Springer. "I think you need a drink, an' so do I."

They rode down the sunny cedar slopes, into a shady ravine skirted by pines, and up to some mossy cliffs from which a spring gushed forth.

Jane was now in the throes of thrilling, bewildering conjectures and fears. Why had Springer followed her? Why had he not sent one of the cowboys? Why did she feel so afraid and foolish? He had always been courteous and kind and thoughtful, at least until she had offended so gregariously. And here he was now. He had fought for her. Would she ever forget? Her heart began to pound. And when he dismounted to take her off her horse, she knew it was to see a scarlet and telltale face.

"Mister Springer, I . . . I thought you were Tex . . . or somebody," she said.

He laughed as he took off his sombrero. His face was warm, and the cuts were still bleeding a little.

"You sure can ride," he replied. "And that's a good little pony."

He loosened the cinches on the horses. Jane managed to hide some of her confusion.

"Won't you walk around a little?" he asked. "It'll rest you. We are fifteen miles from home."

"So far?"

Then presently he lifted her up and stood beside her with a hand on her horse. He looked up frankly into her face. The keen eyes were softer than usual. He seemed so fine and strong and splendid. She was afraid of her eyes and looked away.

"When the boys found you were gone, they all saddled up to find you," he said. "But I asked them if they didn't think the boss ought to have one chance. So they let me come."

Something happened to Jane's heart just then. She was suddenly overwhelmed by a strange happiness that she must hide, but could not. It seemed there was a long silence. She felt Springer there, but she could not look at him.

"Do you like it out here in the West?" he asked presently.

"Oh, I love it! I'll never want to leave it," she replied impulsively.

"I reckon I'm glad to hear that."

Then there fell another silence. He pressed closer to her and seemed now to be leaning on the horse. She wondered if he heard the weird knocking of her heart against her side.

"Will you be my wife an' stay here always?" he asked simply. "I'm in love with you. I've been lonely since my mother died. . . . You'll sure have to marry some one of us. Because, as Tex says, if you don't, ranchin' can't go on much longer. These boys don't seem to get anywhere with you.

Have I any chance . . . Jane . . . ?"

He possessed himself of her gloved hand and gave her a gentle pull. Jane knew it was gentle because she scarcely felt it. Yet it had irresistible power. She was swayed by that gentle pull. She was slipping sidewise in her saddle. She was sliding into his arms.

A little later he smiled up at her and said: "Jane, they call me Bill for short. Same as they call me boss. But my two front names are Frank Owens."

"Oh!" cried Jane, startled. "Then you . . . you . . . ?"

"Yes, I'm the guilty one," he replied happily. "It happened this way. My bedroom, you know, is next to my office. I often heard the boys poundin' the typewriter. I had a hunch they were up to some trick. So I spied upon them . . . heard about Frank Owens an' the letters to the little schoolmarm. At Beacon I got the postmistress to give me your address. An', of course, I intercepted some of your letters. It sure has turned out great."

"I . . . I don't know about you or those terrible cowboys," replied Jane dubiously. "How did *they* happen on the name Frank Owens?"

"Sure, that's a stumper. I reckon they put a job up on me."

"Frank . . . tell me . . . did *you* write the . . . the love letters?" she asked appealingly. "There were two kinds of letters. That's what I could never understand."

"Jane, I reckon I did," he confessed. "Somethin' about your little notes just won me. Does that make it all right?"

"Yes, Frank, I reckon it does," she returned, leaning down to kiss him.

"Let's ride back home an' tell the boys," said Springer gaily. "The joke's sure on them. I've corralled the little schoolmarm from Missouri."

Over the Northern Border

Max Brand®

Fredrick Schiller Faust (1892–1944) was born in Seattle, Washington. He wrote over 500 average-length books (300 of them Westerns) under nineteen different pseudonyms, but Max Brand—"the Jewish cowboy", as he once dubbed it—has become the most familiar and is now his trademark. Faust was convinced very early that to die in battle was the most heroic of deaths, and so, when the Great War began, he tried to get overseas. All of his efforts came to nothing, and in 1917, working at manual labor in New York City, he wrote a letter that was carried in *The New York Times* protesting this social injustice. Mark Twain's sister came to his rescue by arranging for Faust to meet Robert H. Davis, an editor at The Frank A. Munsey Company.

Faust wanted to write—poetry. What happened instead was that Davis provided Faust with a brief plot idea, told him to go down the hall to a room where there was a typewriter, only to have Faust return some six hours later with a story suitable for publication. That was "Convalescence", a short story that appeared in *All-Story Weekly* (3/31/17) and that launched Faust's career as an author of fiction. Zane Grey had recently abandoned the Munsey publications, *All-Story Weekly* and *The Argosy*, as a market for his Western serials, selling them instead to the slick-paper *Country Gentleman*.

The more fiction Faust wrote for Davis, the more convinced this editor became that Faust could equal Zane Grey in writing a Western story.

The one element that is the same in Zane Grey's early Western stories and Faust's from beginning to end is that they are psycho-dramas. What impact events have on the soul, the inner spiritual changes wrought by ordeal and adversity, the power of love as an emotion and a bond between a man and a woman, and above all the meaning of life and one's experiences in the world conspire to transfigure these stories and elevate them to a plane that shimmers with nuances both symbolic and mythical. In 1920 Faust expanded the market for his fiction to include Street & Smith's *Western Story Magazine* for which throughout the next decade he would contribute regularly a million and a half words a year at a rate of 5¢ a word. It was not unusual for him to have two serial installments and a short novel in a single issue under three different names or to earn from just this one source $2,500 a week.

In 1921 Faust made the tragic discovery that he had an incurable heart condition from which he might die at any moment. This condition may have been in part emotional. At any rate, Faust became depressed about his work, and in England in 1925 he consulted H. G. Baynes, a Jungian analyst, and finally even met with C. G. Jung himself who was visiting England at the time on his way to Africa. They had good talks, although Jung did not take Faust as a patient. Jung did advise Faust that his best hope was to live a simple life. This advice Faust rejected. He went to Italy where he rented a villa in Florence, lived extravagantly, and was perpetually in debt. Faust needed his speed at writing merely to remain solvent. Yet what is most amazing about him is not that he wrote so much, but that he wrote so much so well!

By the early 1930s Faust was spending more and more time in the United States. Carl Brandt, his agent, persuaded him to write for the slick magazines since the pay was better and, toward the end of the decade, Faust moved his family to Hollywood where he found work as a screenwriter. He had missed one war; he refused to miss the Second World War. He pulled strings to become a war correspondent for *Harper's Magazine* and sailed to Europe and the Italian front. Faust hoped from this experience to write fiction about men at war, and he lived in foxholes with American soldiers involved in some of the bloodiest fighting on any front. These men, including the machine-gunner beside whom Faust died, had grown up reading his stories with their fabulous heroes and their grand deeds, and that is where on a dark night in 1944, hit by shrapnel, Faust expired, having asked the medics to attend first to the younger men who had been wounded.

Faust's Western fiction has nothing intrinsically to do with the American West, although he had voluminous notes and research materials on virtually every aspect of the frontier. *The Untamed* (Putnam, 1919) was his first Western novel and in Dan Barry, its protagonist, Faust created a man who is beyond morality in a Nietzschean sense, who is closer to the primitive and the wild in Nature than other human beings, who is both frightening and sympathetic. His story continues, and his personality gains added depth, in the two sequels that complete his story, *The Night Horseman* (Putnam, 1920) and *The Seventh Man* (Putnam, 1921).

Those who worked with Faust in Hollywood were amazed at his fecundity, his ability to plot stories. However, for all of his incessant talk about plot and plotting, Faust's Western fiction is uniformly character-driven. His plots emerge from the characters as they are confronted with conflicts and frustrations. Above all, there is his humor—the hilarity of the opening chapters of *The Return of the Rancher* (Dodd, Mead, 1933), to give only one instance, is sustained by the humorous contrast between irony and naïveté. So many of Faust's characters are truly unforgettable, from the most familiar, like Dan Barry and Harry Destry, to such marvelous creations as José Ridal in *Blackie and Red* (Chelsea House, 1926) or Gaspar Sental in *The Return of the Rancher*.

Too often, it may appear, Faust's plots are pursuit stories and his protagonists in quest of an illustrious father or victims of an Achilles' heel, but these are premises and conventions that are ultimately of little consequence. His characters are in essence psychic forces. In Faust's fiction, as Robert Sampson concluded in the first volume of *Yesterday's Faces* (Bowling Green University Popular Press, 1983), "every action is motivated. Every character makes decisions and each must endure the consequences of his decisions. Each character is gnawed by the conflict between his wishes and the necessities of his experience. The story advances from the first interactions of the first characters. It continues, a fugue for full orchestra, ever more complex, modified by decisions of increasing desperation, to a climax whose savagery may involve no bloodshed at all. But there will be psychological tension screaming in harmonics almost beyond the ear's capacity."

Faust's finest fiction can be enjoyed on the level of adventure, or on the deeper level of psychic meaning. He knew in his heart that he had not resolved the psychic conflicts he projected into his fiction, but he held out hope to the last that the resolutions he had failed to find in life and in his stories might somehow, miraculously, be achieved on the higher plane of the poetry that he continued to write. Yet Faust is not the first writer, and will not be the last, who treasured least what others have come to treasure most. It may even be possible that a later generation, having read his many works as he wrote them (and they are now being restored after decades of inept abridgments and rewriting), will find Frederick Faust to have been, truly, one of the most significant American literary artists of the 20th Century. Much more about Faust's life, his work, and critical essays on various aspects of his fiction of all kinds can be found in *The Max Brand Companion* (Greenwood Press, 1996).

I

"It ain't hard at all," said the sheriff. "Most likely he thinks that nobody seen him because of the dark. And he's right when he thinks that nobody could make out his face. But the point is that there's lots of ways of identifying a gent, and one of the ways is by the hoss that he rides. And old Jeffreys is willing to swear that he made out the gray gelding of Bill Vance, the high-headed fool of a hoss that young Vance has been riding around lately. So all I'm going to do, boys, is to wait till the moon comes up and then slip out to the Vance place. The reason that I want you fellows to come along is because I never can tell when the Vance people will put up a fight. They got the spirit of a load of dynamite, and any old spark is lightning enough to set them off and blow the tar out of everything within reach."

"Till the moon comes up?" queried one of his men. "Well, that won't be more'n half an hour, I guess, at the most and. . . ."

But Jack Trainor, sitting in the next room of the hotel and hearing every syllable that was spoken because the wall between was of a thickness hardly rivaling cardboard, waited to hear no more. He had made out, from what passed before in their talk, that the sheriff had gathered the half dozen men in the next room to conduct an inquiry into the stage robbery that had occurred the night before. And now he had been struck rigid with horror by the mention of the name of Bill Vance, his brother-in-law.

Trainor had left Bill's house the previous evening after a

visit of a fortnight. It seemed impossible that young Vance should have committed the robbery, but on second thought Jack remembered that his host had been absent during the entire first half of the night, pleading a business call across the hills. Moreover, he knew that Vance was desperately hard pressed for money. He had made considerable loans to Bill in the past, but all that he could raise on a cowpuncher's pay had been little enough, considering the needs of a growing family. However that might be, he had no time to argue about possibilities. The important thing for him to do was to rush back to Bill's house and learn the truth from him and deliver the warning about the coming of the sheriff.

That was what he did. Five minutes later he was out of the hotel and on his horse galloping hard along the road. As he swung out of the saddle before the door, he saw the white rim of the moon slide up above the eastern hills. The house was black. The family slept. And yet, at the first rap at the door, there was an answering stir.

Did a guilty conscience make the sleep of Bill Vance light?

"It's me, Bill," he called softly, and a moment later the door was opened to him by his brother-in-law, the moonlight shining fully on his face and making him seem old and pale.

"What's wrong?" gasped out Vance.

"How d'you know that there's anything wrong?" demanded Jack Trainor sternly. "Who said that there was anything wrong?"

"I don't know . . . only. . . ."

"Bill," commanded Jack, "you got to tell me the whole truth. Did you stick up the Norberry stage?"

There was another gasp from the wretched Bill. Confession of his guilt, and his despair for the consequences of his act that now confronted him, showed at once in his face.

"It was only because I. . . ." He stopped short. "Who says I did it?" he asked.

"You're guilty, Bill," said Trainor. "And they know it. They know that the gent that stuck up the stage rode a gray horse. They recognized that high-headed young gray of yours, that Mike horse that you been riding lately."

"They co-couldn't," stammered Bill. "It was dark and. . . ."

"You did it, then?"

"Lord help me," groaned Bill.

"Better start by helping yourself. Bill, they'll be here in twenty minutes. They were to start by moonrise and then. . . ."

"I'll stay here."

"You're crazy, Bill. That'll be ruin. They'll get you sure. You ain't got the face to stand up before a jury. They'll see through you as clear as day."

"I don't care what they do to me. It would be ruin if I ran for it. What would become of Mary and the kids if I ran for it?"

The heavy truth of that statement bore in upon the mind of Jack Trainor. He regarded his sister's husband bitterly.

"Does Mary know that I've come back?" he asked.

"No. She's sound asleep, I guess."

"Then I'll tell you what I'll do. I'll take the gray horse and make a getaway. You stay here where you are and, if they ask, tell them that I was out last night, you don't know where, and that I've gone out again tonight, and that both times I took the gray horse. Understand?"

"Good Lord, Jack, you don't mean that you'll take the crime on your own head? Man. . . ."

"Shut up that talk. We ain't got the time for it. You got a family, and it's the needs of the family that made you do it . . .

but you'll never try it again, I guess."

"Never, so help me. . . ."

"Help yourself, Bill," said the other sternly. "You been looking around to the Lord and other folks for help long enough."

"But I can't let you . . . I'm not a low-enough hound to let you step in and take the blame for this."

"You got to let me. You got three people depending on you. I got none."

"But Mary knows that you didn't leave the house. . . ."

"She'll let it go as I want her to do . . . she knows that the family mustn't be ruined."

"But this may wreck your life, Jack."

"My life is young. If it's wrecked now, I got time to make a new life over again. Stop arguing and help me get the gray and throw a saddle over him."

Ten minutes later, on the back of gray Mike, he wrung the hand of his brother-in-law.

"They'll think that I started back for town and registered for a room at the hotel just as a bluff. Meantime, I'm going to ride for Jerneyville and show myself, and, when I get through at Jerneyville, there won't be any doubts about me being the man that done the stick-up of the stage last night. Good bye, Bill. Go straight. And put every cent of that money you got by the hold-up in such a place that it will be found and returned to them that lost it. A gent can't get on by taking things that he don't own by rights. So long!"

And, as he gave the gray his head, they could hear the drumming of many hoofs far down the road coming out from town. But Jack Trainor regarded them not. He had under him a fresh horse with a fine turn of speed, and, by the time the posse had finished making its examination of Bill Vance, he would be so far away that they could never hope to head him off without a change of horses.

So he swung toward Jerneyville, keeping the gray well in hand, and at an easy pace cantered down the main street of the village at midnight. There he picked out the bank, which was well guarded, he knew, dismounted, broke in the back door, making noise enough to attract the attention of an army, and, of course, he was promptly encountered by the watchman.

He knew that worthy, a fat and harmless fellow with a smile as bland as a summer sky. He had often thought that thieves who could not handle such a watchman as he must be stupid villains, indeed. Now Trainor tested his theory and found that it was perfectly workable. He stopped the first yell of the fat watchman with a blow of his fist and then knocked the gun out of the hand of the other.

It exploded as it struck the floor, while the half-strangled shriek of the fat man echoed through the village: "Murder! Robbery! Jack Trainor is robbing the bank!"

With that hubbub behind him, and the grim knowledge that he had certainly established his reputation as a criminal and been identified as such, Trainor hurried outdoors, sprang into his saddle, and let the eager gray show some of the speed that had been going into the steady pull at the bit earlier in the night.

II

The cry that the fat man raised in the bank at Jerneyville proved to be louder and longer than Trainor had dreamed. It struck up echoes that, so it seemed, raised men out of the ground for hundreds of miles. He rode southward at first, aiming at the Río Grande and safety in the confusion beyond that muddy little river. But the first four days brought twice that many brushes with pursuing posses.

The first day of his flight went by well enough. The second day it ceased to be a joke. The third day, hard pressed on two sides, he became a criminal in fact as well as in theory by stealing a horse, even though he left behind him the worn-out gray of twice the value of the animal he took in exchange. The law had no time to waste on such trifles as this. The point was that he now rode on property that was not his. The written law of the land would send him to prison for the act, and the unwritten law of the Southwest would hang him for the same reason.

It was on the third night that he decided that the trail southward was growing entirely too hot for him. The trouble was that they knew exactly what his goal was. 200 miles away flowed the Río Grande, but every mile of the 200 would be policed with men ready to shoot to kill.

There was another border to the north, ten times as far away, but, since his pursuers never dreamed that he would strike in that direction, he might safely reach it. So that night he turned his pinto north and west and rode like mad for the railroad. Before dawn he was beside the tracks. In the gray of the early morning light he was lying stretched on the rods of a thundering freight that shot him northward, covering a day's ride for a horse in the space of a single hour.

Yet all was not smooth on that trip to the Northland. By no means! Before it ended, he knew the hardness of the fists of a brakeman, and many a shack knew the hardness of the quick fists of Jack Trainor. He knew other things, also, but, at the end of ten days of fighting and starving and freezing, with the bitter weather biting him more and more, he found himself at length flung from a speeding train that was roaring through a mountain pass.

He turned a dozen somersaults when he struck the ground, but he sat up, sound in body and bone, although sadly bruised. And then he watched the train thunder away out of view down the pass. He was left alone, half frozen, with the cold of an early winter night numbing his body, and the Canadian Rockies soaring up on every side toward the cold shining of the stars. And never in his life had he felt such loneliness, such a sense of utter helplessness. To him, home meant the wide silence of the desert with hills rolling softly against the horizon. Such monster forest trees as those that marched in ragged ranks up these mountainsides were almost like human beings to Jack Trainor.

Yet, he must trust to fortune to strike through those same dark and forbidding trees and attempt to find food, for he was desperately hungry. Thirty-six hours of exposure without food of any kind gave him the appetite of a wolf, and like a wolf he stalked up the slope among the trees, bent on finding game.

A rising moon made the cold visible, so to speak, and gave it teeth to pierce to the very heart of the scantily clad cowpuncher. He trudged on up hill and down dale, feeling that, if he paused, the cold would numb his muscles so that they could not be used. And yet there was no sign of life before him or on any side.

The white moonshine was displaced by an ugly dawn, for no sooner did the sun show its edge than the sky was covered by a mass of clouds driving rapidly before the wind, and the day came up dim with the storm howling through the trees. A sort of madness came on Trainor. He had put many a long mile behind him, and now he decided that there was no chance of coming across the habitation of man in this direction, for he had reached not the slightest sign of a trail in all the distance he had covered. Therefore, he determined to turn back toward the tracks. Only madness could have given him that determination, for he was long past the point where he had sufficient strength to bring him to the spot from which he started during the night. Moreover, even if he wished to get back, that was now becoming increasingly difficult, for whirls of snow began to appear on the wind, blowing through the branches above him softly, and spotting the solid black of the evergreens with white. This fall of snow was quickly transformed into such a downpouring as he had never dreamed of in his southland. It was like the descent of a myriad of gigantic moths flying down on noiseless wings and piling up on the ground.

Before an hour passed he was staggering through drifts knee high, where the wind had whipped and piled them on the edges of the open places. The air in front of him was filled with white. His senses began to reel; long since, he had lost all sense of direction. In fact, he had reached that point at which many a man would have given up, but pride kept him going. He could not admit defeat, no matter to what extreme he were pushed, and, just as he would have fought a human enemy to the bitter end, so he fought on mutely against weariness, cold, and devastating hunger.

Once he stumbled. He roused himself later to find that he had fallen into a profound sleep. And he was numb to the elbows and the knees. He got up and beat the circulation back in a frenzy, and then rushed blindly ahead, for he knew that, if he paused once again to rest in that fashion, the exhaustion of nearly three days without sleep would, combined with the cold, destroy him.

But now he found that his senses were swimming. He could not distinguish the way that he kept. Sometimes, he crashed into the trunks of trees. Sometimes, when he hooked an arm across his face to protect himself from the thicket that he seemed about to plunge into, he found that there was nothing but empty air and the rushing of the snow before him.

Every step he was taking now was straight away from the railroad. Indeed, ever since he started, save for a brief half hour, he had been working on a line due north from the tracks. And now a mere chance floored him, so greatly was he reduced. He slipped on a stone under the lee of a great tree, struck his head violently against the trunk, and collapsed to the ground. Had he possessed a tithe of his ordinary strength, he would not have minded that fall and blow on the head at all, but in his present condition of exhaustion it was enough to throw him into the deep oblivion of senselessness.

He was roused from that senselessness as from a profound sleep by a huge voice that called to him out of an immense distance. He smiled and shook his head. It seemed to him that someone was calling to him to get up and start a day's work in the pitiless cold of the world—someone was asking him to leave a cozy bed.

But the voice thundered over him again. He felt himself being shaken. Cruelly he was wrenched to his feet. He was beaten and thumped, and ever that immense voice roared at him. Then suddenly the veil dropped from his eyes, and he beheld himself standing in the midst of a forest full of blowing snow with a monstrous man looming above him, pommeling him with one fist while with the other arm he held him erect, and all the while shouting to him to make him regain his senses.

That glimpse of the startling truth ended in a mist of blackness again, and he crumpled into a deep sleep once more. But, just before the sleep came on, he felt himself lifted and pitched over the shoulder of the stranger.

It seemed to him that a nightmare journey began. Sometimes, he was enduring another of those beatings. Again, he was being carried on by the giant, although this was obviously folly. What man was large enough to carry him through such a bitter storm as this, while the wind plucked at them and swung them back and forth?

After that a longer sleep ensued, and it was broken, at length, with a sense of burning in his throat and burning, also, of his feet and his face and his hands. He opened his eyes and looked up. Brandy had been poured down his throat. He was swathed in hot blankets. He was lying beside a red-hot stove. Then, as his senses cleared still further, he saw above him the strange giant of the storm, black-bearded, with bright, bright eyes, rosy cheeks, and a tangle of uncombed hair. Out of his throat issued a great roar, that familiar voice of his dreams: "Hello . . . hello . . . hello!"

The voice fairly drowned the mind of Jack Trainor, but he managed to smile faintly. "I'm here, right enough," he said.

At that, the big man slumped into a chair and heaved a great sigh. Jack saw that the other was on the point of collapse from exhaustion. Sweat was running down his face. The rosy cheeks were veined with purple from overexertion.

"Lord, Lord," groaned the big man. "I thought that you'd never come 'round. I thought you was going. . . ."

He did not finish his suggestion, but lolled back more heavily in his chair, laughing weakly and making a gesture to Jack to signify that all was well.

The man of the cattle ranges of the southland heaved himself up on his elbow and looked about him. He found that he was in a small cabin, the walls of which were of massive logs, with a small stove in the center, a bunk on one side, and guns, traps, and fishing tackle covering the walls. Plainly it was a trapper who had blundered upon him. Then it occurred to him with a start that he weighed a full 180 pounds.

"How far did you carry me?" he asked.

"Three miles . . . I guess," gasped the other.

"Three miles?" echoed Jack, and then, looking more closely at his companion, he saw that it was indeed possible. The man was a giant, standing several inches above six feet, and weighing twenty or thirty pounds above 200—and all of this solid muscle.

But now the prostrate giant recovered himself. He rose from his chair and staggered to a corner from which he began to produce bacon and flour, and in a few minutes he had the beginnings of a meal smoking on top of the stove. As for Jack, he felt that, had he been 100 miles away and soundly asleep, his nose would have brought him these tidings of food and roused him.

Sitting up to throw back his covers, he found that he was astonishingly weak. He had to lean back against the side of the cabin again, and the big man, reeling with weakness as though from liquor, laughed joyously at him.

"The last mile pretty near finished me," he declared. "I thought I was gone, my friend, I promise you. But I prayed to the good Lord. He gave me strength. And so here we are, both of us!" And he laughed again.

There was something at once so kindly and so childishly simple in what he said, and in his manner of saying it, that Jack felt his very heart warmed by the big man.

"Partner," he said, and found that his voice was strangely small and husky, "you've saved my life. Nobody else that I know of could've carried me the way you carried me."

"I?" said the other, shaking his head violently. "What I have done is nothing . . . nothing. But only think of the luck . . . that I saw the toe of your boot sticking up through the surface of the snow, and that I knew it was not a branch showing."

Jack Trainor shuddered and caught his breath. Had he been as near to death as that? Had the snow entirely drifted over him?

He held out his hand to the big man. "What's your name? I'm Jack Trainor."

"And I, Joseph Bigot."

"Joseph, before I come to the end of my life, I'll show you how I appreciate what you've done for me."

"*Tush,*" said the other, flushing a brighter red. "You talk about such things later. Now I got no time!"

And he resolutely turned his back upon his guest and went ahead with the preparation of the food.

III

A month had passed. The mountains were covered with a thick white crust that would bear the weight of a man. And behold a new Jack Trainor, whistling down the mountain trail! He was clad in a clumsy fur garment that obviously had been made for a bigger man than he. His appearance was that of a monster in a sagging skin. But he walked freely and easily on the far side of the trail, he entered the cabin, and he exhibited the duster of pelts that he had carried in.

Big Joseph Bigot sat cross-legged on the floor, working over the last broken trap that he had stayed at home to repair that day. His practiced eye looked swiftly over the catch of the day, and he shook his head.

"No more days like yesterday . . . but then, my friend, that is enough luck for one season, eh?"

"Sure," said Jack, smiling, "luck enough, I guess. And here's another that I forgot to throw in with the rest."

And, so saying, he threw down a dark and shining pelt, a fox skin, the fur of which was like blowing feathers, so soft and light was it. It brought a shout from Bigot. He plunged to his feet and seized the skin. He sprang to the door with it. He let the gray light fall upon it. Then he whirled and executed about the cabin a clumsy bear dance that threatened to wreck the place.

"Ah," he cried when he could speak, "ah, Jack, it is true, what I told you yesterday when we brought in the catch! You have beginner's luck! If we keep on, we shall be rich. You hear? Rich!"

Jack Trainor regarded his companion with a great deal of curiosity and even a trace of scorn. According to his own code, it was far better to conceal all traces of emotion. As for the bit of soft fur that he had taken from the trap, and that he now had shown, he had known that it was a particularly fine one to look at and to touch. But why it should bring such rejoicing from the trapper he could not imagine.

"I dunno," he said slowly, "but it looks to me like a pretty far cry from this here fur to being rich."

"Does it?" said Joseph Bigot. "Man alive, d'you know what that fur is?"

"What?"

"It's blue fox! It's the finest fur that a man can get. It's what every trapper dreams about. If I told you that a thousand dollars would be. . . ."

"A thousand dollars," gasped Jack, amazed.

"I dunno what the market will be," said Joseph Bigot, "but I know this one thing . . . that I'm going to write to the girl today and tell her that in the spring we can get married." He cast up both of his long arms and shook his fists at the ceiling. "The time's come!" he said. "I've waited twelve years, and now the time's come!"

Jack Trainor forgot about the fox skin and the price it might bring. Instead, he could think of nothing but the last statement of the big Canadian.

"D'you mean to say that you've been engaged to the same girl for twelve years?" he breathed.

Bigot laughed. "Twelve years I have waited," he answered enigmatically. "First I wait for one, and then I wait for the other . . . twelve years altogether."

And he would say no more about it until they had cooked and eaten their supper and cleaned up the tins. After that, they sat around for the long, bleak evening. Outside, the freezing sap in the trees was bursting with loud reports from time to time, for the thermometer had dropped fully thirty degrees since midday. At midday it had been cold enough, a wind at ten below zero coursing over the summit and shrieking through the trees. That wind had the edges of icy knives to go through and through even the thickest furs, and the only way to keep from being frozen was to stir about. Now, at night, there was not a stir of the air. The big pale moon moved up a cloudless sky. The mountains, under its light, were either black with forest and shadow or glistening in strange blue-white. And the cold was so terrible that it needed no wind to drive it home.

In the sides of the little cabin it found crevices and cracks through which to slide like rapier points, stabbing every living thing it struck. The stove roared, and the wood within it kept up a steady hissing of sap and humming, while the top of the stove was red hot. All the air in the room above the top of that stove was clear and warm. All the air below the surface of that stove was glittering with hoar frost. The upper parts of the bodies of the men were almost too warm, but below the knees they were slowly freezing. One could feel the sharply defined borderline between the upper and the lower strata of atmosphere by passing the hand through the air. It was almost like moving the hands from warm water into ice water.

Jack Trainor, in fact, had not stopped trembling during the first three weeks of his stay. But, after that, as he grew hardened exteriorly to the biting weather, and, as his body accumulated the natural protection of a thin layer of fat over its entire surface, he began to fare better. And now, thoroughly accustomed to the heavy weight of the thick clothes and the furs with which the generous Bigot had equipped him, inured to the drafts and the bitter sweep of the winds, Jack had commenced to enjoy his strange surroundings and his new life.

He had been of little use to Bigot at first, but by constant study he made himself a sufficient master of the work to tend a line of traps after Bigot had set them out, and in this fashion he was able to double the amount of ground that the big man covered with his lines. To be sure, he could never be more than a very clumsy amateur, for to become a really fine trapper one must begin in childhood to study animals and the ways of taking them. More than that, one must be born with a certain gift.

Merely by his ability to cover ground was he useful when it came to tending the traps. There were other ways in which he was of greater service, and chief among these was his skill as a hunter. To be sure, the hunting in the snow-covered mountains was quite a different thing from the hunting in the southern deserts. But, once a hunter, always a hunter, no matter in what climate or country or for what game. A man who can shoot deer will, up to a certain point, be an excellent hunter of anything else from coyotes to tigers. And Jack Trainor guarded the trap lines from those terrible enemies of the trapper that prowl through the night and devour before the dawn the prizes that the steel jaws have taken. Many a bobcat and lynx he dropped with his quick rifle, and Bigot, a most second-rate marksman in spite of a life spent in practice, wondered at these successes of his new ally.

As for the work he was doing, Bigot promised a share in the profits when the spring came and they returned to the lowlands, but the profits meant nothing to Jack Trainor. He was glad to have a haven during this winter. Moreover, he was beginning to see that the resolution he had so lightly taken, to sacrifice himself in the interests of his brother-in-law, was apt to lead to most lasting and disastrous results. During this winter, he was more or less free, for the stern weather and the inaccessible mountains would shut him off from discovery.

They had almost no communication with the outer world. Once a fortnight, Bigot tramped down to the nearest little town and post office. There he sent out his mail and collected what had come for him, purchased needed supplies—as much as he could carry upon his back—and turned again into the stern trail that led over the peaks to his little cabin. Other than this fortnightly touch with the world, they were utterly isolated. But what would happen when the spring came and the trails were opened? The arm of the law was long, and the servants of the law were fleet.

So it was that many a solemn thought drifted slowly through the mind of Jack Trainor as he sat on this evening in the cabin and listened to the booming of the frozen trees and felt the cold numbing his feet. Also, he was much amused by the actions of the trapper. Joe had brought out writing materials and placed them upon the little homemade table. He was sitting, with his pencil poised above the paper, the expression upon his face that of one determined to do or die, and feeling that death was nearer than accomplishment.

He felt that this time Bigot would welcome an opportunity to talk, and therefore he asked again: "And what about that story you started to tell me, Joe, about the twelve-year engagement? What's the yarn behind that?"

As he had half expected, Joe Bigot laid down his pencil with a sigh of relief and turned upon his companion.

IV

"You see," said Bigot, "up to the time that I was twenty, I didn't bother the girls none. I had other work, my friend, and I let them go their way while I went mine. But one day Nora Cary came walking by, and I turned around and looked after her. Ever since then I've never felt the same."

He paused, tamped his pipe, then frowned at the floor.

"Next week," he said, "I asked Nora to marry me. She laughed at me."

"And you forgot her, I hope?" said Jack fiercely. "If a girl laughed at me, I'd cut out my heart rather'n foller her."

"I guess that maybe you would," responded the trapper mildly. There was much about Jack that he did not understand, and that he made no pretense of understanding. "But I didn't. Next summer I asked her again, and she said no. Next winter I asked her again, and she stopped to think."

Jack Trainor swore softly. He was beginning to see in the steady patience of the big man a force that would easily wear down the patience, and impose upon the mind of a woman.

"I asked her the next spring again, and she said yes," went on the trapper, refilling his pipe. "After that I was happy for a couple of years, working all the time and saving up money until I had a lot of it put by. I had enough made to build a house and furnish it, and everything was all ready for the wedding next summer. But, when the time for the wedding came, Nora Cary wasn't there."

He began smoking so furiously that his face was almost totally obscured behind the fog.

"She'd run off with Bergen, that went to school with the both of us. They come back that fall and settled down, and next summer Nora had a baby."

He seemed entirely serene after that brief outburst of smoking. Jack Trainor leaned and listened to him with the most profound attention. He felt an actual awe of the big man, a mental awe as well as a physical one for the giant.

"Things kept on like that," said Bigot.

"You mean you never stopped loving Nora?"

Bigot looked at him in mild amazement.

"I said she was married," he said in quiet rebuke.

"I know . . . I know," said Jack impatiently, "but I mean . . . you were pretty fond of her just the same. You didn't pay much attention to any of the other girls in the town, eh?"

"I ain't got much time for girls," said Bigot without emotion. "That is, for girls outside of Nora. Three years ago she died."

Jack started. It was like the shock that comes when we hear of the death of a person we know. He had visualized Nora. He had been thinking of her, on this bitter night, in a well-warmed room in some village in the lowlands. And now, suddenly, he knew that she was long since dead. It took his mind with a wrench back to the stolid face of Bigot.

There was something so heart-wringing to him about that placid face that he rose and crossed the room with his quick, nervous step and dropped his hand upon the thick and heavily muscled shoulder of the trapper.

"Good old Joe," he said heartily and softly. "Good old Joe."

But Joe looked up to him in immense surprise.

"What is it?" he asked.

"Nothing," said Trainor, and turned and walked slowly back to his former place. When he faced the trapper again, all the signs of emotion were gone from his face.

"After Nora died," said Bigot, "I had my sister take the little ones."

"You did? Would her husband let you do that?"

"Him? He went away," said the trapper tersely.

The character of the dead woman's husband was blazoned in sudden light to the mind of Trainor.

"Children cost a good deal," explained Bigot.

"But what's this marriage in the spring?" asked, Jack, bewildered.

"Nora has a sister," said the trapper.

There was another gasp from the cowpuncher. "Well," he said with feeling, "I'll be eternally lost. You beat all get out with a tin hat on it, Joe. But go on. She has a sister, eh? And you're going to marry the sister so's she can take care of the kids that Nora left behind her when she died?"

This question the big man considered for a time with great care.

"She has the same eyes that Nora had," he replied after a time, "bright, snapping ones. They are black."

It was another blow to Jack.

"How old is she?" he asked.

"Twenty."

"Twenty. And you're thirty-two. That's a good deal of difference in the ages, isn't it?"

"I suppose it is. But what difference does time make?"

Again Jack was staggered. He had thought, before he began this conversation, that he knew the other from A to Z. Now he began to feel that he knew nothing except about the surface of Joe Bigot. Time meant nothing to Joe. Why should it mean anything to other persons?

"There is a funny thing," said Joe, sighing. "She must have letters. Every week she must have a letter."

"I've seen you writing them. But why? The mail only leaves once in two weeks."

"Why? I didn't ask her," replied the trapper. "All I know is that she wants me to write to her every week, a separate letter. And so I do it." Sorrow spread over his face darkly. "I write a letter every week," he reiterated. He said it as a man might speak of a plague. "It is very hard," and he sighed. "But, you see, it angers her when she doesn't get the letters, and yet it angers her when she gets them. Look!"

He took out his wallet. From it he removed a sheaf of letters written upon very thin white paper. He selected one of these letters and presented it to Jack. The letter under his hand showed a swift-moving and rather delicate script flowing across the page. It was a "dashed-off" hand, so to speak. He read:

Dear Joe:

I was away last Saturday at Jessie Haines's place. When I came back, I got three letters from you in a bunch. Oh, Joe, why do you write such letters?

I could sit in this room and write more about the mountains in five minutes, and more about love, too, than you write in a whole winter.

I know you're brave and strong and good, but a girl can't live forever on courage and strength and goodness. She needs something else.

Alice

Jack lowered the letter with a black scowl and passed it back to Bigot.

"So, you see," said Bigot, "that is why I am glad that I have the blue fox . . . that we have it, rather. It will be something for her to live on, eh?"

"You think that's what she meant . . . that she wanted money?" said Jack.

"Now you are laughing at me?" queried Bigot pathetically. "I know I am stupid. When people talk, I feel like when I was a little boy at the end of the line and they played crack the whip. That's the way when people talk, sometimes. I go sailing off into nothing. I don't understand what they are saying."

Jack Trainor, still smiling in spite of himself, shook his head. "I wouldn't mock you, Joe. In the first place, I like you too well. In the second place, I respect you too much. In the third place, I'm afraid to."

"Afraid to?" echoed the big man. He laughed softly. "You, Jack, fear nothing. You don't know what fear is."

"You think not?"

"I know it. Otherwise, you would never have walked into the mountains in that thin suit without food."

Jack Trainor shook his head. He had long before discovered that it was useless to argue with the trapper on this point. Joseph Bigot had decided to his own satisfaction that Trainor was a daredevil, and he could not be convinced to the contrary. He would have it that the braving of winter in the mountains, by a man to all intents and purposes unclothed and helpless, was a sign of sublime daring rather than ignorance.

"We'll drop that, then," said Jack. "But this Alice Cary . . . Joe, she sure knows what she wants and what she doesn't want, and one of the things that she doesn't want is the sort of letter that you write to her. I'd like to see one of 'em if it wasn't so personal you couldn't show it to me."

"Personal?" echoed the mild-eyed giant. "Why, Jack, why

shouldn't you see it? Here's a couple of 'em here."

"Ones you didn't send?"

"I sent 'em just the way they stand, except that I copied 'em clean."

He handed the two to Trainor, and the second one read:

Dear Alice:

I was glad to get your last letter. I hope you are feeling well now. I am getting along pretty well now. Last week I caught three red foxes and eighteen. . . .

"Say, Joe," called Trainor, "doesn't it strike you that she might be interested in something a pile more than she'd be interested in the sort of furs you collected?"

"In what, then? Ain't that what we got to live on?"

"Forget what you got to live on," said Jack. "A girl ain't interested in that. She'll live on grass seed and hope and be plumb happy, so long as she's got a gent around handy to tell her every once in a while that he's mighty fond of her. That's the way a woman is put together."

Joe Bigot sighed. "You know pretty near everything, Jack," he said. "If I had you to coach me, maybe I could write a letter that would keep her interested. Would you show me how it's done?"

"Why, look here"—Jack chuckled—"I ain't no professional slinger of fancy English. The best I can do is to work up an interest talking about what I want and why I want it."

"But," began Joe, "that won't help me."

"Why won't it?"

"What d'you mean?"

"Joe, tell me just why you want to marry Alice. Is it simply because she's her sister's sister?"

The big man pondered. "She's prettier than Nora ever

was," he decided. "And she's brighter. And she's kinder."

"Did you ever tell her all those things?" asked Jack.

"Ain't she got a mirror? Can't she look in her mirror and see a pile more than I could ever tell her?"

"That right there," cried Jack, "would be good enough to put into a letter! The thing for you to do is to loosen up. You got plenty to say. But you're like a good pitcher at the beginning of the season . . . you're afraid to put any stuff on the ball in the cold weather. Thing for you to do, Joe, is to thaw out. Show a few signs of spring. . . ."

"In January?" said Joseph Bigot, bewildered. "Spring in January? I don't know what you mean, my friend Jack."

Trainor threw up his hands. "Here," he said. "Are you dead certain that Alice Cary is more interested in you than she is in any other young gent down in those parts?"

"She has promised to be my wife," said Joe with an air of conclusiveness.

Jack sighed. "Because she gave you a promise," he said, "that's a pretty good reason for her to want to change her mind . . . or for her to think about changing her mind . . . ain't it? Man, man, when you tie up a dog with a rope, don't that make the dog want to get away, even if the place you tied him is all covered with marrow bones?"

"If he has the bones to eat," said Joe, "why should the dog wish to go? Such a dog would be a fool, my friend Jack."

Jack Trainor studied his friend's face with the air of one somewhere between anger and amusement and despair. At length he said: "If I sit down and work out a letter for you, will you use it to sort of get you started on a letter of your own?"

"Sure," said Joe. "Why not? Good Lord, Jack, that would be more than gold in my pocket."

"Then give me her picture, will you?"

Joe Bigot drew out the picture, and his companion sat for

some time studying it intently.

"Who's the young gent down in the plains," he said, "that she likes the best?"

"That'd be young Larry Haines," said Joe. "He was courting her ever since she was a little one."

"Well," said Jack, "this is where we start in giving Larry the outside edge of an outside chance. We're going to freeze him out!"

Jack Trainor walked briskly to the table. He sat down and for ten or fifteen minutes stared constantly at the picture. Then he began to write, and Joe Bigot forgot to smoke, so great was his wonder at the oiled smoothness with which the pen of the smaller man fled across the paper.

.

V

It was rolling ground, but not enough to limit the horizon with higher summits here and there. That sheet of green swept away eternally. It washed off to the ends of the earth, and through that clear air, indeed, one felt that the ends of the earth were well nigh visible. Only to the far westward there arose a cloud of pale and indefinite blue, wavering low against the sky. One had to be told to know that those were the Canadian Rockies. Standing on this high place in the low country, all at first seemed monotony. There was the marvelous green of the earth and the marvelous blue of the sky and the pure, pure white of the clouds that blew here and there. There was only the sky and the earth and, in between, a great space of freedom for the mind and the soul to wander. There were few trees. No trees were wanted. No hills were wanted. The smoother and the barer, the better. One did not wish for walls or checks of any kind.

There was a great sense of life in that illimitable plain. One felt it when there was no moving thing in view save the swift clouds. It was a fruitful land. One knew that the soil was rich without seeing the patch of black, yonder, that the plow had turned up not later than that morning, and that was beginning to dry out to a fallow gray as the sun and the wind worked on it. There was such wealth of soil, indeed, that the careless proprietors rather chose to let the land produce as it would than encourage it with the plow to any great extent.

There were groupings and dottings of cattle, also, wandering here and there, swinging their heads up and down slowly, while their mellow voices came booming, now in loud single calls, and now in more distant and more musical choruses. Toward the farther horizon, one could make out two small towns, each a blur of red roofs wonderfully pleasant between sky and green earth. Nearer at hand was another town—or, rather, just a chance cluster of houses.

On the top of the hill the girl had halted her horse, and her companion had followed suit, although both his horse and he manifested impatience at the pause. But Alice Cary was enjoying every minute, as was attested by the way in which she threw back her head and smiled. She looked from the green hills to the blue sky, and from the wide limitless sky back to the flowing hills.

"Ah, Larry," she said, "maybe you have to have other things, but I like this pretty well. Maybe you have to have Montreal, but I like this for my part."

His horse was dancing. He allowed the high-headed creature to prance in front of the horse of Alice. Thereby he cut off her view and forced her to consider him more closely.

"But that isn't answering me, Alice," he said. "And for the last week you've been dodging me. And . . . and you know that he's apt to be back almost any time now. I don't want to doubt you, but . . . but it sounds mighty as if you'd changed your mind."

His horse here worked past and threatened the roan of Alice with a flirt of his hoofs, whereat she reined her mount back deftly. She rode in divided skirts with a bold and swinging style that was extremely mannish in its pattern and extremely feminine in its effect. Her dress, too, with the cowboy red bandanna at her throat, her loose blouse, her heavy leather gloves, and the sombrero on her head was masculine in plan but wonderfully girlish in its results.

"Larry Haines," she said, "suppose I should tell you

that I had changed my mind?"

The horse of Larry Haines was changed to a statue, so closely did it follow the will of its master! Larry Haines, also, gained two inches in height as he jerked himself to rigidity. His lean, handsome face turned to iron, and his eyes glared at her. More than once before, he had half terrified her in this manner. Indeed, it was a part of the mystery and the charm of the man that attracted her. She knew Jessie Haines as well as she knew herself—or better. She knew herself like a book that had been carefully read. But Larry Haines, although she had grown up with him, remained unknown to her. He never shrouded himself with mystery, but there was about him a native strength that thrust other persons to a distance and kept them away from him. He had never wasted much time on girls until he had met her. And then his sudden burst of attentions, beginning only a short while after her engagement to the former suitor of her sister, had fairly swept her off her feet. She was frankly flattered, because the attentions of Larry Haines made her the envied and the wondered at among the girls of the village.

How he kept up that insistent siege; how, at length, in the absence of the big trapper, she had been won over and had given her promise to leave her home and run away with Larry to be married in the distant city of Montreal—all of these things made up a long story. And now she trembled as she faced the youth.

He took it very quietly. She might have known that he would act in this manner. And yet his quietness was worse than the angry shouting of another man.

"If you told me that you had changed your mind," he said, "I should believe you, that's all. You're free. You're independent. There's no reason why you shouldn't change your mind if you see cause for it."

But, while he spoke, the color went out of his cheeks and left them yellow—an unhealthy sallow. By that sign and the fixed glittering of his eyes she could guess at the emotion within him, but just the emotion was beyond her. It might be wild grief. Or it might be jealous rage. Or it might be simply injured vanity. But one could never tell what actually happened in the brain of Larry. Of his devilish temper, there could be no doubt. Since childhood, he had been a victim to silent bursts of rage that were dangerous to all around him. Now that he was grown older, his skill with weapons and the persistence of that same fierce temper made him dreaded by men of his own age. They actually shunned him. Wherever he went, he went alone. Strange to say, his dangerous qualities made him acceptable only in a company of girls, or old men and old women.

Why this should be, Alice had often wondered. But now she understood. Always, before, she had never come closer to the darker side of Larry than the reports that others made of him. But today it was easy to see the panther in him stirring under the surface. All the time that he was attributing perfect freedom to her to do as she pleased, she knew that madness was growing in his brain.

"You know that I wouldn't change my mind easily, Larry, where you're concerned?"

"You flatter me," said Larry

She looked fixedly at him. No doubt he was mocking both her and himself.

"I've never been easy about it . . . you know that," she said at length. "I've always felt that it was a sin to leave poor Joe in this way."

"A fellow that has to be pitied isn't worth thinking about!" exclaimed Larry Haines fiercely. "But let that go."

"You know what he's done and what he's been." said the

girl. "He's never changed. He was true to poor Nora when everyone was laughing at him. And then he took her babies. He took them just as tenderly as though he had been their father! A man like that . . . why, how could I refuse him when he asked me to marry him, Larry?"

"I don't suppose that you could," said Larry slowly. "I suppose he's fond of you just for the sake of your sister. But I see that makes no difference with you. You don't care to be loved for your own sake."

She raised her hand. His malevolence showed through too plainly. It made her wince.

"I admit," she said, "that I may have made up my mind to marry him for some such reason. But lately, Larry, I. . . ."

"Ah!" he exclaimed suddenly. "Lately you've been thinking about him, and, because he was a long distance from you, you suddenly began to make a hero out of him, you began to make him romantic!"

She flushed hotly and made no answer. He realized that he had gone much too far and instantly changed his tactics. His tone altered to the most soothing smoothness.

"It's because you're too good for him or for any other man," he said gently. "You see, Alice, you are ashamed of yourself because you can't love him. You think it's your duty. You don't see that he's exactly what he seems . . . a great clod of a man, Alice! There's no spark of real feeling in him. There's no fire in him! Why, you'd be miserable with him!"

She shook her head and smiled at him in such a cocksure and confident manner that he was amazed. Her flush, also, had changed in quality. There was a misty touch to her eyes that alarmed young Haines.

"I thought just what you think about Joe Bigot," she answered. "I've thought it all my life. I'll even confess now, Larry, that the reason I first became engaged to Joe was because I pitied him, and because I felt, if he were so willing to raise Nora's babies, I should at least try to do my share. I thought, too, that the only reason he cared for me at all was simply because I'm Nora's sister. But. . . ." She paused.

"Well?" asked Larry Haines impatiently. "Well?"

"But a few weeks ago there was a change. The letters I have been getting from Joe Bigot would have driven a saint mad. He told me about the weather. He told me about the number of furs he was taking. And that was about all. Any plowman could have written such letters. Then there was a change! You see, all the time, from the very first, I had been half hoping that behind the dull exterior there might be fire. And it turned out that I was right . . . I was right! It was like the breaking of a dam. I opened a letter, and his words picked me up on a flood and carried me out of myself! Oh, I wish I could show you that letter!"

"I wish you could," said Larry dryly. "I'd sure like to see Bigot's poetry."

"That's exactly what it was. It was poetry. The words had actually a rhythm to them. They keep running through my mind . . . not the real words, you know, but the tune of them."

"I see," said Larry in the tone of one who does not see and does not wish to see.

"He began in just the way he usually began a letter . . . except that there was a little difference in between the words that took my breath away. He began by talking about the cold and the hoar frost and the bursting trees around the cabin and the sense in the air that the world was freezing to death. And, after he had made such a picture of it that I started to shiver myself, he went on to talk about what the mountains would be like when the spring came. And he made such a picture, Larry, such a picture." Her words failed her; her voice trembled. "And all at once, toward the end of the letter, Larry, he told me that he felt he had been frozen all of his life, and that he had never been able to say what he felt, because he was really asleep . . . in a wintertime, so to speak. But now he felt a change. It was a thawing, a coming of spring. That was the first letter. It set me tingling to my fingertips to read it. I kept saying to myself . . . is the giant going to wake up? Oh, Larry, when I opened the next letter, I knew that he had. And all at once the spring was there! It seems that he loved Nora, or thought he did. But that is nothing to the way he cares for me. It isn't true that I only shine by her reflected light. And. . . ."

"In one word, you love him at last, Alice."

"Yes!"

"Then there's no more to be said about Montreal, of course."

"But, Larry, I'm terribly sorry."

"Of course you are. You're too nice a girl not to be sorry, Alice."

"Are you sarcastic now?"

"I?"

"I never know. I never can quite tell what's going on in you."

"That's because I'm so simple."

"At least, I know you'll forget me quickly."

"Perhaps you hope so."

"And I'm right, Larry."

"You're wrong. You know what I think of marriage."

"Marriage? You mean that a man should never marry more than once . . . that it's sacrilege to marry more than once? But what has that to do with mere love?"

"Mere love? It means just this . . . that a man, if he really is in love, can only love once. It's nonsense to talk about any second affairs. It's nonsense. It's Continental, no doubt, but it's not true. I tell you, my dear, that I shall never care for another woman."

"Oh, Larry!"

He was silent.

"I know it can't be true. You are only bitter and angry now. A month from today in Montreal you'll be smiling when you remember me off here in the grasslands."

"A month from today I'll still be here."

"Do you mean that?"

"I do."

"Larry, does it mean that there's going to be trouble between you and poor Joe?"

He started to deny it, then changed his mind, and there was a wicked gleam in his eye.

VI

They had shipped the pelts. Now they were ready to start eastward into the lowlands.

"But why," said Jack Trainor, "should I go with you?"

Joe Bigot blinked. "How else will you get your share of the money?" he said simply. "Unless you want me to send it after you."

"Money is nothing," said the cowpuncher. "Don't you lie awake worrying about me and money. We'll get on."

Bigot shook his head. "A quarter of that coin is coming to you . . . it belongs to you. If you don't take it, I'll put it in a jug and let it rest there until you come. I'll never touch it."

Trainor slapped him on the shoulder and laughed. "Well," he said, "let it rest in the jug, then. But I can't go home with you."

"You've got work some place?"

"I've got work all the time, now that the roads are opened up. I've got to keep moving, Joe. The law is behind me."

And he told the big man, for the first time, the true story about his flight to the North. At least, he told the truth from the point where he climbed onto the rods of the freight that took him on his first stage toward the Northland. But he left Joe to infer that the charges against him were true. When he had finished, he waited and studied the face of Joe with great curiosity. For all the simplicity of the big man, he was never able to tell exactly how Joe would act. He had not long to doubt.

"I'm sorry," said Bigot, "but when they come for you, we'll give them a hard job, the two of us. Why, Jack, you can't go off by yourself. You wouldn't have anybody to guard your back if they came at you from two sides at once."

Trainor was so touched that the tears sprang into his eyes, but he laughed it off. "But suppose she should guess that I wrote these letters for you? If I go, we must arrange a story, Joe. We must pretend that you and I met when you were coming down from the mountains, eh?"

It was so arranged. That simple lie would do harm to nobody. But the subject of the letters was a sore one with poor Joe. They made up the first real lie he had ever told in his life. He could not get over the fact that he had signed his name to words that he had not written.

"Forgery," he used to say, "that's what it is!"

"Bah!" Jack Trainor would answer. "It isn't a check, Joe."

But all of his persuading could never quite lift the cloud from the brows of Bigot.

"The only reason I can do it," he used to say, "is because I feel all the things you have said for me. I feel all those things, Jack, but I can't put them down in words. Because I feel them, it isn't altogether a lie if I let you write the letters for me, is it?"

And Jack, of course, would insist that it was a mere nothing. He himself had been passing through a strange time of trial. It had grown a peculiar pleasure and a peculiar torment to sit down before the picture of Alice Cary once a week and write to her as though he loved her. Not that the letters were hard to write, for, indeed, there was nothing easier. That faint smile of the girl in the picture was enough to keep his pen working forever, he felt. But, now that he was to see her in the flesh—what?

There were two dangers. The first, and what he felt to be

the more imminent, danger was that she would not be a tithe so charming as she was in the photograph. That would mean the destruction of a pleasant dream that, otherwise, he might have taken with him to his grave. The second danger, although it was one that he declared to himself over and over would never become an actuality, was that when he saw her she might be a thing of beauty even greater than the picture promised. And in that case, what would happen to his poor head, already swimming from too much thinking of her? And what would happen to his friendship for the man who had saved his life, great-hearted, unsuspicious, gentle Joe Bigot?

He knew his own impulsive nature well enough to fear what he might do. He dreaded seeing her because seeing her might make him desire to marry her. And once he desired to marry her, he felt that he would not be able to exercise any control. He would be gone in a flash.

Because of this, he had dreaded going home with Joe Bigot. But now he succumbed to the temptation. It was decided that he would be described, in the village, as a man who Joe had simply encountered on his way down from the mountains, and who he had brought back to help him work his little farm. With this plan in mind, they started home.

There was much to be done, however, before that journey was pressed on. In the first place, Jack Trainor must have a horse. Joe was equipped with a mighty-boned Canadian gray that was capable of carrying a ton on its back. Jack Trainor, a large man himself, was by no means content with such an animal.

"I've got to have speed," he declared to Joe, and for speed they started looking through the little town into which they had dropped out of the hills. They found what they wanted in the mid-afternoon on the place of a French-Canadian, 2,000 miles away from his beloved Quebec, cursing the land he farmed and caring nothing for the bad-tempered four-year-old that, as he said: "Eats the head off all day, and, when it is for riding . . . *mon Dieu! . . . le bon Dieu!* . . . it is a wild tornado!"

He offered the colt and the saddle for hardly more than the price of the latter alone, and straightway Jack saddled the lithe-limbed bay tornado and gave it its head. There followed five savage minutes. When the tornado was breathless, Jack raked a spur down its neck—not cruelly, but with an eye to the future.

It brought out another frantic effort. That effort did not avail to unseat the rider. And so Jack Trainor paid the price, swung into the saddle, and jogged onto the long East Road.

"I've seen good riding," said Joe Bigot, "but I never dreamed that a man could stay on a horse when a horse done what the bay has just finished doing."

"Bah!" Jack Trainor grinned. "This hoss means mighty well when it comes to bucking, but he ain't been rode enough to get any practice in fancy bucking. And it takes practice to make a good bucker, just the way it takes practice to make a man a good shot."

"There's exceptions to that."

"There are?"

"I know one man who's a dead shot, but he never practices hardly at all."

"You know such a man?"

"Larry Haines. He can shoot as straight as an eagle looks. He never misses. But he ain't had much practice."

"I'd like to meet up with him," said Jack slowly. "I've heard such a lot about him that I'd like to meet up with him. These dead shots . . . I've heard about 'em here and there, but I've never seen 'em pan out when it came to a showdown. Maybe this Larry Haines will be different."

Such was the mood in which they started. But as they journeyed on, and day after day, they struck farther and farther into the green heart of the cattle ranges of Canada, and Jack stopped pondering the question of Haines and the girl. He was too much occupied with the beauty of the country through which they were traveling.

"We'll go first," said Joe, "straight for the hill that looks over the town. It ain't very high, but it's high enough to give us a look over the country."

And so, on the last day, they struck for the hill, and, when they came in view of it, they could plainly make out, upon the top, the forms of two riders sitting their horses quietly there. Those forms grew into a woman and a man and these in turn grew more and more distinct, until Joe Bigot uttered a shout and spurred his horse into full speed.

"It's Alice!" he cried. "Come on, Jack!"

Now there was enough speed in the long legs of the bay colt to lay a circle around the big gray, but Jack Trainor held his mount in. He felt that it was too important a crisis simply to be rushed upon.

And so the face of the girl grew out slowly upon him until at length, with a cry of excitement, she started her horse on to meet her lover. Then Jack Trainor knew that the test would be even grimmer than he had expected, for she was far more lovely than the photograph had been able to hint.

VII

He passed the two at a trot. They were in a flurry of exclamations and laughter, and even big Joe Bigot seemed to have found his tongue. For that matter, Jack Trainor declared to himself that she would have roused a dying man to eloquence and foolishness. Another great question was settled in his mind. How would she greet the big trapper when he came down to her? After the letters that had been poured upon her, how would she reconcile their eloquence—and Jack felt that they were eloquent indeed—with the slow-moving mind of the big man? One glance at her excited face as he moved past the two settled that matter. She was thinking of nothing except that he had returned to her. There was no doubt about him in any respect.

But, in the meantime, the attention of Jack began to center around another figure, the companion of Alice Cary who had remained in the background. One glance at that sallow, handsome face, now strangely pinched and drawn as he looked down upon the girl greeting Bigot, and Jack felt sure that he had an answer to the riddle. It was Larry Haines, the invincible fighter, the sullen and dark-minded youth.

He saw Larry, now, produce the makings and roll a cigarette in spite of the blowing wind and the emotion that, Jack guessed, would have reduced any other man to trembling. The cigarette was lighted despite the gale, and then, as the issuing cloud of smoke hung for a moment and was dashed by the breeze, Jack Trainor came up to the smoker.

"Only the lucky ones," said Jack with great good cheer,

"have someone waiting for them, eh?"

Larry Haines turned toward him with an indecipherable expression.

"That sounds as though it might be true," he said. "Are you a friend of Joe's?"

"Just met him when he was coming down out of the hills. We drifted this way together."

"That's a pretty long drift, eh?" suggested Larry Haines.

"All depends," answered Jack. "It's long for some and short for some . . . I mean, for those that keep moving and don't care much where they get."

"I don't know that kind," replied Haines coldly.

"That's your misfortune," answered Jack in the same tone. "Those that keep moving like the road. They can't see any point in standing still the rest of a man's life."

He was disliking Haines heartily. He could gather from the expression of the other that the feeling was mutual. That distaste seemed founded upon nothing but chance. In the meantime, Joe and the girl had come slowly up the hill toward them, and Trainor gave his attention to the young couple

Alice Cary was obviously entirely happy. They had been talking about everything—nothing. She had had no chance to make comparisons or conduct an investigation. As for Joe Bigot, the big man was actually trembling with joy. And now and again he fixed upon Trainor a glance that was burning with gratitude.

The smile with which she acknowledged her introduction to Jack Trainor went through and through him, and then he found that she and Bigot and Haines and he were riding four abreast down the hill and toward the little red-roofed village in the distance. On the way Jack thought to himself: *She's sharp as a fox, for all of her careless ways. And Haines is sharp as a fox. Between them, it will be a close squeeze if they don't find out the truth. The thing for me to do is simply to get out of the town before they find any clues to work on. That would be the finish of poor Joe with the girl. And, no matter how beautiful she may be, he's too good for her.*

He was roused from this meditation by the voice of the girl saying: "Look at that tree yonder. What sort of a tree is it, Joe? But see the way it's budding, just like points of light on the tips of the twigs. I'll never see a tree bud after this, Joe, without thinking of something that you said about it."

Larry Haines twisted his head sharply toward Bigot. The idea of Bigot's having said something about budding trees apparently stunned him.

"Something I said? I don't remember," said Joe innocently.

The girl frowned. Had she not been in the saddle, she would probably have stamped, Jack decided. She did not want to go further into the matter. It was a reference Joe, if he were a true lover, should have caught up at once like a burning brand passed to him. It should have set him on fire, and now it seemed that he did not even remember having said it.

"Not said . . . but something you wrote. I suppose that's the same thing," said Alice Cary.

Her smile was a thin veneer over her anger, it seemed to observant Jack Trainor.

"I disremember," said Joe Bigot as heavily as before.

In the cabin in the mountains, he had formed the habit of looking to Jack for counsel whenever he was mentally cornered by a difficulty. Now his eye rolled toward his friend again, and the flash of Trainor's glance brought him up with an almost visible start.

"In a letter," he said. "Yes, I sort of vaguely remember it."

This brought a dark frown to the forehead of Alice, for it

was something that he should more than casually remember. If it had been an utterance out of his soul, as it had seemed, it should never be forgotten.

Jack Trainor, gnawing his lips with anxiety at one side of the little troop, remembered it well enough.

"It was about the winter being like night, and the spring being like day, and the budding of the trees the sunshine of the day . . . it was something like that," said the girl. "I thought it was beautiful, Joe."

Joe stirred under her reproachful glance, and then, feeling the ferret-like glance of Larry Haines upon him, he turned a bright crimson.

But Jack Trainor knew that there was a vital part of the simile left out—the part that referred to her in the same breath with the buds. It had been a comparison that had come out of his heart, seeing the faint smile of the girl in the photograph play like sunshine indeed in the dark, cold interior of the cabin. But now there was danger ahead in very fact. The suspicions of Larry Haines must be by this time fully aroused. No matter how the girl may have passed over the eloquence of her big lover and accepted it as real, Larry Haines would instantly know that Joe was perfectly incapable of saying such a thing as this—of conceiving such fanciful and complicated figures of speech.

But Haines said not a word to attempt to draw a confession from Joe. For that, Trainor respected his prowess and feared him the more. A man capable of playing a waiting game is always to be dreaded when it comes to a pinch. With all of his soul, Jack wished them well and safely out of the difficulty.

Luckily the down pitch of the hill—almost the only considerable incline in the entire vicinity—had urged the horses to a gallop, and now the whole troop fled down the slope at a round pace that blew the color back into the cheeks of Alice and sent the light gleaming into her eyes. She was laughing again when they reached the level once more, and so the party continued in the most perfect good humor until they reached the silent little street of the village.

All that way Larry Haines had said not a word.

Yes, decided Jack, *I must certainly move on this very night!* But, just as this conclusion became definite in his mind, Haines spoke for the first time.

"There's a man you ought to know, Joe," he said. "That old chap yonder. He's a trapper, too, and he spent the season up in the mountains pretty close to you. I think he went out from the same town to his trap line."

He watched Joe keenly as he spoke. Trainor watched the big man with no less attention to see how he would endure the test. And he was glad to note that Bigot neither changed color nor started visibly. There had not been one chance in a thousand that a trapper from the far-distant Rockies would come into the vicinity of the little town. It was like leaving someone in Peking and meeting him again in the middle of the Arizona desert. It was an unlucky chance, to say the least. But even at that, the probabilities were great that the old fellow ahead of them, just now in the act of sauntering across the street, had never even heard the name of Joe Bigot in the mountains unless he actually stumbled across a mutual friend.

However, it was necessary to make inquiries and follow up the remark of Haines. Trainor marked with pleasure that Bigot saw the need and accepted the risk. His face was unchanged except for a slight bulging of the heavy muscles at the angle of the jaw, and that small sign was enough to tell Jack of the spiritual strain under which the poor trapper was laboring. He veered his horse to the side, nevertheless, and paused beside the old man, whose bent body was token of the labor he had endured.

"Hello, stranger," said Joe. "The boys tell me that you been up trapping around Crampton. I been working a trap line up that way myself."

The other nodded, running his fingers thoughtfully through his short tangle of gray beard. But his face remained a blank. For that Jack was profoundly grateful.

"Look here, Minter," broke in Haines, "you must be a good deal of a hermit if you never ran across Joe Bigot in the mountains and yet you got your provisions from the same place."

"Joe Bigot?" echoed the old man slowly. "Joe Bigot?"

Here, as his face suddenly cleared under the light of knowledge, the heart of Trainor failed him.

"Sure I've heard of you, Bigot. I recollect the storekeeper talking about you. Used to say that you always took out enough grubstakes to've done two ordinary men. But then, a man can see in half a glance that you ain't ordinary, not by seventy pounds, I'd say."

He laughed heartily at his rather thin jest, his eyes snapping and glittering with enjoyment under their white brows.

"A man has to eat," said Joe good-naturedly. "And I reckon I do my share. But I walked my share of line, too."

"I guess maybe you did," said the old man enviously. "You got the legs for it, man! I guess you kept an extra measure of traps this winter, eh?"

"Extra lot of traps?" echoed poor old Joe Bigot feebly, feeling that the blow was about to fall.

"Why, yes. They told me you had a man out with you . . . somebody that wandered into your shack during a storm, and. . . ."

The cat was out. Could it be whistled back into the bag?

VIII

"In your cabin this winter?" cried Alice Cary with great eyes of astonishment.

"In my cabin? Why, yes," said Joe. "But, come to think about it, I guess I didn't write that he was there."

Jack Trainor was utterly astonished. He had never dreamed that the big, honest trapper had such possibilities. Taking it all in all, it was as roundly delivered a lie as he had ever heard told. And this from slow Joe Bigot!

"Write to me about him? You certainly didn't! But how long was he there?"

That vital question was avoided deftly by Joe Bigot. Just as it began, he blurted out some remark to the trapper about the severity of the winter and then expressed a desire to see him soon and declared that he would look him up. With that and a farewell wave, they passed on. Alice Cary repeated her question.

"How long was the stranger with you, Joe, and who was he? And what was he doing in a storm in the mountains?"

Again Jack Trainor was breathless. Again he felt the eyes of Bigot fumble hopelessly toward him, then, realizing that there was no succor in his companion, he searched about in his own brain for a sufficient answer. How much better it would have been if, at all costs, those letters had never been written, and if the pure truth could be told!

"He was a Russian, I think," said Joe Bigot. "His name was Rasmussen. He was running a line of traps up north of mine. But he was new to the country. One day a norther caught him out when he was hunting south, away off from his line. He'd seen my smoke, so he decided that it would be easier to make for my place than it would be to turn around and buck the wind and the snow to get back to his own lean-to. So he came down my way and got there just about froze."

"Poor fellow!" cried Alice. "Was he very far gone?"

Jack Trainor heaved a faint sigh of relief. It seemed that the great crisis was passed. Then he turned a little and looked at Larry Haines. That worthy had fastened his ferret eyes upon the face of Joe Bigot, and, although he never spoke, a subtle disbelief, a subtle mockery, had overspread his features. Apparently he had arrived at more of a conclusion than the girl had been able to come to in seeing through the untruths that Joe was telling.

Joe Bigot was continuing his new story with a great deal of fluency that more and more surprised Jack Trainor.

"He wasn't very far gone. But he thought he was. He wasn't used to the cold, you see."

"Not used to the cold! But I thought you said that he was a Russian?"

"I did. But he came out of the south of Russia."

"But don't they have cold winters every place in Russia?"

"Not down by Turkey, I think," put in Trainor calmly.

Larry Haines, who had been pricking his ears during these remarks, now flashed upon Jack an absolutely wolfish glance, and then forced his eyes deliberately away, as though he feared to reveal too much of his own malignance through that look.

"He came out of the south of Russia, down by Turkey," went on the big man glibly with a flash of gratitude toward Jack. "He wasn't used to the cold, and he was scared because he'd got numbed in places. But I brought him around. It didn't take long. There's some think that the only thing to do when folks are frozen is to rub them with snow. But I've always figured that to be fool talk. First I use cold water, and then I take water that's a little warmer and a little warmer, and that way I get the circulation going gradual again. I've tried rubbing with snow, and I've tried the other way. There ain't any comparison, I think. He came around fine, and after that I saw a good deal of him."

"He lived with you . . . and left his own trap line? That old fellow said that somebody was really living with you."

"Yes, I told them about it at the store once."

That unlucky day when he had told the storekeeper of the arrival of the stranger! How many details did the other trapper in the town know?

"He left his trap line because he thought that it was worth his while to learn what he could about setting out traps from me. Him and me used to walk my line of traps together, and so he picked up a good deal that I knew and that he didn't."

Here the girl laughed. "Joe," she confessed, "when he spoke at first about somebody being with you, I thought that there was a secret about it."

"Secret?" muttered Joe Bigot with an assumption of a vast innocence. "Why should there be any secret about it?"

Indeed, more and more Trainor began to feel that there had been possibilities of intelligence and quick wit in Bigot that he had completely overlooked. He had quite smoothed the matter over for Alice Cary, so it seemed, and it only remained to see how far Larry Haines could press his suspicions.

On the whole, Jack would have been happier had Haines taken an opportunity to cross-question the big trapper on the spot. But this he showed no intention of doing. He made no effort to corner Bigot. But the tiger was nevertheless in view

111

in the face that Trainor saw. Sooner or later he would get on the trail of Joe, and then he would be merciless should he run him down.

A moment later, Haines parted from them, shaking hands with Joe again and saying that he was glad to see him back, and shaking hands with Trainor, also. But he did this silently, and the eyes that they raised to each other were dark with enmity.

After that, they went on to the girl's house, and there they would both stay for supper. They were alone for a moment when she ran in while they were putting up their horses.

"I'm done for!" gasped Joe Bigot, turning white the instant they were by themselves.

"You're not done for," said Trainor hotly. "You're as safe as though you'd never told anything but the truth if you stick to what you've said. Keep going over it until you've got it safe in your head. Remember what you said . . . Rasmussen is a good name. It sounds like the sort of name that a man would never make up. The trouble with it is that it's a hard name to remember and keep straight. Then there's the yarn about Russia. Why the devil you had to make him a Russian, I can't tell."

"I can't, either," said Joe wretchedly. "That name Rasmussen . . . it popped out of somewhere in my head. After I'd used it, I thought that I'd have to explain it. So I just said that he was a Russian. You see? And then the stuff about his trap line. . . ."

"That's all right, because you had to have some reason for him being out there in the snows. And, taking it all in all, Joe, I want to say right here that it was about the best lying that I've heard in my life." He laughed softly at the thought. "I've been cornered myself once or twice, but I've never been able to invent things as fast as you did today, Joe. Why in the name of the devil, though, didn't you tell me that you'd mentioned me to somebody?"

"It was the storekeeper. I spoke about you after that first time. And then I plumb forgot what I'd said. Storekeeper went right out of my head. Talking to him ain't like talking to other folks, anyway. Sort of takes it for granted that when you go into the store you'll tell him everything you know. It's like talking to yourself. And listening to him talk is just like reading a newspaper. Nobody would ever think of wondering where he learned what he knows. He just seems to get all the gossip out of the air. But now the point is that it's done and can't be helped. I've told 'em that I've only knowed you a couple of days. What's to be done now? Jack, hadn't I better confess everything to Alice?"

"What!" roared Jack.

"I know. Sounds queer. And she'd be mighty mad! But I can't get along very well carrying this lie on my shoulders, Jack. I don't feel no ways nacheral."

"Listen to me," said Trainor solemnly. "If she finds out about this, she'll be through with you for good. You think that the lie is a terrible thing to her. I don't agree with you. She sort of would admire a man with the brains to get away with a good lie once in a while. And I don't think that she'd be any too much shocked if she knew that you'd told something that wasn't true but had had the brains to cover it up pretty well. It'd open up a new side of you to her. And, Joe, what she's looking for, it seems to me, is excitement."

"And that's where she'll find me out," said the unfortunate trapper. "I can never keep her entertained."

"I dunno," answered Jack. "Seems to me that you've made a pretty good start." He grinned as he spoke. "Haines is the rat that we've got to watch," he went on, "or he'll gnaw a hole in the ship and sink you before you know it."

"Aye, he hates me," said Joe, "I could see that."

"That ain't the important thing. The important thing is that he loves Alice. And he'd sell his soul to spoil your chances with her."

"If he should do that," said the trapper slowly, "I would kill him, Jack, I'm afraid."

That quietly spoken sentence stayed in the ear of Trainor with a strange ring. It was as though the threat had been spoken to him in person. It showed him, in a glimpse, other and unexpected depths in the nature of the giant. And the ability to hate profoundly was apparently one of these.

At the supper table that night, Trainor found that the girl's family was hardly distinguishable from many families that he had known in his own country. A sort of happy-go-lucky carelessness pervaded the talk and the manners. The talk this evening, of course, turned very largely upon Joe and his experiences during the winter. Most of all, the questions were directed toward the strange Russian who had appeared in the storm. But upon this one subject, strangely, Joe was very reticent, not as though reluctant to talk about the Russian, but as though the subject wearied him.

The meal was concluded happily enough, then Jack started for his hotel, and Joe walked part of the way with him.

"Tonight," said Trainor as they went down the quiet street with the dim sounds of voices coming from the houses on either side, "Joe, I've got to get under way. I've got to leave town."

"Tonight?" protested Joe eagerly. "But you can't do that, partner. I can't let you. You haven't had a chance to get to know folks. You haven't had a chance to get to know Alice."

"I've seen enough of her," said Jack with a peculiar heaviness of voice that caused the other to look at him in amazement. "I've seen enough," he went on, qualifying his statement, "so's I can get a good picture of her when I've gone along. I know how happy you'll be with her, partner."

At this, Joe clapped him on the shoulder. Still he could not understand the purpose of Jack in leaving at once.

"It's Haines," explained Jack. "It's Haines that bothers me. I can't get him out of my head."

"Haines? I thought he was perfectly quiet."

"That's it. Too quiet. He bothers me for that reason. He's got some plan in his head, and, when that plan begins to take shape, I think it'd be better for me to be out of town. I know too much. He's liable, some way, to corner you about me. Better for me to be gone, son."

Joe Bigot nodded. "He's a bad one," he admitted. "But you'll come back, Jack?"

"Sure," lied Trainor. "I'll be back. Keep a thought for me, Joe."

"I'll never forget you," said Joe Bigot simply. "I'll think of you every minute of my life. And if I marry Alice, I'll know that it's been on account of you. But still, it looks as though I'm getting something I don't deserve."

And with that he turned and went slowly up the street.

IX

To Jack Trainor, following with his eyes as the gigantic trapper swung down the street, it seemed that he was watching Joe Bigot march ahead to a great happiness, the greatest that had come to any man he had ever known. For himself, he felt that he was doing the only honorable thing in leaving the town and leaving it forever. It was not Haines. Haines was only a partial reason, although a strong reason, at that. But the real impulse came from the thought that he must not see too much of the girl. She was too beautiful for him to feel safe. He could not trust himself. There was a dash of headlong recklessness in his nature that had not been checked by the freedom of his life during the past few months, and that recklessness was tingling in his soul now. He knew that, given a fair opportunity, he would be swept off his feet.

It was this knowledge that made him go. But, in obeying all that was best in his heart, he was gloomy indeed as he turned around and faced the little shack of a building that did duty as a hotel in the little town. He had not yet reached the doorway of the small building when a hand was laid gently upon his shoulder. He whirled like a shot and found himself looking into the face of no other person than Larry Haines himself.

Larry Haines had apparently recovered from his deep gloom.

"I've a story to tell you," he said, "and there's such a laugh to it that I guess you'll forgive me for stopping you in the street with it."

"Go ahead," answered Jack, and waited uneasily. On the whole, he felt that he would have preferred frowns or even open threats to this continual smiling.

"Well," said Larry, "I'd better put it up to you to decide for yourself. When a bear goes off and starts barking like a fox, is it reasonable to suppose that he has actually turned into a fox, or sha'n't we conclude that there is a fox at hand doing the barking for him?"

"I don't get the drift of that," said Trainor coldly.

"I didn't think you would. But you'll get a laugh out of it by tomorrow at the latest."

There was such an open and defiant insolence under this apparent good nature that Trainor saw the other was simply aching for a fight and was perfectly confident of his ability to end the battle in his favor. It brought a flush into the head of Jack. Never in his life—and he had done many a deed of violence in his time—had he been so desirous of annihilating a man root and branch. But two things held him back. The first was a sudden knowledge sweeping over him that poor Joe Bigot would never get married to Alice Cary so long as this cunning devil was around to interfere. The second, speaking very frankly, was a decided doubt as to his ability to cope with Haines. He decided that he must not venture a battle until his back was against the wall. But first of all, he must find out what Haines knew and what he merely guessed. That was of the very greatest importance.

"Maybe I'll be laughing tomorrow, then," he said. "But I don't get the bear story."

Haines nodded. "I can't make you understand," he declared, "so I'll drop the fable and get down to facts. My friend, I've made up my mind to several things. The first is that Mister Rasmussen of wintry memory is a myth."

"Rasmussen? Well, that's strange. But why would

117

Bigot invent a yarn like that?"

Haines shook his head. "You are Rasmussen," he said. "That's plain, whatever your real name may be."

"Wait a minute," said Trainor. "I don't keep up with you. I'm a Russian trapper, you say? Well, Haines, I guess I'll get my laugh out of you without waiting until tomorrow."

"Bah!" snapped Haines, suddenly in dead earnest. "You know what I mean. I mean that you're the man who stayed with Bigot this winter. You must think I'm a fool not to see through it? You're the man who wrote the letters."

"Partner," said Trainor softly, "something has happened to your head. What letters?"

"All right," said Haines. "I was going to make a little proposition to you. But, if I can't do that, I'll turn around and go to Alice Cary in the morning and tell her what I suspect."

"And that is?"

"Why, simply that you were marooned in a storm, found Joe's cabin, had good reasons for wanting to stay quiet during a month or two, and so remained with him. While you were there, Joe tells you what a hard time he's having keeping up his end of the correspondence with Alice. You offer to take a hand. He tells you about her. You get interested. He shows you her picture. You sit down and start writing love letters on your own account, you might say, and you let him copy them and sign his name."

The narrative was so wonderfully faithful, so nearly exactly the truth, that Trainor was floored. He could neither laugh nor grow angry for an instant, and during that moment he knew that the ferret eyes of Haines had burrowed into his face and seen the truth in his confusion.

"By thunder!" cried Haines. "It is true, then. It's more than a guess. I couldn't believe it. But now I know that it's true."

Trainor ground his teeth. He had mistaken Larry's assumption of certainty for the fact. Now he must pay the penalty.

"And what's more," went on Haines, thinking aloud now, "if you stayed all winter with Joe, you did have a reason for it. And, if there was a reason for you to stay there, maybe there's a reason for other people to want you somewhere else, eh?" He was fairly rushing upon a complete discovery. "I think," continued Haines, "that, if I were to telegraph to certain places in the States, they'd be pretty interested in a description of you, eh?"

Trainor meditated quickly. It was plain that Haines felt his first step in destroying Bigot's influence with the girl must be to get rid of Joe's new friend. No matter if he intended to leave the next day and never return again. Haines would not believe that, and straightway he would bring the powers of the law down upon the head of Trainor. But what could he do to checkmate the younger man?

"Haines," he said, "you'd never find out anything in time to stop the wedding."

Haines started. "You admit everything, then?"

"That's not the point. I say you've started on the trail too late."

"Not a bit too late."

"What could you do? How could you stop things from going on the way they've started now?"

"Very easy. I get Joe Bigot and the girl together. Then I tell them that you have confessed, and I recount the whole story. Do you think that old pig-headed Bigot will have brains enough to laugh the story down? No, he'll blurt out a confession of his own and leave Alice and me laughing at him."

Jack Trainor saw that it was not more than the truth. Still he fought against that belief.

"You forget," he said, "that Joe's improving. Look at the

nice little series of lies he's just told today. And he was taken by surprise, at that. But now I'll get him prepared for you. I'll even work up his counter story."

"No," said Larry Haines. "You'll do nothing like that."

"No?"

"Certainly not. You and I, my friend, are coming to an understanding!"

"Impossible, Haines. I'm Bigot's friend.

"You are? You'll be more my friend than you are his before I'm through with you."

Trainor shrugged his shoulder. A slight chill was creeping over him. He could not estimate what strength the other might have in reserve.

"I can pay a high price," went on Haines calmly.

"You can? Not high enough," answered Jack.

"Good!" said Haines. "I'm glad to see that you're not going to start by talking virtue and end up by talking dollars. I'd rather have the dollars talk from the first. It's cheaper that way. I can begin, you see, by offering to keep away from the telegraph."

"You start with that. What that means I can't tell."

"I'm not asking you to confess anything about that. I'm asking you simply to listen to reason after you've heard me state my terms. The first of them is that I won't try to get the law on your shoulders. The second one is that I'll give you a fat little stake for yourself. Understand?"

"A stake for myself and no jail," said Trainor curtly. "That sounds good to me!"

"Now we're beginning to talk business, eh?"

"Looks that way. How much of a stake, though?"

Haines hesitated. "A thousand . . . ," he began.

Trainor laughed. "I thought we were going to talk business?" he said.

"How much do you want?"

"A pile more than a thousand."

"Why should you get it?"

"Because I'm going to give you a signed confession telling you everything from the first."

Haines jerked back his head and laughed softly to himself.

"I'll boost it over a thousand, then," he said. "Nobody has ever had to call me a miser."

"How high above? Remember, you're bidding for a wife."

There was an angry snarl from the other at this implication, but he said no articulate word.

"I'll make that two thousand dollars cold, my friend! Will that do you?"

"That's about right. That gives me a little leeway." He paused. "Suppose you give me a check for that right now?"

"Well, I can give you my note for it. Step into the hotel.

"Come up to my room. I've got to get a room, and we can talk things over there, eh?"

Accordingly Larry Haines followed into the hotel where Jack secured a room and went up to it in the company of the other. There he sat down to the little table in the center of the room and took paper and pen and ink out of the drawer.

"Now," he said, "I'll sit here and watch you do it, and you sit right over there, opposite, and write out the confession. And, when you're through with it, I'll give you an I.O.U. Will that do?"

"Certainly," said Trainor.

He stepped to the table, dragged up a chair, and stooped as though to sit down. Instead of lowering himself into the chair, however, he shot out his right fist. It landed high along the side of Larry's head. The latter had seen the shadow of the arm dart out across the top of the table and had flinched. Even in that infinitely slight moment, he had been able to reach the gun that he wore concealed in his clothes, for, when he toppled to the floor and Jack rushed around the table to pick him up, he found that the long Colt was lying in the loose fingers of the fallen man. It was such a tribute to his speed that it sent the shivers again flying up Trainor's back. Suppose it had been gun play?

X

If he felt any scruples, however, they were short lived. He had, to be sure, tricked the man shamefully. But all things were fair, so it seemed, in combating one who did not hesitate to purchase a wife, and who, on the way to that end, thought nothing of buying the honor of another man. In the meantime, he had need for speed of hand rather than debates of conscience. Quickly he ripped up a sheet, and with the bands he bound Larry hand and foot and gagged him. All this he accomplished before the latter opened his eyes. The blow had landed just back of the temple where the skull is softest and thinnest and a great purple blur was beginning to show up where the hair did not cover it.

He had hardly ended this task when there was a trample of feet in the hall and then the rap and the voice of the landlord at the same instant. The door opened, but Jack Trainor was there, barring the entrance.

"Something fell," said the landlord. "I heard something drop. Anything wrong?"

"I was tilted back in my chair," said Trainor glibly, "and it fell over backward with me. I've got a bruised back. That's all that's been injured."

The landlord looked as though he would enter, but presently he nodded, and then withdrew. Trainor closed and locked the door and returned to his victim.

He found that Haines was in the act of struggling weakly to a sitting position, his eyes blank and troubled, but, at the first glimpse of Trainor, the face of Haines flooded with intelligence and hatred.

"Now," said Jack, drawing his revolver and laying it ostentatiously upon the table, "the time has come for us to talk business of a different kind from what you've expected, I guess. In the first place, I want to tell you that you're right. I'm wanted. And I'm wanted for murder." The lie came easily from his tongue. "Murder, Haines, and I want you to know it so you'll understand that I'm ready to go the limit up here if you press me. A man can't be hung more than once, and he'll be hung as easy for one killing as for fifty." It was evident that Haines was impressed. "And so," said Jack, "I think I can trust you not to holler for help if I take the gag out of your mouth."

He did as he said. Haines gasped violently to recover his choked-off wind, and then he stared steadily at Trainor with such a consuming rage that the larger man shuddered.

"What's coming now?" asked Haines.

"The first thing is that I'm going to free your right arm and let you sit at that table to write a little note to your home saying that you're going to be kept out pretty late, and that you may sleep at the hotel. You hear?"

There was a snarl from Haines, but he carefully softened the tone so that it would not carry beyond the room in which he was imprisoned.

"I'll do what you want," he said. "I know that I've been a fool. I've trusted a stranger for the first time and the last time in my life. No matter what it costs me, I can't pay too high for it."

"Not even the woman you love?"

"Not even the loss of her is too high a price," insisted Larry Haines, although he lost his color as he spoke. Accordingly Jack freed his arm, and then helped him to the table and saw him take pen and paper and write:

Dear Dad:

I'm kept out. I have to talk about some new business with Joe Bigot, who just got back today from the mountains. I may have to stay at the hotel all night. Don't worry.

Larry

This note he then sealed in an envelope and handed to Jack, who got a servant and dispatched the message. Then he turned once more to the other and secured his right hand firmly. After that, he went on to tie Larry Haines hand and foot, so swathing him with bandages that he was well nigh like an Egyptian mummy.

"Because," he said, when a faint protest was wrung from Haines, "I've got to leave, and, if I leave, I've got to make sure of you. There's one safe way, Haines, and that's a tap on the head. Then I need not waste all this time. If you were in my boots, that's what you'd do, eh?"

The suggestion brought a quick and indescribably cruel smile across the lips of the other man, and then he made his face impassive once more.

"Well, that's a chance that may come my way one of these days. In the meantime, you lie here, partner, and keep thinking about what's going on outside. When they come up in the morning and let you loose, you'll find that Alice Cary and Joe Bigot are man and wife. No matter what you tell her then, the damage will be done, and in the end she'll be glad that she married him."

He moved the gag toward the lips of Haines, but the latter stopped him again.

"It seems a queer thing to me, stranger," he said to Jack,

"that a fellow like you would stand by and see such a girl as Alice Cary marry a blockhead like Bigot without lifting your hand. Why, man, she's on fire with brains and energy. She's the sort of girl. . . ."

"That I'd like to marry myself," said Jack. "That what you're driving at?"

"I tell you this, that she's fallen in love. She thinks that she's in love with Joe Bigot. But I know that she isn't. The man she's in love with is the man who wrote those letters out of the mountains . . . and you're the man."

Jack shook his head. "It won't work, Haines," he said. "You certainly hate Bigot, eh? But you can't make me do it. I don't say that couldn't be done. She's like prairie grass in August. It wouldn't take much to set her on fire, as you say. But the very things that make her incline to laugh at Joe are the things that will make her love him more in the end. Why, he's twice the man that you and I are put together. He doesn't talk as much, that's all. And what does a lot of chatter mean?"

"What's he done for you?" asked the other suddenly, making no effort to reply to this sudden flood of words.

"He saved my life."

"I thought it was that. Well, I'll stop talking. But I'd rather see her married to any man in the world than to Bigot."

After that, without a struggle, he allowed Jack to affix the gag between his teeth. Jack stood back, made sure that all the bonds were so fast that the victim could hardly lift his head, to say nothing of banging upon the floor in any manner, and then turned upon his heel and strode rapidly from the room.

Downstairs he found the proprietor and told him that he would be out for some time, and that Mr. Haines, in the room above, must not be disturbed at any cost, because he was doing some important work. Then, knowing that the door to that room was locked, and that the key was in his pocket, he

126

hurriedly sought Joe Bigot in the house of Alice Cary.

There was only one light burning in the old house when he arrived. But he knew perfectly well that it was the room of Alice in which the light burned and never the room of his friend. Alice's room it was, where she sat with her thoughts chasing through the clouds. She was full of the return of her lover, but that lover was by this time fast asleep and smiling.

Jack Trainor shrugged his shoulders. He could barely understand such a man. But at least he knew enough of Joe to be aware that the latter's apathy did not always spring from indifference. No matter how calm his exterior might be, his calmness was no true sign that there was a lack of fire in his heart. That he loved the girl with a quiet and enduring love, Trainor was certain.

He reached the house. In a minute he was in the room where Bigot slept, and roused him by dropping his hand upon the shoulder of the sleeper. Instantly Joe was up and grappling him with a bear-like power. It was a moment before he recognized the protesting voice of Jack and gasped out, as he relaxed his hold: "I thought it was Larry Haines come with a gun to get me because he couldn't stop me any other way."

It was such a basically true dream, in spite of its falsity, that Jack was amazed.

"Why does Haines hate you so, much?" he asked at length.

"Once him and me and two others sat in at a game of poker. I caught Haines cheating. I didn't say anything right then, but the next day, when I paid him what I'd lost to him, I told him what I knew. Ever since then he's hated me. He thinks that I try to tell about that game to everybody. But you're the first human being that's heard me speak of it."

It was such a tribute to the patient honesty of the big man that the heart of Jack Trainor softened suddenly. For years, perhaps, Joe had kept in perfect secrecy tidings about his greatest enemy that would have brought about the detestation of the rest of the acquaintances of the younger man. What motive of clemency had influenced him to this end? Once again, as so often before, Jack felt that he was brought into the presence of a fineness of heart of which he himself would be incapable.

He communicated the purpose of his errand at once. Larry Haines suspected everything. All must be put to the torch now. Tomorrow would be too late. If he loved Alice Cary—if he really felt that he could make her happy to the end of her life—he must prepare to push matters, for, in the morning, Larry Haines would be at liberty, and he would reveal the deception in the writing of the letters. Before morning dawned, Alice must be the wife of Joe Bigot.

Poor Joe listened to the storm of words and bowed his head. It was the result of the first real lie he had ever lived and acted.

"Go to her now," urged Jack softly. "Tell her that you've got to marry her now. And you can do it. You can have a minister here in no time. You can have everything fixed right away, eh?"

Joe Bigot, for answer, went to the window and leaned out into the cooler and the more placid air of the night.

XI

The man-of-all-work who took the letter from Larry Haines to his home hitched a horse to a cart, jogged the two miles into the country to the farmhouse of the Haines family, and then, having delivered the envelope, turned about and jogged peacefully back toward the village, his head jerking forward sleepily as the cart wriggled down the road. He had no idea of the hubbub that broke out behind him in the Haines house when he delivered the letter.

It was opened by a gray-haired lady, and, when she scanned the contents, she frowned, and then rose from her seat and began to walk the floor anxiously, very much as men do when they are in trouble. As a matter of fact, Larry Haines had managed to write into that apparently harmless note the message that all was not well with him. It had been done in an entirely simple manner, and it had succeeded because Jack Trainor knew nothing of the domestic history of the Haines family. The alarm note lay entirely in the opening address— **Dear Dad,** read Mrs. Haines—and caught her breath. Her husband had died ten years before!

It was one of those things that could not indicate a lapse of mind. One does not carelessly write down at the head of a letter a familiar name for someone who has been dead for ten years and in a quiet grave.

She read the note through. It was certainly sanely phrased. There was no evidence of liquor in it. Besides that, she knew that her boy did not drink. Moreover, it was his handwriting, or it seemed to be his handwriting. But, when she looked at the handwriting again, she said to herself that it was changed. And changed it certainly was, for with consummate art Larry Haines had altered some of the small details of his script. They had to be small things, and they had to be swiftly and smoothly done, for every line that he made was under the inspection of the hawk eye of the victor. What he managed to change was the method of crossing the Ts, not curling a line back from the bottom of the letter and swirling it over the top, making a separate and straight line through the letter to complete it. It was not hard, also, to follow the same method throughout the note. Every letter he formed with greater care than usual, leaving out all of those lazy little flourishes that tell where a careless writer's pen has trailed across the paper.

Mrs. Haines stared eagerly at the letter, and then she went to her desk and took out a letter that her son had written from Montreal the year before. One glance was sufficient to sweep all of the color from her face.

"Boys!" she cried, and dropped into her chair almost in a faint.

It happened by the grace of Providence that two tall nephews were at that moment laughing and jesting in the next room. They came hurrying to her, and she thrust the two letters into their hands.

"Larry is in danger . . . Larry is in danger!" she cried. "Henry . . . Bob . . . help him!"

They stared at her as though she might have lost her mind. What danger could have overtaken clever Larry Haines, whose prowess with his fists and with weapons of all kinds they knew only too well?

"It's a forged letter!" cried the poor mother. "Don't you see? It's addressed to his father . . . ten years dead! And look at the handwriting . . . forgery!"

The two crowded their heads close together, and they stared at the two letters.

"It is a forgery," said Bob suddenly. "It's got the swing of Larry's writing, but all the little touches are left out. Come on, Henry. We'll ride in to the hotel."

Five minutes later they were in the saddle, and their horses' hoofs were roaring down the hard road toward the village. They rode recklessly, for they were come of a reckless race. They covered the two miles before them in hardly more time than it had taken them to catch and saddle their horses, and then they flung out of their stirrups and rushed into the hotel.

"Where's Larry Haines?" they asked. "Seen him around here?"

"Sure," said the proprietor. "What's happened? Is his house on fire? He's right upstairs writing!"

Bob and Henry exchanged embarrassed looks.

"We'll be drifting back, then," growled Bob.

"Better see him and make sure, first," said Henry. "You never can trust anything until you've seen it with your own eyes. I've heard that said a pile of times."

He led the way up the stairs, and at the designated door they saw the filtering of light through the crack at its edges. They tapped, but there was no response.

"He'll be mighty mad when we come in," muttered Bob. "You know how he hates to be bothered. We better go back."

"I'd rather have him mad at me," insisted Henry, "than go back and face Aunt Marie without having seen him. I sure would!"

The fear of Aunt Marie made them knock again, and then call softly to tell Larry who was there.

Still there was no answer. They then tried the knob of the door and found that it was locked. Next they beat heavily against the door, and, when that summons brought no answer, they exchanged half-frightened, half-grim looks and in silence both put their strong shoulders to the door.

Something was certainly wrong when a light burned in a room where the door was locked and no one gave an answer. Down went the door with a crash, and, stepping over the threshold, they found the object of their quest lying near the bed, helpless with his bonds and nearly choked by the gag that had worked deeply into his mouth.

That was removed. Their knives slashed the strips of sheet away. For a moment he could only gasp for air, and then he managed to say: "Not a word of this . . . not a word of how you found me here. You understand? Otherwise, I'll do a murder on you!"

The injury done to his vanity was, after all, of the first importance in the eyes of Larry. But now, in another moment, he had regained his breath and could speak and act. His first move was to tear the revolver out of Henry's holster.

Then, briefly and savagely, he told them what he knew—that a conspiracy had been formed against Alice Cary—that she might at this very moment be in the midst of a ceremony that was making her the wife of the wrong man!

The mention of the name of the pretty girl and a wrong done to her sent the others into a fury. In a trice they were down the stairs. It was only a short distance down the street to the house of Alice Cary, but they traveled that distance on horseback, with Larry clinging beside Bob.

They reached the house. They rushed inside and shouted for Alice. The shout brought her sleepy father who, amazed, repeated the call for the girl, received no answer, and then threw her door open. But Alice was gone! Her bed had not been slept in!

He shouted these strange tidings down to the group below

and was answered by a wail of fury.

Out of the house they sped and to their horses.

"Try the minister's . . . try him at his house!" cried Larry.

And down the road they went at the full speed of the laboring, sweating, terrified horses. They flung themselves off when they reached the little vine-covered house of the man of God. And there, shining through the vines that tangled in front of his study window, was a light.

Yet he might be up reading. No, for they could hear other voices sounding in the room!

They crashed through the front door, and, almost in the same leap, they found themselves herding into the narrow, low-ceilinged room. The aged minister stood with his book in his hand and his eyes raised to heaven. Kneeling before him were Joe Bigot and Alice Cary. Behind stood the minister's wife and his man-of-all-work. At the trio's entrance, the witnesses withdrew.

"It's wrong!" cried Larry Haines, struck sick and white by this sight. "Alice, will you give me two minutes to tell you what I know . . . ?"

"Rise up," said the minister, "you are man and wife." He turned upon the intruders. "You have come too late," he said. "You should have spoken before. Hold your peace forever!"

But Larry cried, writhing in his passion: "There's been foul play! I've been bound and gagged to keep me from coming here and telling Alice what I know to. . . ."

"Wait, Larry," said Alice.

She spoke with such a perfect coolness in front of his excitement that he was abashed in spite of himself.

"I know everything," she said.

"Perhaps you think you do, but. . . ."

"I know everything," she answered, "about the letters."

"When . . . ?"

"Tonight. In the middle of the night Joe came and told me everything, just before he asked me to marry him. It wasn't what you would have done, I suppose, if you'd been in his place. And it wasn't even what that clever friend of his would have done . . . but it was the best thing, Joe."

She stepped a little closer to Larry Haines, her eyes suddenly sparkling.

"It took the knife out of your hands. But up to this very moment I wouldn't believe that you really intended to use it."

Color rushed into the face of Larry. He saw himself baffled, shamed. For an instant he glared around him, seeking some equal foe on whom he could work his vengeance. But, seeing none, he turned and rushed out into the night.

On that far-off hill that was the only elevation overlooking the beautiful little Canadian village, Jack Trainor halted his horse and looked back. He could make out two or three lights still burning in the town, but, even as he drew rein, one of these went out, then another. He waited for a few long minutes. At length the third light also disappeared, and no one could have told where the village lay in the deep blackness which covered the plain.

It was the blotting out of a great adventure for Jack. And, as he turned away, there was a weight of melancholy and a joy mingled with it, for he knew that he had learned to give more than he could ever take. For, as he said to himself, what did one added sorrow matter when, at the price of it, he could give great happiness to two?

Riders of the Dawn

Louis L'Amour

Louis Dearborn LaMoore (1908-1988) was born in Jamestown, North Dakota. He left home at fifteen and subsequently held a wide variety of jobs although he worked mostly as a merchant seaman. From his earliest youth, L'Amour had a love of verse. His first published work was a poem, "The Chap Worth While", appearing when he was eighteen years old in his former hometown's newspaper, the *Jamestown Sun*. It is the only poem from his early years that he left out of *Smoke From This Altar* that appeared in 1939 from Lusk Publishers in Oklahoma City, a book that L'Amour published himself; however, this poem is reproduced in *The Louis L'Amour Companion* (Andrews and McMeel, 1992) edited by Robert Weinberg. L'Amour wrote poems and articles for a number of small circulation arts magazines all through the early 1930s and, after hundreds of rejection slips, finally had his first story accepted, "Anything for a Pal" in *True Gang Life* (10/35). He returned in 1938 to live with his family where they had settled in Choctaw, Oklahoma, determined to make writing his career. He wrote a fight story bought by Standard Magazines that year and became acquainted with editor Leo Margulies who was to play an important rôle later in L'Amour's life. "The Town No Guns Could Tame" in *New Western* (3/40) was his first published Western story.

135

During the Second World War, L'Amour was drafted and ultimately served with the U.S. Army Transportation Corps in Europe. However, in the two years before he was shipped out, he managed to write a great many adventure stories for Standard Magazines. The first story he published in 1946, the year of his discharge, was a Western, "Law of the Desert Born", in *Dime Western* (4/46). A call to Leo Margulies resulted in L'Amour's agreeing to write Western stories for the various Western pulp magazines published by Standard Magazines, a third of which appeared under the byline Jim Mayo, the name of a character in L'Amour's earlier adventure fiction. The proposal for L'Amour to write new Hopalong Cassidy novels came from Margulies who wanted to launch *Hopalong Cassidy's Western Magazine* to take advantage of the popularity William Boyd's old films and new television series were enjoying with a new generation. Doubleday & Company agreed to publish the pulp novelettes in hard cover books. L'Amour was paid $500 a story, no royalties, and he was assigned the house name Tex Burns. L'Amour read Clarence E. Mulford's books about the Bar-20 and based his Hopalong Cassidy on Mulford's original creation. Only two issues of the magazine appeared before it ceased publication. Doubleday felt that the Hopalong character had to appear exactly as William Boyd did in the films and on television, and thus even the first two novels had to be revamped to meet with this requirement prior to publication in book form.

L'Amour's first Western novel under his own byline was *Westward the Tide* (World's Work, 1950). It was rejected by every American publisher to which it was submitted. World's Work paid a flat £75 without royalties for British Empire rights in perpetuity. L'Amour sold his first Western short story to a slick magazine a year later, "The Gift of Cochise", in *Collier's* (7/5/52). Robert Fellows and John Wayne purchased screen rights to this story from L'Amour for $4,000, and James Edward Grant, one of Wayne's favorite screenwriters, developed a script from it, changing L'Amour's Ches Lane to Hondo Lane. L'Amour retained the right to novelize Grant's screenplay, which differs substantially from his short story, and he was able to get an endorsement from Wayne to be used as a blurb, stating that *Hondo* was the finest Western Wayne had ever read. *Hondo* (Fawcett Gold Medal, 1953) by Louis L'Amour was released on the same day as the film, *Hondo* (Warner, 1953), with a first printing of 320,000 copies.

With *Showdown at Yellow Butte* (Ace, 1953) by Jim Mayo, L'Amour began a series of short Western novels for Don Wollheim that could be doubled with other short novels by other authors in Ace Publishing's paperback two-fers. Advances on these were $800, and usually the author never earned any royalties. *Heller with a Gun* (Fawcett Gold Medal, 1955) was the first of a series of original Westerns L'Amour had agreed to write under his own name following the success of *Hondo* for Fawcett. L'Amour wanted even this early to have his Western novels published in hard cover editions. He expanded "Guns of the Timberland" by Jim Mayo in *West* (9/50) to make *Guns of the Timberlands* (Jason Press, 1955), a hard cover Western for which he was paid an advance of $250. Another novel for Jason Press followed and then *Silver Canyon* (Avalon Books, 1956) for Thomas Bouregy & Company. These were basically lending library publishers, and the books seldom earned much money above the small advances paid.

The great turn in L'Amour's fortunes came about because of problems Saul David was having with his original paperback Westerns program at Bantam Books. Fred Glidden had been signed to a contract to produce two original paperback

Luke Short Western novels a year for an advance of $15,000 each. It was a long-term contract, but, in the first ten years of it, Glidden only wrote six novels. Literary agent Marguerite E. Harper then persuaded Bantam that Fred's brother, Jon Glidden, could help fulfill the contract, and Jon was signed for eight Peter Dawson Western novels. When Jon died suddenly before completing even one book for Bantam, Harper managed to engage a ghost writer at the Disney studios to write these eight "Peter Dawson" novels, beginning with *The Savages* (Bantam, 1959). They proved inferior to anything Jon had ever written, and what sales they had seemed to be due only to the Peter Dawson name.

Saul David wanted to know from L'Amour if *he* could deliver two Western novels a year. L'Amour said he could, and he did. In fact, by 1962 this number was increased to three original paperback novels a year. The first L'Amour novel to appear under the Bantam contract was *Radigan* (Bantam, 1958). It seemed to me, after I read all of the Western stories L'Amour ever wrote in preparation for my essay, "Louis L'Amour's Western Fiction" in *A Variable Harvest* (McFarland, 1990), that by the time L'Amour wrote "Riders of the Dawn" in *Giant Western* (6/51), the short novel he later expanded to form *Silver Canyon*, he had almost burned out on the Western story, and this was years before his fame, wealth, and tremendous sales figures. He had developed seven basic plot situations in his pulp Western stories, and he used them over and over again in writing his original paperback Westerns. *Flint* (Bantam, 1960), considered by many to be one of L'Amour's better efforts, is basically a reprise of the range-war plot which, of the seven, is the one L'Amour used most often. L'Amour's hero, Flint, knows about a hide-out in the badlands (where, depending on the story, something is hidden: cattle, horses, outlaws, etc.). Even certain episodes within his basic plots are repeated again and again. Flint scales a sharp V in a cañon wall to escape a tight spot as Jim Gatlin had before him in L'Amour's "The Black Rock Coffin Makers" in .44 *Western* (2/50) and many a L'Amour hero would again.

Basic to this range-war plot is the villain's means for crowding out the other ranchers in a district. He brings in a giant herd that requires all the available grass and forces all the smaller ranchers out of business. It was this same strategy Bantam used in marketing L'Amour. *All* of his Western titles were continuously kept in print. Independent distributors were required to buy titles in lots of 10,000 copies if they wanted access to other Bantam titles at significantly discounted prices. In time L'Amour's paperbacks forced almost everyone else off the racks in the Western sections. L'Amour himself comprised the other half of this successful strategy. He dressed up in cowboy outfits, traveled about the country in a motor home, visiting with independent distributors, taking them to dinner and charming them, making them personal friends. He promoted himself at every available opportunity. L'Amour insisted that he was telling the stories of the people who had made America a great nation, and he appealed to patriotism as much as to commercialism in his rhetoric.

His fiction suffered, of course, stories written hurriedly and submitted in their first draft and published as he wrote them. A character would have a rifle in his hand, a model not yet invented in the period in which the story was set, and, when he crossed a street, the rifle would vanish without explanation. A scene would begin in a saloon and suddenly the setting would be a hotel dining room. Characters would die once and, a few pages later, die again. An old man for most of a story would turn out to be in his twenties.

Once, when we were talking and Louis had showed me his topographical maps and his library of thousands of volumes that he claimed he used for research, he asserted that, if he claimed there was a rock in a road at a certain point in a story, his readers knew that, if they went to that spot, they would find the rock just as he described it. I told him that might be so, but I personally was troubled by the many inconsistencies in his stories. Take *Last Stand at Papago Wells* (Fawcett Gold Medal, 1957). Five characters are killed during an Indian raid. One of the surviving characters emerges from seclusion after the attack and counts *six* corpses.

"I'll have to go back and count them again," L'Amour said, and smiled. "But, you know, I don't think the people who read my books would really care."

All of this notwithstanding, there are many fine, and some spectacular, moments in Louis L'Amour's Western fiction. I think he was at his best in the shorter forms, especially his magazine stories, and the two best stories he ever wrote appeared in the 1950s, "The Gift of Cochise" early in the decade and "War Party" in *The Saturday Evening Post* in 1959. The latter was later expanded by L'Amour to serve as the opening chapters for *Bendigo Shafter* (Dutton, 1979). That book is so poorly structured that Harold Kuebler, senior editor at Doubleday & Company to whom it was first offered, said he would not publish it unless L'Amour undertook extensive revisions. This L'Amour refused to do, and, eventually, Bantam started a hardcover publishing program to accommodate him when no other hardcover publisher proved willing to accept his books as he wrote them. Yet the short novel that follows possesses several of the characteristics in purest form that, I suspect, no matter how diluted they ultimately would become, account in largest measure for the loyal following Louis L'Amour won from his readers: a strong male character who is single and hence marriageable; and the powerful, romantic, strangely compelling vision of the American West that invests L'Amour's Western fiction and makes it such a delightful escape from the cares of a later time —in this author's words: "It was a land where nothing was small, nothing was simple. Everything, the lives of men and the stories they told, ran to extremes."

I

I rode down from the high blue hills and across the brush flats into Hattan's Point, a raw bit of spawning hell, scattered hit or miss along the rocky slope of a rust-topped mesa. Ah, it's a grand feeling to be young and tough with a heart full of hell, strong muscles and quick, flexible hands! And the feeling that somewhere in town there's a man who would like to tear down your meat house with hands or gun.

It was like that, Hattan's Point was, when I swung down from my buckskin and gave him a word to wait with. A new town, a new challenge, and, if there were those who wished to take me on, let them come and be damned.

I knew the whiskey of this town would be the raw whiskey of the last town, and of the towns behind it, but I shoved through the batwing doors and downed a shot of rye and looked around, measuring the men along the bar and at the tables. None of these men did I know, yet I had seen them all before in a dozen towns. The big, hard-eyed rancher with the iron-gray hair who thought he was the bull of the woods, and the knife-like man beside him with the careful eyes who would be gun slick and fast as a striking snake. The big man turned his head toward me, as a great brown bear turns to look at something he could squeeze to nothing, if he wished.

"Who sent for you?"

There was harsh challenge in the words. The cold demand of a conqueror, and I laughed within me. "Nobody sent for me. I ride where I want and stop when I want."

He was a man grown used to smaller men who spoke softly to him, and my answer was irritating. "Then ride on," he said, "for you're not wanted in Hattan's Point."

"Sorry, friend," I said. "I like it here. I'm staying, and maybe in whatever game you're playing, I'll buy chips. I don't like being ordered around by big frogs in such small puddles."

His big face flamed crimson, but before he could answer, another man spoke up, a tall young man with white hair. "What he means is that there's trouble here, and men are taking sides. Those who stand upon neither side are everybody's enemy in Hattan's Point."

"So?" I smiled at them all, but my eyes held to the big bull of the woods. "Then maybe I'll choose a side. I always did like a fight."

"Then be sure you choose the right one"—this was from the knife-like man beside the bull—"and talk to me before you decide."

"I'll talk to you," I said, "or any man. I'm reasonable enough. But get this, the side I choose will be the right one."

The sun was bright on the street and I walked outside, feeling the warm of it, feeling the cold from my muscles. Within me I chuckled, because I knew what they were saying back there. I'd thrown my challenge at them for pure fun; I didn't care about anyone. And then suddenly I did.

She stood on the boardwalk straight before me, slim, tall, with a softly curved body and magnificent eyes and hair of deepest black. Her skin was lightly tanned, her eyes an amazing green, her lips full and rich.

My black leather chaps were dusty, and my gray shirt was sweat-stained from the road. My jaws were lean and unshaven, and under my black, flat-crowned hat my hair was black and rumpled. I was in no shape to meet a girl like that, but there she was, the woman I wanted, my woman.

In two steps I was beside her. "I realize," I said as she turned to face me, "the time is inopportune. My presence scarcely inspires interest, let alone affection and love, but this seemed the best time for you to meet the man you are to marry. The name is Mathieu Sabre. Furthermore, I might as well tell you now. I am of Irish and French extraction, have no money, no property but a horse and the guns I wear, but I have been looking for you for years, and I could not wait to tell you that I was here, your future mate and husband." I bowed, hat in hand.

She stared, startled, amazed, and then angry. "Well, of all the egotistical. . . ."

"Ah." My expression was one of relief. "Those are kind words, darling, wonderful words. More true romances have begun with those words than any other. And now, if you'll excuse me?"

Taking one step back, I turned, vaulted over the hitching rail, and untied my buckskin. Swinging into the saddle, I looked back. She was standing there, staring at me, her eyes wide, and the anger was leaving them. "Good afternoon," I said, bowing again. "I'll call upon you later."

It was time to get out and away, but I felt good about it. Had I attempted to advance the acquaintance, I should have gotten nowhere, but my quick leaving would arouse her curiosity. There is no trait women possess more fortunate for men than their curiosity.

The livery stable at Hattan's Point was a huge and rambling structure that sprawled lazily over a corner at the beginning of the town. From a bin I got a scoop of corn, and, while the buckskin absorbed this warning against hard days to come, I curried him carefully. A jingle of spurs warned me, and, when I looked around, a tall, very thin man was leaning against the stall post, watching me.

When I straightened up, I was looking into a pair of piercing dark eyes from under shaggy brows that seemed to overhang the long hatchet face. He was shabby and unkempt, but he wore two guns, the only man in town who I'd seen wearing two except for the knife-like man in the saloon. "Hear you had a run in with Rud Maclaren."

"Run in? I'd not call it that. He suggested the country was crowded, and that I move on. So I told him I liked it here, and, if the fight looked good, I might choose a side."

"Good. Then I come right on time. Folks are talkin' about you. They say Canaval offered you a job on Maclaren's Bar M. Well, I'm beatin' him to it. I'm Jim Pinder, ramroddin' the CP outfit. I'll pay warrior wages, seventy a month an' found. All the ammunition you can use."

My eyes had strayed beyond him to two men lurking in a dark stall. They had, I was sure, come in with Pinder. The idea did not appeal to me. Shoving Pinder aside, I sprang into the middle of the open space between the rows of stalls.

"You two!" My voice rang in the echoing emptiness of the building. "Get out in the open! Start now or start shootin'!"

My hands were wide, fingers spread, and right then it did not matter to me what way they came. There was that old jumping devil in me, and the fury was driving me as it always did when action began to build up. Men who lurked in dark stalls did not appeal to me, or the men who hired them.

They came out slowly, hands wide. One of them was a big man with black hair and unshaven jowls. He looked surly. The other had the cruel, flat face of an Apache. "Suppose I'd come shootin'?" the black-haired man sneered.

"Then they'd be plantin' you at sundown." My eyes held him. "If you don't believe that, cut loose your wolf right now."

That stopped him. He didn't like it, for they didn't know me and I was too ready. Wise enough to see that I was no half-baked gunfighter, they didn't know how much of it I could back up and weren't anxious to find out.

"You move fast." Pinder was staring at me with small eyes. "Suppose I had cut myself in with Blacky and the 'Pache?"

My chuckle angered him. "You? I had that pegged, Jim Pinder. When my guns came out, you would have died first. You're faster than either of those two, so you'd take yours first. Then Blacky, and after him"—I nodded toward the Apache—"him. He would be the hardest to kill."

Pinder didn't like it, and he didn't like me. "I made an offer," he said.

"And you brought these coyotes to give me a rough time if I didn't take it? Be damned to you, Pinder! You can take your CP outfit and go to blazes!"

His lips thinned down and he stared at me. I've seldom seen such hatred in a man's eyes. "Then get out!" he said. "Get out fast! Join Maclaren, an' you die!"

"Then why wait? I'm not joining Maclaren so far as I know now, but I'm staying, Pinder. Any time you want what I've got, come shooting. I'll be ready."

"You swing a wide loop for a stranger. You started in the wrong country. You won't live long."

"No?" I gave it to him flat and face up on the table. "No? Well, I've a hunch I'll handle the shovel that throws dirt on your grave, and maybe trigger the gun that puts you there. I'm not asking for trouble, but I like it, so whenever you're ready, let me know."

With that I left them. Up the street there was a sign:

MOTHER O'HARA'S COOKING
MEALS FOUR BITS

With the gnawing appetite of me, that looked as likely a direction as any. It was early for supper, and there were few at table. The young man with white hair and the girl I loved, and a few scattered others who ate sourly and in silence.

When I shoved the door open and stood there with my hat shoved back on my head and a smile on my face, the girl looked up, surprised, but ready for battle. I grinned at her, and bowed. "How do you do, the future Missus Sabre? The pleasure of seeing you again so soon is unexpected, but real."

The man with her looked surprised, and the buxom woman of forty-five or so who came in from the kitchen looked quickly from one to the other of us.

The girl ignored me, but the man with the white hair nodded. "You've met Miss Maclaren, then?"

So? Maclaren it was? I might have suspected as much. "No, not formally. But we met briefly on the street, and I've been dreaming of her for years. It gives me great wonder to find her here, although when I see the food on the table, I don't doubt why she is so lovely if it is here she eats."

Mother O'Hara liked that. "Sure 'n' I smell the blarney in that," she said sharply. "But sit down, if you'd eat."

My hat came off, and I sat on the bench opposite my girl, who looked at her plate in cold silence.

"My name is Key Chapin." The white-haired man extended his hand. "Yours, I take it, is Sabre?"

"Matt Sabre," I said.

A grizzled man from the foot of the table looked up. "Matt Sabre from Dodge, once marshal of Mobeetie, the Mogollon gunfighter?"

They all looked from him to me, and I accepted the cup of coffee Mother O'Hara poured. "The gentleman knows me," I said quietly. "I've been known in those places."

"You refused Maclaren's offer?" Chapin asked.

"Yes, and Pinder's, too."

"Pinder?" Chapin's eyes were wary. "Is he in town?"

"Big as life." I could feel the girl's eyes on me. "Tell me what this fight is about?"

"What are most range wars about? Water, sheep, or grass. This one is water. There's a long valley east of here called Cottonwood Wash, and running east out of it is a smaller valley or cañon called the Two Bar. On the Two Bar is a stream of year-around water with volume enough to irrigate land or water thousands of cattle. Maclaren wants that water. The CP wants it."

"Who's got it?"

"A man named Ball. He's no fighter and has no money to hire fighters, but he hates Maclaren and refuses to do business with Pinder. So there they sit with the pot boiling and the lid about to blow off."

"And our friend Ball is right smack in the middle."

"Right. Gamblers around town are offering odds he won't last thirty days, even money that he'll be dead within ten."

That was enough for now. My eyes turned to the daughter of Rud Maclaren. "You can be buying your trousseau, then," I said, "for the time will not be long."

She looked at me coolly, but behind it there was a touch of impudence. "I'll not worry about it," she said calmly. "There're no weddings in boot hill."

They laughed at that, yet behind it I knew there was the feeling that she was right, and yet the something in me that was me told me no, it was not my time to go. Not by gun or horse or rolling river—not yet.

"You've put your tongue to prophecy, darlin'," I said, "and I'll not say that I'll not end in boot hill, where many another good man has gone, but I will say this, and you sleep on it, daughter of Maclaren, for it's a bit of the truth. Before I sleep in boot hill, there'll be sons and daughters of yours and mine on this ground. Yes, and believe me"—I got up to go—"when my time comes, I'll be carried there by six tall sons of ours, and there'll be daughters of ours who'll weep at my grave, and you with them, remembering the years we've had."

When the door slapped shut behind me, there was silence inside, and then through the thin walls I heard Mother O'Hara speak. "You'd better be buyin' that trousseau, Olga Maclaren, for there's a lad as knows his mind!"

This was the way of it then, and now I had planning to do, and my way to make in the world, for although I'd traveled wide and far, in many lands not my own, I'd no money or home to take her to. Behind me were wars and struggles, hunger, thirst, and cold, and the deep, splendid bitterness of fighting for a cause I scarcely understood, because there was in me the undying love of a lost cause and a world to win. And now I'd my own to win, and a threshold to find to carry her over.

And then, as a slow night wind moved upon my cheek and stirred the hair above my brow, I found an answer. I knew what I would do, and the very challenge of it sent my blood leaping, and the laughter came from my lips as I stepped into the street and started across it.

Then I stopped, for there was a man before me. He was a big man, towering above my six feet and two inches, broader and thicker than my 200 pounds. He was a big-boned man and full of raw power, unbroken and brutal. He stood there, wide-legged before me, his face wide as my two hands, his big head topped by a mat of tight curls, his hat missing somewhere.

"You're Sabre?" he said.

"Why, yes," I said, and he hit me.

Never did I see the blow start. Never even did I see the balled fist of him, but it bludgeoned my jaw like an axe butt, and something seemed to slam me behind the knees, and I felt myself going. He caught me again before I could fall, and then dropped astride of me and began to swing short, brutal blows to my head with both big fists. All of 260 pounds he must have weighed, and none of it wasted by fat. He was naked, raw, unbridled power.

Groggy, bloody, beaten, I fought to get up, but he was astride me, and my arms were pinned to my sides by his great knees. His fists were slugging me with casual brutality. Then, suddenly, he got up and stepped back and kicked me in the ribs. "If you're conscious," he said, "hear me. I'm Morgan Park, and I'm the man who marries Olga Maclaren!"

My lips were swollen and bloody. "You lie!" I said, and he kicked me again, then stepped over me and walked away, whistling.

Somehow I got my arms under me. Somehow I dragged myself against the stage station wall, and then I lay there, my head throbbing like a great drum, the blood slowly drying on my split lips and broken face. It had been a beating I'd taken, and the marvel of it was with me. I'd not been licked since I was a lad, and never in all my days had I felt such blows as these. His fists were like knots of oak, and the arms behind them like the limbs of a tree.

I had a broken rib, I thought, but one thing I knew. It was time for me to travel. Never would I have the daughter of Maclaren see me like this!

My hands found the building corner and I pulled myself to my feet, and, staggering behind the buildings, I got to the corner of the livery stable. Entering, I got to my horse, and somehow I got the saddle on him and led him out of the door. And then I stopped for an instant in the light.

Across the way, on the stoop of Mother O'Hara's, was Olga Maclaren!

The light was on my face, swollen, bloody, and broken. She stepped down off the porch and came over to me, looking up, her eyes wide with wonder. "So it's you. He found you then. He always hears, and this always happens. You see, it is not so simple a thing to marry Olga Maclaren." There seemed almost regret in her voice. "And now you're leaving."

"Leaving? That I am, but I'll be back!" The words fumbled through my swollen lips. "Have your trousseau ready, daughter of Maclaren. I mean what I say. Wait for me. I'll be coming again, darlin', and, when I do, it will be first to tear down Morgan Park's great hulk, to rip him with my fists."

There was coolness in her voice, shaded with contempt. "You boast! All you have done is talk . . . and taken a beating!"

That made me grin, and the effort made me wince, but I looked down at her. "It's a bad beginning at that, isn't it? But wait for me, darlin', I'll be coming back."

I could feel her watching me ride down the street.

II

Throughout the night I rode into wilder and wilder country, always with the thought of what faced me. At daybreak, I bedded down in a cañon tall with pines, resting there while my side began to mend. My thoughts returned again and again to the shocking power of those punches I had taken. It was true the man had slugged me unexpectedly, and once pinned down I'd had no chance against his great weight. Nonetheless, I'd been whipped soundly. Within me there was a gnawing eagerness to go back—and not with guns. This man I must whip with my hands.

The Two Bar was the key to the situation. Could it be had with a gun and some blarney? The beating I'd taken rankled, and the contempt of Olga Maclaren, and with it the memory of the hatred of Jim Pinder and the coldness of Rud Maclaren. On the morning of the third day I mounted the buckskin and turned him toward the Two Bar.

A noontime sun was darkening my buckskin with sweat when I turned up Cottonwood Wash. There was green grass here, and trees, and the water that trickled down was clear and pure. The walls of the wash were high and the trees towered to equal them, and the occasional cattle looked fat and lazy, far better than elsewhere on this range. The path ended abruptly in a gate bearing a large sign in white letters against a black background.

TWO BAR GATE RANGED FOR A SPENCER .56 SHOOTING GOING ON HERE

Ball evidently had his own ideas. No trespasser who got a bullet could say he hadn't been warned. Beyond this gate a man took his own chances. Taking off my hat, I rose in my stirrups and waved it toward the house.

A gun boomed, and I heard the sharp *whap* of a bullet whipping past. It was a warning shot, so I merely waved once more. That time the bullet was close, so I grabbed my chest with both hands and slid from the saddle to the ground. Speaking to the buckskin, I rolled over behind a boulder. Leaving my hat on the ground in plain sight, I removed a boot and placed it to be seen from the gate. Then I crawled into the brush, from where I could cover the gate.

Several minutes later, Ball appeared. Without coming through the gate, he couldn't see the boot was empty. He was a tall old man with a white handlebar mustache and shrewd eyes. No fool, he studied the layout carefully, but to all appearances his aim had miscalculated and scored a hit. He glanced at the strange brand on the buckskin and at the California bridle and bit. Finally he opened the gate and came out, and, as he moved toward my horse, his back turned toward me. "Freeze, Ball! You're dead in my sights!"

He stood still. "Who are you?" he demanded. "What you want with me?"

"No trouble. I came to talk business."

"I got no business with anybody."

"You've business with me. I'm Matt Sabre. I've had a run in with Jim Pinder and told off Maclaren when he told me to leave. I've taken a beating from Morgan Park."

Ball chuckled. "You say you want no trouble with me, but, from what you say, you've had it with ever'body else."

He turned at my word, and I holstered my gun. He stepped back far enough to see the boot, then he grinned. "Good trick. I'll not bite on that one again. What you want?"

Pulling on my boot and retrieving my hat, I told him. "I've no money. I'm a fighting man and a sucker for the tough side of any scrap. When I rode into Hattan's Point, I figured on trouble, but when I saw Olga Maclaren, I decided to stay and marry her. I've told her so."

"No wonder Park beat you. He's run off the local lads." He studied me curiously. "What did she say?"

"Very little, and, when I told her I was coming back to face Park again, she thought I was loud-mouthed."

"Aim to try him again?"

"I'm going to whip him. But that's not all. I plan to stay in this country, and there's only one ranch in this country I want or would have."

Ball's lips thinned. "This one?"

"It's the best, and anybody who owns it stands in the middle of trouble. I'd be mighty uncomfortable anywhere else."

"What you aim to do about me? This here's my ranch."

"Let's walk up to your place and talk it over."

"We'll talk here." Ball's hands were on his hips and I had no doubt he'd go for a gun if I made a wrong move. "Speak your piece."

"All right. Here it is. You're buckin' a stacked deck. Gamblers are offerin' thirty to one you won't last thirty days. Both Maclaren and Pinder are out to get you. What I want is a fighting, working partnership. Or you sell out and I'll pay you when I can. I'll take over the fight."

He nodded toward the house. "Come on up. We'll talk this over."

Two hours later the deal was ironed out. He could not stay awake every night. He could not work and guard his stock. He could not go to town for supplies. Together we could do all of it.

"You'll be lucky if you last a week," he told me. "When they find out, they'll be fit to be tied."

"They won't find out right away. First I'll buy supplies and ammunition, and get back here."

"Good idea. But leave Morgan Park alone. He's as handy with a gun as his fists."

The Two Bar controlled most of Cottonwood Wash and on its eastern side opened into the desert wilderness with only occasional patches of grass and much desert growth. Maclaren's Bar M and Pinder's CP bordered the ranch on the west, with Maclaren's range extending to the desert land in one portion, but largely west of the Two Bar.

Both ranches had pushed the Two Bar cattle back, usurping the range for their own use. In the process of pushing them north, most of the Two Bar calves had vanished under Bar M or CP brands. "Mostly the CP," Ball advised. "Them Pinders are pizen mean. Rollie rode with the James boys a few times, and both of them were with Quantrill. Jim's a fast gun, but nothin' to compare with Rollie."

At daylight, with three unbranded mules to carry the supplies, I started for Hattan's Point, circling around to hit the trail on the side away from the Two Bar. The town was quiet enough, and the day warm and still. As I loaded the supplies, I was sweating. The sweat trickled into my eyes and my side pained me. My face was still puffed, but both my eyes were now open. Leading my mules out of town, I concealed them in some brush with plenty of grass, and then returned to Mother O'Hara's.

Key Chapin and Canaval were there, and Canaval looked up at me. "Had trouble?" he asked. "That job at the Bar M is still open."

"Thanks. I'm going to run my own outfit." Foolish though

it was, I said it. Olga had come in the door behind me, her perfume told me who it was, and even without it something in my blood would have told me. From that day on she was never to be close to me without my knowledge. It was something deep and exciting that was between us.

"Your own outfit?" They were surprised. "You're turning nester?"

"No. Ranching." Turning, I swept off my hat and indicated the seat beside me. "Miss Maclaren? May I have the pleasure?"

Her green eyes were level and measuring. She hesitated, then shook her head. Walking around the table, she seated herself beside Canaval.

Chapin was puzzled. "You're ranching? If there's any open range around here, I don't know of it."

"It's a place over east of here," I replied lightly. "The Two Bar."

"What about the Two Bar?" Rud Maclaren had come in. He stood, cold and solid, staring down at me.

Olga glanced up at her father, some irony in her eyes. "Mister Sabre was telling us that he is ranching . . . on the Two Bar."

"What?" Glasses and cups jumped at his voice, and Ma O'Hara hurried in from her kitchen, rolling pin in hand.

"That's right." I was enjoying it. "I've a working partnership with Ball. He needed help, and I didn't want to leave despite all the invitations I was getting." Then I added: "A man dislikes being far from the girl he's to marry."

"What's that?" Maclaren demanded, his eyes puzzled.

"Why, Father"—Olga's eyes widened—"haven't you heard? The whole town is talking of it. Mister Sabre has said he is going to marry me."

"I'll see him in hell first!" Maclaren replied flatly. "Young man, you stop using my daughter's name or you'll face me."

"No one," I said quietly, "has more respect for your daughter's name than I. It's true that I've said she was to be my wife. That is not disrespectful, and it's certainly true. As for facing you, I'd rather not. I'd like to keep peace with my future father-in-law."

Canaval chuckled and even Olga seemed amused. Key Chapin looked up at Rud. "One aspect of this may have escaped you. Sabre is now a partner of Ball. Why not make it easy for Sabre to stay on, then buy him out?"

Maclaren's head lifted as he absorbed the idea. He looked at Sabre with new interest. "We might do business, young man."

"We might," I replied, "but not under threats. Nor do I intend to sell out my partner. Nor did I take the partnership with any idea of selling out. Tomorrow or the next day I shall choose a building site. Also, I expect to restock the Two Bar range. All of which brings me to the point of this discussion. It has come to my attention that Bar M cattle are trespassing on Two Bar range. You have just one week to remove them. The same goes for the CP. You've been told and you understand. I hope we'll have no further trouble."

Maclaren's face purpled with fury. Before he could find words to reply, I was on my feet. "It's been nice seeing you," I told Olga. "If you care to help plan your future home, why don't you ride over?"

With that, I stepped out the door before Maclaren could speak. Circling the building, I headed for my horse.

Pinder's black-haired man was standing there with a gun in his hand. Hatred glared from his eyes. "Figured you pulled a smart one, hey?" he sneered. "Now I'll kill you!"

His finger started to whiten with pressure, and I hurled myself aside and palmed my gun. Even before I could think, my gun jarred in my hand. Once. Twice.

Blacky's bullet had torn my shirt collar and left a trace of blood on my neck. Blacky stared at me, then lifted to his toes and fell, measuring his length upon the hard ground.

Men rushed from the buildings, crowding around. "Seen it," one man explained quietly. "Blacky laid for him with a drawed gun."

Canaval was among the men. He looked at me with cool, attentive gaze. "A drawn gun? That was fast, man."

Ball was at the gate when I arrived. "Trouble?" he asked quickly.

My account was brief. "Well, one less for later," said Ball. "If it had to be anybody, it's better it was Blacky, but now the Pinders will be after you."

"Where does Morgan Park stand?" I asked. "And what about Key Chapin?"

"Park?" Ball said. "He's fixin' to marry the Maclaren girl. That's where his bread's buttered. He's got him a ranch on the Arizona line, but he don't stay there much. Chapin publishes the *Rider's Voice*, a better newspaper'n you'd expect in this country. He's also a lawyer, plays a good hand of poker, an' never carries a gun. If anybody isn't takin' sides, it's him."

Mostly I considered the cattle situation. Our calves had been rustled by the large outfits, and, if we were to prosper, we must get rid of the stock we now had and get some young stuff. Our cattle would never be in better shape, and would get older and tougher. Now was the time to sell. A drive was impossible, for two of us couldn't be away at once, and nobody wanted any part of a job with the Two Bar. Ball was frankly discouraged. "No use, Matt. They got us bottled up. We're through whenever they want to take us."

An idea occurred to me. "By the way, when I was drifting

down around Organ Rock the other day, I spotted an outfit down there in the hills. Know 'em?"

Ball's head came up sharply. "Should have warned you. Stay away. That's the Benaras place, the B Bar B brand. There's six in the family that I know of, an' they have no truck with anybody. Dead shots, all of 'em. Few years back some rustlers run off some of their stock. Nobody heard no more about it until Sheriff Will Tharp was back in the badlands east of here. He hadn't seen hide nor hair of man nor beast for miles when suddenly he comes on six skeletons hanging from a rock tower."

"Skeletons?"

Ball took the pipe from his mouth and spat. "Six of 'em, an' a sign hung to 'em readin' . . . 'They rustled B Bar B cows.' Nothin' more."

But quite enough! The Benaras outfit had been let strictly alone after that. Nevertheless, an idea was in my mind, and the very next morning I saddled up and drifted south.

It was wild and lonely country, furrowed and eroded by thousands of years of sun, wind, and rain. A country tumbled and broken as if by an insane giant. Miles of raw, unfleshed land with only occasional spots of green to break its everlasting reds, pinks, and whites. Like an oasis, there appeared a sudden cluster of trees, green fields, and fat, drifting cattle. "Whoever these folks are, Buck," I commented to my horse, "they work hard."

The *click* of a drawn back hammer froze Buck in his tracks, and carefully I kept my hands on the saddle horn. "Goin' somewhar, stranger?" Nobody was in sight among the boulders at the edge of the field.

"Yes. I'm looking for the boss of the B Bar B."

"What might you want with him?"

"Business talk. I'm friendly."

The chuckle was dry. "Ever see a man covered by two Spencers that wasn't friendly?"

The next was a girl's voice. "Who you ridin' for?"

"I'm Matt Sabre, half owner of the Two Bar, Ball's outfit."

"You mean that ol' coot took a partner? You could be lyin'."

"Do I see the boss?"

"I reckon." A tall boy of eighteen stepped from the rocks. Lean and drawn, his hatchet face looked tough and wise. He carried his Spencer as if it was part of him. He motioned with his head.

The old man of the tribe was standing in front of a house built like a fort. Tall as his son, he was straight as a lodgepole pine. He looked me up and down, then said: "Get down an' set."

A stout motherly woman put out some cups and poured coffee. Explaining who I was, I said: "We've some fat stock about ready to drive. I'd like to make a swap for some of your young stuff. We can't make a drive, don't dare even leave the place or they'd steal it from us. Our stock is in good shape, but all our young stuff has been rustled."

"You're talkin'." He studied me from under shaggy brows. He looked like a patriarch right out of the Bible, a hard-bitten old man of the tribe who knew his own mind and how to make it stick. He listened as I explained our set-up and our plans. Finally he nodded. "All right, Sabre. We'll swap. My boys will help you drive 'em back here."

"No need for that. Once started down the cañons, I'll need no help. No use you getting involved in this fight."

He turned his fierce blue eyes on me. "I'm buyin' cows," he said grimly. "Anybody who wants trouble over that, let 'em start it!"

"Now, Paw!" Mother Benaras smiled at me. "Paw figures he's still a-feudin'."

Old Bob Benaras knocked out his pipe on the hearth. "We're beholden to no man, nor will we backwater for any man. Nick, roust out an' get Zeb, then saddle up an' ride with this man. You ride to this man's orders. Start no trouble, but back up for nobody. Understand?" He looked around at me. "You'll eat first. Maw, set up the table. We've a guest in the house." He looked searchingly at me. "Had any trouble with Jim Pinder yet?"

It made a short tale, then I added: "Blacky braced me in town a few days ago. Laid for me with a drawn gun."

Benaras stared at me and the boys exchanged looks. The old roan tamped tobacco into his pipe. "He had it comin'. Jolly had trouble with that one. Figured soon or late he'd have to kill him. Glad you done it."

All the way back to the Two Bar we watched the country warily, but it was not until we were coming up to the gate that anyone was sighted. Two riders were on the lip of the wash, staring at us through a glass. We passed through the gate and started up the trail. There was no challenge. Nick said suddenly: "I smell smoke!"

Fear went through me like an electric shock. Slapping the spurs to my tired buckskin, I put the horse up the trail at a dead run, Nick and Zeb right behind me. Turning the bend in the steep trail, I heard the crackle of flames and saw the ruins of the house!

All was in ruins, the barn gone, the house a sagging, blazing heap. Leaving my horse on the run, I dashed around the house. "Ball!" I yelled. "Ball!" And above the crackle of flames, I heard a cry.

He was back in a niche of rock near the spring. How he had lived this long I could not guess. His clothes were charred and it was obvious he had somehow crawled, wounded, from the burning house. He had been fairly riddled with bullets.

His fierce old eyes were pleading. "Don't let 'em git . . . git the place. Yours . . . it's yours now." His eyes went to Nick and Zeb. "You're witnesses. I leave it to him. Never to sell . . . never to give up!"

"Who was it?" For the first time in my life I really wanted to kill. Although I had known this old man for only a few days, I had come to feel affection for him and respect. Now he was dying, shot down and left for dead in a blazing house.

"Pinder." His voice was hoarse. "Jim an' Rollie. Rollie, he . . . he was dressed like you. Never had no chance. Fun . . . funny thing. I . . . I thought I saw . . . Park."

"Morgan Park?" I was incredulous. "With the Pinders?"

His lips stirred, but he died forming the words. When I got up, there was in me such hatred as I had never believed was possible. "Everyone of them!" I said. "I'll kill every man of them for this!"

"Amen!" Zeb and Nick spoke as one. "He was a good man. Pappy liked him."

"Did you hear him say Morgan Park was with the Pinders?"

"Sounded like it," Zeb admitted, "but 'tain't reasonable. He's thick with the Maclarens. Couldn't have been him."

Zeb was probably right. The light had been bad, and Ball had been wounded. He could have made a mistake.

The stars went out and night moved in over the hills and gathered black and rich in the cañons. Standing there in the darkness we could smell the smoke from the burned house and see occasional sparks and flickers of tiny flames among the charred timbers. A ranch had been given me, but I had lost a friend. The road before me stretched dark and long, a road I must walk alone, gun in hand.

163

III

For two days we combed the draws and gathered cattle, yet at the end of the second day we had but 300 head. The herds of the Two Bar had been sadly depleted by the rustling of the big brands. On the morning of the third day we started the herd. Neither of the men had questioned me, but now Zeb wanted to know: "You aim to leave the ranch unguarded? Ain't you afraid they'll move in?"

"If they do, they can move out or be buried here. That ranch was never to be given up, and, believe me, it won't be!"

The cañon channeled the drive and the cattle were fat and easy to handle. It took us all day to make the drive, but my side pained me almost none at all, and only that gnawing fury at the killers of the old man remained to disturb me. They had left the wounded man to burn, and for that they would pay.

Jonathan and Jolly Benaras helped me take the herd of young stuff back up the trail. Benaras had given me at least fifty head more than I had asked, but the cattle I had turned over to him were as good as money in the bank, so he lost nothing by his generosity.

When we had told him what had happened, he had nodded. "Jolly was over to Hattan's Point. It was the Pinders, all right. That Apache tracker of theirs along with Bunt Wilson and Corby Kitchen an' three others. They were with the Pinders."

"Hear anything about Morgan Park?"

164

"No. Some say Lyell, that rider of Park's, was in the crowd."

That could have been it. Ball might have meant to tell me it was a rider of Park's. We pushed the young stuff hard to get back, but Jonathan rode across the drag before we arrived. "Folks at your place. Two, three of 'em."

My face set cold as stone. "Bring the herd. I'll ride ahead."

Jonathan's big Adam's apple bobbed. "Jolly an' me, we ain't had much fun lately. Cain't we ride with you?"

An idea hit me. "Where's their camp?"

"Foot of the hill where the house was. They got a tent."

"Then we'll take the herd. Drive 'em right over the tent!"

Jolly had come back to the drag. He chuckled. "Why, sure!" He grinned at Jonathan. "Won't Nick an' Zeb be sore? Missin' all the fun?"

We started the herd. They were young stuff and still full of ginger, ready enough to run. They came out of the cañon not more than 400 yards from the camp and above the gate. Then we really turned them loose, shooting and shouting; we started that herd on a dead run for the camp. Up ahead we saw men springing to their feet, and one man raced for his rifle. They hadn't expected me to arrive with cattle, so they were caught completely off guard. Another man made a dive for his horse and the startled animal sprang aside, and, as he grabbed again, it kicked out with both hoofs and started to run.

Running full tilt, the herd hit the camp. The man who lost his horse scrambled atop a large rock and the others lit out for the cliffs, scattering away from the charging cattle. But the herd went through the camp, tearing up the tent, grinding the food into the earth, smearing the fire, and smashing the camp utensils into broken and useless things under their charging hoofs.

One of the men who had gotten into the saddle swung his horse and came charging back, his face red with fury. "What goes on here?" he yelled.

The horse was a Bar M. Maclaren's men had beaten the CP to it. Kneeing my horse close to him. I said: "I'm Matt Sabre, owner of the Two Bar, with witnesses to prove it. You're trespassin'. Now light a shuck!"

"I will like hell!" His face was dark with fury. "I got my orders, an' I. . . ."

My fist smashed into his teeth and he left the saddle, hitting the ground with a *thud*. Blazing with fury, I lit astride him, jerking him to his feet. My left hooked hard to his jaw and my right smashed him in the wind. He went down, but he got up fast and came in swinging. He was a husky man, mad clear through, and for about two minutes we stood toe to toe and swapped it out. Then he started to back up and I caught him with a sweeping right that knocked him to the dust. He started to get up, then thought the better of it. "I'll kill you for this!"

"When you're ready," I said, then turned around. Jonathan and Jolly had rounded up two of the men and they stood waiting for me. One was a slim, hard-faced youngster who looked like the devil was riding him. The other was a stocky redhead with a scar on his jaw. The redhead stared at me, hatred in his eyes. "You ruined my outfit. What kind of a deal is this?"

"If you ride for a fighting brand, you take the good with the bad," I told him. "What did you expect when you came up here? A tea party? You go back and tell Maclaren not to send boys to do a man's job and that the next trespasser will be shot."

The younger one looked at me, sneering. "What if he sends me?" Contempt twisted his lips. "If I'd not lost my gun in the scramble, I'd make you eat that."

"Jolly. Lend me your gun."

Without a word, Jolly Benaras handed it to me.

The youngster's eyes were cold and calculating, but wary now. He suspected a trick, but could not guess what it might be.

Taking the gun by the barrel, I walked toward him. "You get your chance," I said. "I'm giving you this gun and you can use it any way you like. Try a border roll or shoot through that open-tip holster. Anyway you try it, I'm going to kill you."

He stared at me, and then at the gun. His tongue touched his lips. He wanted that gun more than anything else in the world. He had guts, that youngster did, guts and the streak of viciousness it takes to make a killer, but suddenly he was face to face with it at close range and he didn't like it. He would learn if he lived long enough, but right now he didn't like any part of it. Yet he wore the killer's brand and we both knew it.

"It's a trick," he said. "You ain't that much of a fool."

"Fool?" That brought my own fury surging to the top. "Why, you cheap, phony would-be badman! I'd give you two guns and beat you any day you like! I'll face you right now. You shove your gun in my belly and I'll shove mine in yours! If you want to die, that makes it easy! Come on, gun slick! What do you say?"

Crazy? Right then I didn't care. His face turned whiter but his eyes were vicious. He was trembling with eagerness to grab that gun. But face to face? Guns shoved against the body? We would both die; we couldn't miss. He shook his head, his lips dry.

My fingers held the gun by the barrel. Tossing it up suddenly, I caught it by the butt, and without stopping the motion I slashed the barrel down over his skull, and he hit the dirt at my feet. Turning my back on them, I returned the pistol to Jolly.

"You!" I said then to the redhead. "Take off your boots!"

"Huh?" He was startled.

"Take 'em off! Then take his off! When he comes out of it, start walking!"

"Walkin'?" Red's face blanched. "Look, man, I'll. . . ."

"You'll walk. All the way back to Hattan's Point or the Bar M. You'll start learnin' what it means to try stealin' a man's ranch."

"It was orders," he protested.

"You could quit, couldn't you?"

His face was sullen. "Wait until Maclaren hears of this! You won't last long! Far's that goes"—he motioned at the still figure on the ground—"he'll be huntin' you now. That's Bodie Miller!"

The name was familiar. Bodie Miller had killed five or six men. He was utterly vicious, and, although lacking seasoning, he had it in him to be one of the worst of the badmen.

We watched them start, three men in their sock feet with twenty miles of desert and mountains before them. Now they knew what they had tackled. They would know what war meant.

The cattle were no cause for worry. They would drift into cañons where there was plenty of grass and water, more than on the B Bar B. "Sure you won't need help?" Jolly asked hopefully. "We'd like t'side you."

"Not now. This is my scrap."

They chuckled. "Well"—Jolly grinned—"they cain't never say you didn't walk in swingin'. You've jumped nearly the whole durned country!"

Nobody knew that better than I, so, when they were gone, I took my buckskin and rode back up the narrow Two Bar

Cañon. It narrowed down and seemed to end, and, unless one knew, a glance up the cañon made it appear to be boxed in, but actually there was a turn and a narrower cañon leading into a maze of cañons and broken lava flows. There was an ancient cliff house back there, and in it Ball and I had stored supplies for a last-ditch stand. There was an old kiva with one side broken down and room enough to stable the buckskin.

At daybreak I left the cañon behind me, riding watchfully, knowing I rode among enemies. No more than two miles from the cañon toward which I was heading, I rounded a bend and saw a dozen riders coming toward me at a canter. Sighting me, they yelled in chorus, and a shot rang out. Wheeling the buckskin, I slapped the spurs to him and went up the wash at a dead run. A bullet whined past my ear, but I dodged into a branch cañon and raced up a trail that led to the top of the plateau. Behind me I heard the riders race past the cañon's mouth, then a shout as a rider glimpsed me, and the wheeling of horses as they turned. By the time they entered the cañon mouth, I was atop the mesa.

Sliding to the ground, Winchester in hand, I took a running dive to shelter among some rocks and snapped off a quick shot. A horse stumbled and his rider went over his head. I opened up, firing as rapidly as I could squeeze off the shots. They scattered for shelter, one man scrambling with a dragging leg.

Several of the horses had raced away, and a couple of others stood ground-hitched. On one of these was a big canteen. A bullet emptied it, and, when the other horse turned a few minutes later, I shot into that canteen, also. Bullets ricocheted around me, but without exposing themselves they could not get a good shot at me, while I could cover their hide-out without trouble.

A foot showed and I triggered my rifle. A bit of leather flew

up and the foot was withdrawn. My position could not have
been better. As long as I remained where I was, they could
neither advance nor retreat, but were pinned down and helpless. They were without water, and it promised to be an intensely hot day. Having no desire to kill them, I still wished to
make them thoroughly sick of the fight. These men enjoyed
the fighting as a break in the monotony of range work, but,
knowing cowhands, I knew they would become heartily sick
of a battle that meant waiting, heat, no water, and no chance
to fight back.

For some time all was still. Then a man tried to crawl back
toward the cañon mouth, evidently believing himself unseen.
Letting go a shot at a rock ahead of him, I splattered his face
with splinters, and he ducked back, swearing loudly.

"Looks like a long hot day, boys!" I yelled. "See what it
means when you jump a small outfit? Ain't so easy as you figured, is it?"

Somebody swore viciously and there were shouted threats.
My own canteen was full, so I sat back and rolled a smoke.
Nobody moved below, but the sun began to level its burning
rays into the oven of the cañon mouth. The hours marched
slowly by, and from time to time, when some thirsty soul grew
restive at waiting, I threw a shot at him.

"How long you figure you can keep us here?" one of them
yelled. "When we get out, we'll get you!"

"Maybe you won't get out!" I yelled back cheerfully. "I
like it here! I've got water, shade, grub, and plenty of smokin'
tobacco! Also," I added, "I've got better than two hundred
rounds of ammunition! You *hombres* are riding for the wrong
spread!"

Silence descended over the cañon and two o'clock passed.
Knowing they could get no water aggravated thirst. The sun
swam in a coppery sea of heat; the horizon lost itself in heat

waves. Sweat trickled down my face and down my body under the arms. Where I lay, there was not only shade but a slight breeze, while down there heat would reflect from the cañon walls and all wind would be shut off. Finally, letting go with a shot, I slid back out of sight and got to my feet.

My buckskin cropped grass near some rocks, well under the shade. Shifting my rifle to my left hand, I slid down the bank, mopping my face with my right. Then I stopped stockstill, my right hand belt high. Backed up against a rock near my horse was a man I knew at once although I had never seen him—Rollie Pinder.

"You gave them boys hell," he said conversationally, "an' good for 'em. They're Bar M riders. It's a shame it has to end."

"Yeah," I drawled, watching him closely. He could be waiting for only one reason.

"Hear you're mighty fast, but it won't do you any good. I'm Rollie Pinder."

As he spoke, he grabbed for his gun. My left hand was on the rifle barrel a few inches ahead of the trigger guard, the butt in front of me, the barrel pointed slightly up. I tilted the gun hard and the stock struck my hip as my hand slapped the trigger guard and trigger.

Rollie's gun had come up smoking, but my finger closed on the trigger a split second before his slug hit me. It felt as if I had been kicked in the side, and I took a staggering step back, a rock rolling under my foot just enough to throw me out of the line of his second shot.

Then I fired again, having worked the lever unconsciously.

Rollie went back against the rocks and tried to bring his gun up. He fired as I did. The world weaved and waved before me, but Rollie was down on his face, great holes torn in his back where the .44 slugs had emerged. Turning, scarcely able to walk, I scrambled up the incline to my former position. My head was spinning and my eyes refused to focus, but the shots had startled the men and they were getting up. If they started after me now, I was through.

The ground seemed to dip and reel, but I got off a shot, then another. One man went down, and the others vanished as if swallowed by the earth. Rolling over, my breath coming in ragged gasps, I ripped my shirt tail off and plugged cloth into my wounds. I had to get away at all costs, but I could never climb back up to the cliff house, even if the way were open.

My rifle dragging, I crawled and slid to the buckskin. Twice I almost fainted from weakness. Pain was gripping my vitals, squeezing and knotting them. Somehow I got to my horse, grabbed a stirrup, managed to get a grip on the pommel, and pulled myself into the saddle. Getting my rifle back into its scabbard, I got some pigging strings and tied myself into the saddle. Then I started the buckskin toward the wilderness, and away from my enemies.

Day was shooting crimson arrows into the vast bowl of the sky when my eyes opened again. My head swam with effort, and I stared about, seeing nothing familiar. Buck had stopped beside a small spring in a cañon. There was grass and a few trees, with not far away the ruin of a rock house. On the sand beside the spring was the track of a mountain lion, several deep tracks and what might be a mountain sheep, but no cow, horse, or human tracks.

Fumbling with swollen fingers, I untied the pigging strings and slid to the ground. Buck snorted and side-stepped, then put his nose down to me inquiringly. He drew back from the smell of stale clothes and dried blood, and I lay there, staring up at him, a crumpled human thing, my body raw with pain and weakness. "It's all right, Buck," I whispered. "We'll pull through. We've got to pull through."

IV

Over me the sky's high gray faded to pink shot with blood-red swords that swept the red into gold. As the sun crept up, I lay there, still beneath the wide sky, my body washed by a sea of dull pain that throbbed and pulsed in my muscles and veins. Yet deep within beat a deeper, stronger pulse, the pulse of the fighting man that would not let me die without fighting, that would not let me lie long without movement.

Turning over, using hand grasps of grass, I pulled myself to the spring and drank deep of the cool, clear, life-giving water. The wetness of it seemed to creep through all my tissues, bringing peace to my aching muscles and life to my starved body. To live I must drink, and I must eat, and my body must have rest and time to mend. Over and over these thoughts went through my mind, and over and over I said them, staring at my helpless hands. With contempt I looked at them, hating them for their weakness. And then I began to fight for life in those fingers, willing them to movement, to strength. Slowly my left hand began to stir, to lift at my command, to grasp a stick.

Triumph went through me. I was not defeated! Triumph lent me strength, and from this small victory I went on to another—a bit of broken manzanita placed across the first, a handful of scraped up leaves, more sticks. Soon I would have a fire.

I was a creature fighting for survival, wanting only to live and to fight. Through waves of delirium and weakness, I dragged myself to an aspen where I peeled bark for a vessel. Fainting there, coming to, struggling back to the place for my fire, putting the bark vessel together with clumsy fingers. With the bark vessel, a sort of box, I dipped into the water but had to drag it to the sand, lacking the strength to lift it up, almost crying with weakness and pain.

Lighting my fire, I watched the flames take hold. Then I got the bark vessel atop two rocks in the fire, and the flames rose around it. As long as the flames were below the water level of the vessel, I knew the bark would not burn, for the heat was absorbed by the water inside. Trying to push a stick under the vessel, I leaned too far and fainted.

When next I opened my eyes, the water was boiling. Pulling myself to a sitting position, I unbuckled my thick leather belt and let my guns fall back on the ground. Then carefully I opened my shirt and tore off a corner of it. I soaked it in the boiling water and began to bathe my wounds. Gingerly working the cloth plugs free of the wounds, I extracted them. The hot water felt good, but the sight of the wound in my side was frightening. It was red and inflamed, but near as I could see, as I bathed it, the bullet had gone through and touched nothing vital. The second slug had gone through the fleshy part of my thigh, and after bathing that wound, also, I lay still for a while, regaining strength and soaking up the heat.

Nearby there was patch of prickly pear, so I crawled to it and cut off a few big leaves, then I roasted them to get off the spines and bound the pulp against the wounds. Indians had used it to fight inflammations, and it might help. I found a clump of *amolilla* and dug some of the roots, scraping them into hot water. They foamed up when stirred and I drank the foamy water, remembering the Indians used the drink to carry off clotted blood, and a man's bullet wounds healed better after he drank it.

Then I made a meal of squaw cabbage and breadroot, not wanting to attempt getting at my saddlebags. Yet, when evening came and my fever returned, I managed to call Buck to me and loosen the girths. The saddle dropped, bringing with it my bedroll and saddlebags. Then I hobbled Buck and got the bridle off.

The effort exhausted me, so I crawled into my bedroll. My fever haunted the night with strange shapes, and guns seemed crashing about me. Men and darkness fought on the edge of my consciousness. Morgan Park—Jim Pinder—Rud Maclaren—and the sharply feral face of Bodie Miller.

The nuzzling of Buck awakened me in the cold light of day. "All right, Buck," I whispered. "I'm awake. I'm alive."

My weakness horrified me. If my enemies found me, they would not hesitate to kill me, and Buck must have left a trail easily followed. High up the cañon wall there was a patch of green, perhaps a break in the rock. Hiding my saddle under some brush, and taking with me my bedroll, saddlebags, rifle, and rope, I dragged myself toward an eyebrow of trail up the cliff.

If there was a hanging valley up there, it was just what I wanted. The buckskin wandered after me, more from curiosity than anything else. Getting atop a boulder, I managed to slide onto his back, then kneed him up the steep trail. A mountain horse, he went willingly, and in a few minutes we had emerged into a high hanging valley.

A great crack in the rock, it was flat-floored and high-walled, yet the grass was rich and green. Somewhere water was running, and before me was a massive stone tower all of sixty feet high. Blackened by age and by fire, it stood beside a spring, quite obviously the same as that from which I had beer drinking below. The hanging valley comprised not over three acres of land seemingly enclosed on the far side, and almost enclosed on the side where I had entered.

The ancient Indians who had built the tower had known a good thing when they saw it, for here was shelter and defense, grass, water, and many plants. Beside the tower some stunted maize, long since gone native, showed there had once been planting here. Nowhere was there any evidence that a human foot had trod here in centuries.

A week went slowly by, and nothing disturbed my camp. Able to walk a few halting steps, I explored the valley. The maize had been a fortunate discovery, for Indians had long used a mush made of the meal as an hourly application for bullet wounds. With this and other remedies my recovery became more rapid. The jerky gave out, but with snared rabbits and a couple of sage hens I managed. And then I killed a deer, and with the wild vegetables growing about I lived well.

Yet a devil of impatience was riding me. My ranch was in the hands of my enemies, and each day of absence made the chance of recovery grow less. Then, after two weeks, I was walking, keeping watch from a look-out spot atop the cliff and rapidly regaining strength. On the sixteenth day of my absence I decided to make an effort to return.

The land through which I rode was utterly amazing. Towering monoliths of stone, long, serrated cliffs of salmon-colored sandstone, and nothing human. It was almost noon of the following day before the buckskin's ears lifted suddenly. It took several seconds for me to discover what drew his attention, and then I detected a lone rider. An hour later, from a pinnacle of rock near a tiny seep of water, the rider was drawing near, carefully examining the ground.

A surge of joy went through me. It was Olga Maclaren.

Stepping out from the shadow, I waited for her to see me, and she did, almost at once. How I must look, I could guess.

My shirt was heavy with dust, torn by a bullet and my own hands. My face was covered with beard and my cheeks drawn and hollow, but the expression on her face was only of relief. "Matt?" Her voice was incredulous. "You're alive?"

"Did you think I'd die before we were married, daughter of Maclaren? Did you think I'd die before you had those sons I promised? Right now I'm coming back to claim my own."

"Back?" The worry on her face was obvious. "You must never go back. You're believed dead, so you are safe. Go away while there's time."

"Did you think I'd run? Olga, I've been whipped by Morgan Park, shot by Rollie Pinder, and attacked by the others, but Pinder is dead, and Park's time is coming. No, I made a promise to a fine old man named Ball, another one to myself, and one to you, and I'll keep them all. In my time I've backed up, I've side-stepped, and occasionally I've run, but always to come back and fight again."

She looked at me, and some of the fear seemed to leave her. Then she shook her head. "But you can't go back now. Jim Pinder has the Two Bar."

"Then he'll move," I promised her.

Olga had swung down from her horse and lifted my canteen. "You've water!" she exclaimed. "They all said no man could survive out there in that waste, even if he was not wounded."

"You believed them?"

"No." She hesitated. "I knew you'd be alive somewhere."

"You know your man then, Olga Maclaren. Does it mean that you love me, too?"

She hesitated and her eyes searched mine, but when I would have moved toward her, she drew back, half frightened. Her lips parting a little, her breast lifting suddenly as she caught her breath. "It isn't time for that now . . . please!"

It stopped me, knowing what she said was true. "You are sure you weren't trailed?"

She shook her head. "I've been careful. Every day."

"This isn't the first day you looked for me?"

"Oh, no." She looked at me, her eyes shadowed with worry. "I was afraid you were lying somewhere, bloody and suffering." Her eyes studied me, noting the torn shirt, the pallor of my face. "And you have been."

"Rollie was good. He was very good."

"Then it was you who killed him?"

"Who else?"

"Canaval and Bodie Miller found him after they realized you were gone from the mesa where you pinned them down. Canaval was sure it had been you, but some of them thought it was the mountain boys."

"They've done no fighting for me although they wanted to. You'd best start back. I've work to do."

"But you're in no shape! You're sick!" She stared at me.

"I can still fight," I said. "Tell your father you've seen me. Tell him the Two Bar was given me in the presence of witnesses. Tell him his stock is to be off that range . . . at once!"

"You forget that I am my father's daughter."

"And my future wife."

"I've promised no such thing!" she flared. "You know I'd never marry you! I'll admit you're attractive, and you're a devil, but marry you? I'd die first!"

Her breast heaved and her eyes flashed and I laughed at her. "Tell your father, though, and ask him to withdraw from this fight before it's too late." Swinging into the saddle, I added: "It's already too late for you. You love me and you know it. Tell Morgan Park that, and tell him I'm coming back to break him with my hands."

V

Riding into Hattan's Point, I was a man well known. Rollie Pinder was dead, and they knew whose gun had downed him. Maclaren's riders had been held off and made a laughingstock, and I had taken up Ball's fight to hold his ranch. Some men hated me for this, some admired me, and many thought me a fool.

All I knew was the horse between my knees, the guns on my thighs, and the blood of me pounding. My buckskin lifted his head high and moved down the dusty street like a dancer, for riding into this town was a challenge to them all. They knew it and I knew it. Leaving my horse behind Mother O'Hara's, I walked to the saloon and went in.

By then I'd taken time to shave, and, although the pallor of sickness was on my face, there was none in my eyes or heart. It did me good to see their eyes widen and to hear my spurs jingle as I walked to the bar. "Rye," I said, "the best you've got."

Key Chapin was there and, sitting with him, Morgan Park. The big man's eyes were cold as they stared at me. "I'm buying, gentlemen," I said, "and that includes you, Morgan Park, although you slug a man when his hands are down."

Park blinked. It had been a long time since anyone had told him off to his face. "And you, Key Chapin. It has always been my inclination to encourage freedom of the press and to keep my public relations on a good basis. And today I might even offer you a news item, something to read like this . . .

179

Matt Sabre, of the Two Bar, was in town Friday afternoon. Matt is recovering from a bullet wound incurred during a minor dispute with Rollie Pinder, but is returning to the Two Bar to take up where he left off."

Chapin smiled. "That will be news to Jim Pinder. He didn't expect you back."

"He should have," I assured him. "I'm back to punish every murdering skunk who killed old man Ball."

All eyes were on me now, and Park was staring, not knowing what to make of me.

"Do you know who they are?" Chapin asked curiously.

"Definitely!" I snapped the word. "Every man of them . . ." I shifted my eyes to Park—"is known . . . with one exception. When Ball was dying, he named a man to me. Only I am not sure."

"Who?" demanded Chapin.

"Morgan Park," I said.

The big man came to his feet with a lunge. His brown face was ugly with hatred. "That's a lie!" he roared.

My shoulders lifted. "Probably a misunderstanding. I'll not take offense at your language, Mister Park, because it is a dead man you are calling a liar, and not I. Ball might have meant that one of your riders, a man named Lyell, was there. He died before he could be questioned. If it is true, I'll kill you after I whip you."

"Whip me?" Park's bellow was amazed. "Whip me? Why, you. . . ."

"Unfortunately, I'm not sufficiently recovered from my wounds to do it today, but don't be impatient. You'll get your belly full of it when the time comes." Turning my back on him, I lifted my glass. "Gentlemen, your health!" And then I walked out of the place.

There was the good rich smell of cooked food and coffee

when I opened the door of Mother O'Hara's. "Ah? It's you, then. And still alive. Things ain't what they used to be around here. Warned off by Maclaren, threatened by Jim Pinder, beaten by Morgan Park, and you're still here."

"Still here an' stayin', Katie O'Hara," I said, grinning at her, "and I've just said that and more to Morgan Park."

"There's been men die, and you've had the killin' of some."

"That's the truth, Katie, and I'd rather it never happened, but it's a hard country and small chance for a man who hesitates to shoot when the time comes. All the same, it's a good country, this. A country where I plan to stay and grow my children, Katie. I'll go back to the Two Bar and build my home there."

"You think they'll let you? You think you can keep it?"

"They'll have no choice."

Behind me a door closed and the voice of Rud Maclaren was saying: "We'll have a choice. Get out of the country while you're alive!"

The arrogance in his voice angered me, so I turned and faced him. Canaval and Morgan Park had come with him. "The Two Bar is my ranch," I said, "and I'll be staying there. Do you think yourself a king that you can dictate terms to a citizen of a free country? You've let a small power swell your head, Maclaren. You think you have power when all you have is money. If you weren't the father of the girl I'm to marry, Maclaren, I'd break you just to show you this is a free country and we want no barons here."

His face mottled and grew hard. "Marry my daughter? You? I'll see you in hell first!"

"If you see me in hell, Maclaren," I said lightly, "you'll be seeing a married man, because I'm marrying Olga, and you can like it or light a shuck. I expect you were a good man once, but there's some that cannot stand the taste of power, and you're one." My eyes shifted to Morgan Park. "And there's another beside you. He has let his beef get him by too long. He uses force where you use money, but his time is running out, too. He couldn't break me when he had the chance, and, when my times comes, I'll break him."

More than one face in the room was approving, even if they glared at me, these two. "The trouble is obvious," I continued. "You've never covered enough country. You think you're sitting in the center of the world whereas you're just a couple of two-bit operators in a forgotten corner."

Turning my back on them, I helped myself to the Irish stew. Maclaren went out, but Park came around the table and sat down, and he was smiling. The urge climbed up in me to beat the big face off him and down him in the dirt as he had me. He was wider than me by inches, and taller. The size of his wrists and hands was amazing, yet he was not all beef, for he had brains and there was trouble in him, trouble for me. He was there to eat and said nothing to me.

When I returned to my horse, there was a man sitting there. He looked up and I was astonished at him. His face was like an unhappy monkey and he was without a hair to the top of his head. Near as broad in the shoulders as Morgan Park, he was shorter than me by inches. "By the look of you," he said, "you'll be Matt Sabre."

"You're right, man. What is it about?"

"Katie O'Hara was a-tellin' me it was a man you needed at the Two Bar. Now I'm a handy all-around man, Mister Sabre, a rough sort of gunsmith, hostler, blacksmith, carpenter, good with an axe. An' I shoot a bit, know Cornish-style wrestlin', an' am afraid of no man when I've my two hands before me. I'm not so handy with a short gun, but I've a couple of guns of my own that I handle nice."

He got to his feet, and he could have been nothing over five feet four but weighed all of 200 pounds, and his shirt at the neck showed a massive chest covered with black hair and a neck like a column of oak. "The fact that you've the small end of a fight appeals to me." He jerked his head toward the door. "Katie has said I'm to go to work for you an' she'd not take it kindly if I did not."

"You're Katie's man, then?"

His eyes twinkled amazingly. "Katie's mon? I'm afraid there's no such. She's a broth of a woman, that one." He grinned up at me. "Is it a job I have?"

"When I've the ranch back," I agreed, "you've a job."

"Then let's be gettin' it back. Will you wait for me? I've a mule to get."

The mule was a dun with a face that showed all the wisdom, meanness, and contrariness that have been the traits of the mule since time began. With a tow sack behind the saddle and another before him, we started out of town. "My name is Brian Mulvaney," he said. "Call me what you like."

He grinned widely when he saw me staring at the butts of the two guns that projected from his boot tops. "These," he said, "are the Neal Bootleg pistol, altered by me to suit my taste. The caliber is Thirty-Five, but good. Now this"—from his waistband he drew a gun that lacked only wheels to make an admirable artillery piece—"this was a Mills Seventy-Five caliber. Took me two months of work off and on but I've converted her to a four-shot revolver. A fine gun," he added.

All of seventeen inches long, it looked fit to break a man's wrists, but Mulvaney had powerful hands and arms. No man ever hit by a chunk of lead from that gun would need a doctor.

Four horses were in the corral at the Two Bar, and the

men were strongly situated behind a log barricade. Mulvaney grinned at me. "What'd you suppose I've in this sack, laddie?" he demanded, his eyes twinkling. "I, who was a miner, also?"

"Powder?"

"Exactly! In those new-fangled sticks. Now, unless it makes your head ache too much, help me cut a few o' these sticks in half." When that was done, he cut the fuses very short and slid caps into the sticks of powder. "Come now, me boy, an' we'll slip down close under the cover o' darkness, an' you'll see them takin' off like you never dreamed."

Crawling as close as we dared, each of us lit a fuse and hurled a stick of powder. My own stick must have landed closer to them than I planned, for we heard a startled exclamation followed by a yell. Then a terrific explosion blasted the night apart. Mulvaney's followed, and then we hastily hurled a third and a fourth.

One man lunged over the barricade and started straight for us. The others had charged the corral. The man headed our way suddenly saw us, and, wheeling, he fled as if the devil was after him. Four riders gripping only mane holds dashed from the corral, and then there was silence. Mulvaney got to his feet, chuckling. "For guns they'd have stood until hell froze over, but the powder, the flyin' rocks, an' dust scared 'em good. An' you've your ranch back."

We had eaten our midday meal the next day, when I saw a rider approaching. It was Olga Maclaren. "Nice to see you," I said, aware of the sudden tension her presence always inspired.

She was looking toward the foundation we had laid for the new house. It was on a hill with the long sweep of Cottonwood Wash before it. "You should be more careful," she said.

"You had a visitor last night."

"We just took over last night," I objected. "Who do you mean?"

"Morgan. He was out here shortly after our boys got home. He met the bunch you stampeded from here."

"He's been puzzling me," I admitted. "Who is he? Did he come from around here?"

"I don't know. He's not talkative, but I've heard him mention places back East. I know he's been in Philadelphia and New York, but nothing else about him except that he goes to Salt Lake and San Francisco occasionally."

"Not back East?"

"Never since we've known him."

"You like him?"

She looked up at me. "Yes, Morgan can be very wonderful. He knows a lot about women and the things that please them." There was a flicker of laughter in her eyes. "He probably doesn't know as much about them as you."

"Me?" I was astonished. "What gave you that idea?"

"Your approach that first day. You knew it would excite my curiosity, and a man less sure of himself would never have dared. If you knew no more about women than most Western men, you would have hung back, wishing you could meet me, or you would have got drunk to work up your courage."

"I meant what I said that day. You're going to marry me."

"Don't say that. Don't even think it. You've no idea what you are saying or what it would mean."

"Because of your father?" I looked at her. "Or Morgan Park?"

"You take him too lightly, Matt. I think he is utterly without scruple. I believe he would stop at nothing."

There was more to come and I was interested.

"There was a young man here from the East," she continued, "and I liked him. Knowing Morgan, I never mentioned him in Morgan's presence. Then one day he asked me about him. He added that it would be better for all concerned if the man did not come around any more. Inadvertently I mentioned the young man's name, Arnold D'Arcy. When he heard that name, he became very disturbed. Who was he? Why had he come here? Had he asked any questions about anybody? Or described anybody he might be looking for? He asked me all those questions, but at the same time I thought little about it. Afterward, I began to believe that he was not merely jealous. Right then I decided to tell Arnold about it when he returned."

"And did you?"

There was a shadow of worry on her face. "No. He never came again." She looked quickly at me. "I've often thought of it. Morgan never mentioned him again, but somehow Arnold hadn't seemed like a man who would frighten easily."

Later, when she was mounting to leave, I asked her: "Where was D'Arcy from? Do you remember?"

"Virginia, I believe. He had served in the Army, and before coming West had been working in Washington."

Watching her go, I thought again of Morgan Park. He might have frightened D'Arcy away, but I could not shake off the idea that something vastly more sinister lay behind it. And Park had been close to us during the night. If he had wanted to kill me, it could have been done, but apparently he wanted me alive. Why?

"Mulvaney," I suggested, "if you can hold this place, I'll ride to Silver Reef and get off a couple of messages."

He stretched his huge arms and grinned at me. "Do you doubt it? I'll handle it or them. Go, and have yourself a time."

And in the morning I was in the saddle again.

VI

High noon, and a mountain shaped like flame. Beyond the mountain and around it was a wide land with no horizons, but only the shimmering heat waves that softened all lines to vagueness and left the desert an enchanted land without beginning and without end.

As I rode, my mind studied the problem created by the situation around Cottonwood Wash. There were at least three, and possibly four sides to the question. Rud Maclaren with his Bar M, Jim Pinder with his CP, and myself with the Two Bar. The fourth possibility was Morgan Park.

Olga's account of Arnold D'Arcy's disappearance had struck a chord of memory. During ten years of my life I had been fighting in foreign wars, and there had been a military observer named D'Arcy, a Major Leo D'Arcy, who had been in China during the fighting there. It stuck in my mind that he had a brother named Arnold.

It was a remote chance, yet a possibility. Why did the name upset Park? What had become of Arnold? Where did Park come from? Pinder could be faced with violence and handled with violence. Maclaren might be circumvented. Morgan Park worried me.

Silver Reef lay sprawled in haphazard comfort along a main street and a few cross streets. There were the usual frontier saloons, stores, churches, and homes. The sign on the Elk Horn Saloon caught my attention. Crossing to it, I pushed through the door into the dim interior. While the bartender served me, I glanced around, liking the feel of the place.

"Rye?" The smooth-pated bartender squinted at me.

"Uhn-huh. How's things in the mines?"

"So-so. But you ain't no miner." He glanced at my cow-hand's garb and then at the guns in their tied-down holsters. "This here's a quiet town. We don't see many gun handlers around here. The place for them is over east of here."

"Hattan's Point?"

"Yeah. I hear the Bar M an' CP both are hirin' hands. Couple of *hombres* from there rode into town a few days ago. One of 'em was the biggest man I ever did see."

Morgan Park in Silver Reef! That sounded interesting, but I kept a tight rein on my thoughts and voice. "Did he say anything about what was goin' on over there?"

"Not to me. The feller with him, though, he was inquirin' around for the Slade boys. Gun slicks both of them. The big feller, he never come in here a-tall. I seen him on the street a couple of times, but he went to the Wells Fargo Bank and down the street to see that shyster, Jake Booker."

"You don't seem to like Booker?"

"Him? He's plumb no good! The man's a crook!"

Once started on Booker, the bartender told me a lot. Morgan Park had been in town before, but never came to the Elk Horn. He confined his visits to the back room of a dive called the Sump or occasional visits to the office of Jake Booker. The only man whoever came with him was Lyell.

Leaving the saloon, I sent off my telegram to Leo D'Arcy. Then I located the office of Booker, spotted the Sump, and considered the situation. Night came swiftly and miners crowded the street, a good-natured shoving, pushing, laughing throng, jamming the saloons and drinking. The crowd relaxed me with its rough good humor, and for the night I fell into it, drifting, joking, listening.

Turning off the street near Louder's store, I passed the street lamp on the corner, and for an instant was outlined in its radiance. From the shadows, flame stabbed. There was a tug at my sleeve, and then my own gun roared, and, as the shot sped, I went after it.

A man lunged from the side of the store and ran staggeringly toward the alley behind it. Pistol ready, I ran after him. He wheeled, slipped, and was running again. He brought up with a crash against the corral bars, and fell. He was crawling to his feet, and I caught a glimpse of his face in the glow from the window. It was Lyell.

One hand at his throat, I jerked him erect. His face was gaunt and there was blood on his shirt front. He had been hit hard by my sudden, hardly aimed shot. "Got you, didn't I?"

"Yes, damn you, an' I missed. Put . . . put me down."

Lowering him to the ground, I dropped to one knee. "I'll get a doctor. I saw a sign up the street."

He grabbed my sleeve. "Ain't no use. I feel it. You got me good. Anyway"—he stared at me—"why should you get a doc for me?"

"I shouldn't. You were in the gang killed Ball."

His eyes bulged. "No! No, I wasn't there! He was a good old man! I wasn't in that crowd."

"Was Morgan Park there?"

His eyes changed, veiled. "Why would he be there? That wasn't his play."

"What's he seeing Booker for? What about Sam Slade?"

Footsteps crunched on the gravel, and a man carrying a lantern came up the alley. "Get a doctor, will you? This man's been shot."

The man started off at a run and Lyell lay quietly, a tough, unshaven man with brown eyes. He breathed hoarsely for several minutes while I uncovered the wound. "The Slades

189

are to get Canaval. Park wants you for himself."

"What does he want? Range?"

"No. He . . . he wants money."

The doctor hurried up with the lantern carrier. Watching him start work, I backed away and disappeared in the darkness. If anybody knew anything about Park's plans, it would be Booker, and I had an idea I could get into Booker's office.

Booker's office was on the second floor of a frame building reached by an outside stairway. Once up there, a man would be fairly trapped if anyone came up those stairs. Down the street a music box was jangling, and the town showed no signs of going to sleep. Studying that stairway, I liked no part of it. Booker had many friends here, but I had none, and going up there would be a risk. Then I remembered all the other times I'd had no friends, so I hitched my guns easier on my thighs and went across the street.

Going up the steps two at a time, I paused at the door. Locks were no problem to a man of my experience and a minute later I was inside a dark office, musty with stale tobacco. Swiftly I checked the tray on the desk, the top drawer, and then the side drawers, lighting my exploration with a stump of candle. Every sense alert, ears attuned to the slightest sound, I worked rapidly, suddenly coming to an assayer's report. No location was mentioned, no notation on the sheet, but the ore had been rich, amazingly rich. Then among some older papers at the bottom of a drawer I found a fragment of a letter from Morgan Park, signed with his name.

You have been recommended to me as a man of discretion who could turn over a piece of property for a quick profit and who could handle negotiations

with a buyer. I am writing for an appointment and will be in Silver Reef on the 12th. It is essential that this business remain absolutely confidential.

It was little enough, but a hint. I left the assayer's report but pocketed the letter. The long ride had tired me, for my wounds, while much improved, had robbed me of strength. Dousing the candle, I returned it to its shelf. And then I heard a low mutter of voices and steps on the stair.

Backing swiftly, I glanced around and saw a closed door that must lead to an inner room. Stepping through it, I closed it just in time. It was a room used for storage. Voices sounded and a door closed. A match scratched, and light showed under the door. "Nonsense! Probably got in some drunken brawl! You're too suspicious, Morgan."

"Maybe, but the man worries me. He rides too much, and he may get to nosing around and find something."

"Did you see Lyell before he died?"

"No. He shot first, though. Some fool saw him take a bead on somebody. This other fellow followed it up and killed him."

The crabbed voice of Booker interrupted. "Forget him. Forget Sabre. My men are lined up and they have the cold cash ready to put on the line! We haven't any time for child's play! I've done my part and now it's up to you! Get Sabre out of the way and get rid of Maclaren!"

"That's not so easy," Park objected stubbornly. "Maclaren is never alone, and, if anybody ever shot at him, he'd turn the country upside down to find the man. And after he is killed, the minute we step in, suspicion will be diverted to us."

"Nonsense!" Booker replied irritably. "Nobody knows we've had dealings. They'll have to settle the estate and I'll step in as representative of the buyers. Of course, if you were married to the girl, it would simplify things. What's the matter? Sabre cutting in there, too?"

"Shut up!" Park's voice was ugly. "If you ever say a thing like that again, I'll wring you out like a dirty towel, Booker. I mean it."

"You do your part," Booker said, "and I'll do mine. The buyers have the money and they are ready. They won't wait forever."

A chair scraped and Park's heavy steps went to the door and out. There was a faint squeak of a cork twisting in a bottleneck, the gargle of a poured drink, then the bottle and glass returned to the shelf. The light vanished and a door closed. Then footsteps grated on the gravel below. Only a minute behind him, I hurried from the vicinity, then paused, sweating despite the cool air. Thinking of what I'd heard, I retrieved my horse and slipped quietly out of town. Bedded down among the clustering cedars, I thought of that, and then of Olga, the daughter of Maclaren, of her soft lips, the warmth of her arms, the quick proud lift of her chin.

Coming home to Cottonwood Wash and the Two Bar with the wind whispering through the greasewood and rustling the cottonwood leaves, I kept a careful watch but saw nobody until Mulvaney himself stepped into sight.

"Had any trouble?" I asked him.

"Trouble? None here," he replied. "Some men came by, but the sound of my Spencer drove them away again." He walked to the door. "There's grub on the table. How was it in Silver Reef?"

"A man killed."

"Be careful, lad. There's too many dying."

When I had explained, he nodded. "Do they know it was you?"

"I doubt it." It felt good to be back on my own place again, seeing the whitefaced cattle browsing in the pasture below, seeing the water flowing to irrigate the small garden we'd started.

"You're tired." Mulvaney studied me. "But you look fit. You've thrown a challenge in the teeth of Park. You'll be backing it up?"

"Backing it up?" My eyes must have told what was in me. "That's one man I want, Mulvaney. He had me down and beat me, and I'll not live free until I whip him or he whips me fair."

"He's a power of man, lad. I've seen him lift a barrel of whiskey at arm's length overhead. It will be a job to whip him."

"Ever box any, Mulvaney? You told me you'd wrestled Cornish style."

"What Irishman hasn't boxed a bit? Is it a sparrin' mate you're wantin'? Sure 'n' it would be good to get the leather on my maulies again."

For a week we were at it, every night we boxed, lightly at first, then faster. He was a brawny man, a fierce slugger, and a powerful man in the clinches. On the seventh day we did a full thirty minutes without a break. And in the succeeding days my strength returned and my speed grew greater. The rough-and-tumble part of it I loved. Nor was I worried about Morgan's knowing more tricks than I—the waterfronts are the place to learn the dirty side of fighting. I would use everything I'd learned there, if Morgan didn't fight fair.

It was after our tenth session with the gloves that Mulvaney stripped them off and shook his head admiringly. "Faith, lad, you've a power of muscle behind that wallop of yours. That last one came from nowhere and I felt it clean to my toes. Never did I believe a man lived that could hit like that."

"Thanks," I said. "I'm ridin' to town tomorrow."

"To fight him?"

"No, to see the girl, Olga Maclaren, to buy supplies, and perhaps to ride him a little. I want him furious before we fight. I want him mad . . . mad and wild."

He nodded wisely at me. "It'll help, for no man can fight unless he keeps his head. But be careful, lad. Remember they are gunnin' for you, an' there's nothin' that would better please them than to see you dead on the ground."

When the buckskin was watered, I returned him to the hitch rail and walked into the saloon. Hattan's Point knew that Lyell was dead, but they had no idea who had done it. Key Chapin was the first man I met, and I looked at him, wondering on which side he stood.

He looked at me curiously and motioned toward the chair across the table from him. Dropping into it, I began to build a smoke. "Well, Sabre, you're making quite a name for yourself."

I shrugged. "That's not important. All I want is a ranch."

"All?"

"And a girl."

"One may be as hard to get as the other."

"Maybe. Anyway, I've made a start on the ranch. In fact, I have the ranch and intend to keep it."

"Heard about Lyell?"

"Killed, wasn't he? Somewhere west of here?"

"At Silver Reef. It's a peaceful, quiet place in spite of being a boomtown. And they have a sheriff over there who believes in keeping it peaceful. They tell me he is working hard to find out who killed Lyell."

"It might be anybody. There was a rumor that he was one of the men in the raid on the Ball Ranch."

"And which you promised to bury on the spot."

What this was building to I did not know, but I was anxious to find out just where Chapin stood. He would be a good friend to have, and a bad enemy, for his paper had a good deal of influence around town.

"You told me when I first came here that the town was taking sides. Which is your side?"

He hesitated, toying with his glass. "That's a harder question to answer since you came," he replied frankly. "I will say this. I am opposed to violence. I believe now is the time to establish a peaceful community, and I believe it can be done. For that reason I am opposed to the CP outfit whose code is violence."

"And Maclaren?"

He hesitated again. "Maclaren can be reasoned with at times. Stubborn, yes, but only because he has an exaggerated view of his own rightness. It is not easy to prove him wrong, but it can be done."

"And Park?"

He looked at me sharply, a cool, measuring glance as if to see what inspired the remark. Then he said: "Morgan Park is generally felt to see things as Maclaren does."

"Is that your opinion?"

He did not answer me, frowning as he stared out the door. Key Chapin was a handsome man, and an able one. I could understand how he felt about law and order. Basically I agreed with him, but when I'm attacked, I can't take it lying down.

"Look, Chapin"—I leaned over the table—"I've known a dozen frontier towns tougher than this one. To each came law and order, but it took a fight to get them. The murderers, cheats, and swindlers must be stamped out before the honest citizens can have peace. And it's peace that I'm fighting for.

You, more than anybody else, can build the situation to readiness for it with your paper. Write about it. Get the upright citizens prepared to enforce it, once this battle is over."

He nodded, then glanced at me. "What about you? You're a gunfighter. In such a community there is no place for such a man."

That made me grin. "Chapin, I never drew a gun on a man in my life who didn't draw on me first, or try to. And while I may be a gunfighter, I'm soon to be a rancher and a solid citizen. Count on me to help."

"Even to stopping this war?"

"What war? Ball had a ranch. He was a peaceful old man who wanted no trouble from anyone, but he was weaker than the Bar M or the CP, so he died. He turned the ranch over to me on the condition that I keep it. If protecting one's property is war, then we'll have it for a long time."

"You could sell out."

"Run? Is that what you mean? I never ducked out of a good fight yet, Chapin, and never will. When they stop fighting me, I'll hang up my guns. Until then, I shall continue to fight." Filling my glass, I added: "Don't look at the overall picture so long that you miss the details."

"What do you mean?"

"Look for motives. What are the origins of this fight? I'd start investigating the participants, and I mean neither Maclaren nor Pinder." Getting up, I put my hat on my head and added: "Ever hear of a man named Booker at Silver Reef? A lawyer?"

"He's an unmitigated scoundrel, and whatever he does he's apt to get away with. If there's a loophole in the law he doesn't know, then nobody knows it."

"Then find out why he's interested in this fight and, when the Slade boys drift into this country, ask yourself why they are here. Also, ask yourself why Morgan Park is meeting Booker in secret."

Olga was not in town, so I turned the buckskin toward the Bar M. A cowhand with one foot bandaged was seated on the doorstep when I rode up. He stared, his jaw dropping.

"Howdy," I said calmly, taking out the makings. "I'm visiting on the ranch and don't want any trouble. As far as you boys are concerned, I've no hard feelings."

"You've no hard feelin's! What about me? You durned near shot my foot off!"

I grinned at him. "Next time you'll stay under cover. Anyway, what are you gripin' about? You haven't done a lick of work since it happened!"

Somebody chuckled. I looked around and saw Canaval. "I reckon he did it on purpose, Sabre."

"*Excuse?*" the injured man roared. Disgusted, he rose and limped off.

"What you want here, Sabre?" Canaval asked, still smiling.

"Just visiting."

"Sure you're welcome?"

"No, I'm not sure. But if you're wondering if I came looking for trouble, I didn't. If trouble comes to me on this ranch now, it will be because I'm pushed and pushed hard. If you're the guardian angel of peace, just relax. I'm courtin'."

"Rud won't take kindly to that. He may have me order you off."

"All right, Canaval, if he does, and you tell me to go, I'll go. Only one thing . . . you keep Park off me. I'm not ready for him, and, when it comes, I'd rather she didn't see it."

"Fair enough." He tossed his cigarette into the yard. "You'll not be bothered under those circumstances. Only"— he grinned and his eyes twinkled—"you might be wrong about Olga. She might like to see you tangle with Park."

Starting up the steps, I remembered something. "Canaval!"

He turned sharply, ready on the instant.

"A friendly warning," I said. "Some of the people who don't like me also want your boss out of here. To get him out, you have to go first. If you hear of the Slades in this country, you'll know they've come for you and your boss."

His eyes searched mine. "The Slades?"

"Yeah, for you and Maclaren. Somebody is saving me for dessert."

He was standing there, looking after me, when I knocked. Inside a voice answered that set my blood pounding. "Come in!"

VII

As I entered, there was an instant when my reflection was thrown upon the mirror beside hers. Seeing my gaze over her shoulder, she turned, and we stood there, looking at ourselves in the mirror—a tall, dark young man in a dark blue shirt, black silk neckerchief, black jeans, and tied-down holsters with their walnut-stocked guns, and Olga in a sea-green gown, filmy and summery-looking.

She turned quickly to face me. "What are you doing here? My father will be furious!"

"He'll have to get over it sometime, and it might as well be right now."

She searched my face. "You're still keeping up that foolish talk? About marrying me?"

"It isn't foolish. Have you started buying your trousseau?"

"Of course not!"

"You'd better. You'll need something to wear, and I won't have much money for a year or two."

"Matt"—her face became serious—"you'd better go. I'm expecting Morgan."

I took her hands. "Don't worry. I promised Canaval there would be no trouble, and there will be none, no matter what Morgan Park wants to do or tries to do."

She was unconvinced and tried to argue, but I was thinking how lovely she was. Poised, her lovely throat bare, she was something to set a man's pulses pounding.

"Matt!" She was angry now. "You're not even listening!

And don't look at me like that!"

"How else should a man look at a woman? And why don't we sit down? Is this the way you receive guests at the Bar M? At the Two Bar we are more thoughtful."

"So I've heard," she said dryly. Her anger faded. "Matt? How do you feel? I mean those wounds? Are they all right?"

"Not all right, but much better. I'm not ready for Morgan Park yet, but I will be soon. He won't be missed much when he's gone."

"Gone?" She was surprised. "Remember that I like Morgan."

"Not very much." I shrugged. "Yes, gone. This country isn't big enough to hold both of us even if you weren't in it."

She sat down opposite me and her face was flushed a little. She looked at me, then looked away, and neither of us said anything for a long minute. "It's nice here," I said at last. "Your father loves this place, doesn't he?"

"Yes, only I wish he would be content and stop trying to make it bigger."

"Men like your father never seem to learn when they have enough."

"You don't talk like a cowhand, Matt."

"That's because I read a book once."

"Key told me you had been all over the world. He checked up on you. He said you had fought in China and South Africa."

"That was a long time ago."

"How did you happen to come West?"

"I was born in the West, and then I always wanted to return to it and have a ranch of my own, but there wasn't anything to hold me down, so I just kept on drifting from place to place. Staying in one place did not suit me unless there was a reason to stay, and there never was . . . before."

Tendrils of her dark hair curled against her neck. The day was warm, and I could see tiny beads of perspiration on her upper lip. She stood up suddenly, uneasily. "Matt, you'd better go. Father will be coming and he'll be furious."

"And Morgan Park will be coming. And it doesn't matter in the least whether they come or not. I came here to see you, and, as long as they stay out of the way, there'll be no trouble."

"But, Matt. . . ." She stepped closer to me, and I took her by the elbows. She started to step back, but I drew her to me swiftly. I took her chin and turned her head slightly. She resisted, but the continued pressure forced her chin to come around. She looked at me then, her eyes wide and more beautiful than I would ever have believed eyes could be, and then I kissed her.

We stood there, clinging together tightly, and then she pulled violently away from me. For an instant she looked at me, and then she moved swiftly to kiss me again, and we were like that when hoofs sounded in the yard. Two horses.

We stepped apart, but her eyes were wide and her face was pale when they came through the door, her breast heaving and her white teeth clinging to her lower lip. They came through the door, Rud Maclaren first, and then Morgan Park, dwarfing Maclaren in spite of the fact that he was a big man. When they saw me, they stopped.

Park's face darkened with angry blood. He started toward me, his voice hoarse with fury. "Get out! Get out, I say!"

My eyes went past him to Maclaren. "Is Park running this place, or are you? It seems to me he's got a lot of nerve, ordering people off the place of Rud Maclaren."

Maclaren flushed. He didn't like my being there, but he disliked Park's usurping of authority even more. "That'll do, Morgan! I'll order people out of my own home!"

201

Morgan Park's face was ugly at that minute, but, before he could speak, Canaval appeared in the door. "Boss, Sabre said he was visitin', not huntin' trouble. He said he would make no trouble and would go when I asked him. He also said he would make no trouble with Park."

Before Maclaren could reply, Olga said quickly: "Father, Mister Sabre is my guest. When the time comes, he will leave. Until then, I wish him to stay."

"I won't have him in this house!" Maclaren said angrily. He strode to me, the veins in his throat swelling. "Damn you, Sabre! You've a gall to come here after shootin' my men, stealin' range that rightly belongs to me, an' runnin' my cattle out of Cottonwood Wash!"

"Perhaps," I admitted, "there's something in what you say, but I think we have no differences we can't settle without fighting. Your men came after me first. I never wanted trouble with you, Rud, and I think we can reach a peaceful solution."

It took the fire out of him. He was still truculent, still wanting to throw his weight around, but mollified. Right then I sensed the truth about Rud Maclaren. It was not land and property he wanted so much as to be known as the biggest man in the country. He merely knew of no way to get respect and admiration other than through wealth and power.

Realizing that gave me an opening. "I was talking to Chapin today. If we are going to be safe, we must stop all this fighting, and the only way it can be done is through the leadership of the right man. I think you're that man, Maclaren."

He was listening, and he liked what he heard.

"You're the big man of the community," I added. "If you make a move for peace, others will follow."

"The Pinders wouldn't listen," he protested. "You know that. You killed Rollie, but if you hadn't, Canaval might have.

Jim will never rest until you're dead. And he hates me and all I stand for."

Morgan Park was listening, his eyes hard and watchful. He had never imagined that Maclaren and I would talk peace, and, if we reached a settlement, his plans were finished.

"If Pinder and the CP were alone, they would have to become outlaws to persist in this fight. If the fight continues, all the rustlers in the country will come in here to run off our herds while we fight. Did it ever fail? When honest men fall out, thieves always profit. Moreover, you'll break yourself paying gunman's wages. From now on they'll come higher."

Olga was listening with some surprise and, I believed, with respect. Certainly I had gone further than I had ever believed possible. My own instinct is toward fighting, yet I have always been aware of the futility of it. Now I could see that, if the fighting ended, all our problems would be simple and easily settled. The joker in the deck was Morgan Park; he had everything to lose by a settlement, and nothing to gain.

Park interrupted suddenly. "I wouldn't trust all this talk, Rud. Sabre sounds good, but he's got some trick in mind. What's he planning? What's he trying to cover?"

"Morgan!" Olga protested. "I'm surprised at you. Matt is sincere and you know it."

"I know nothing of the kind," he replied shortly. "I'm surprised that you would defend this . . . this killer."

He was looking at me as he spoke, and it was then I said the one thing I had wanted to say, the hunch I could not prove. "At least," I replied, "my killings have been in fair fights, by men trying to kill me. I've never killed a man who had no gun, and who would have been helpless against me in any case."

Morgan Park stiffened and his face grew livid. Yet I knew from the way his eyes searched my face that he detected the undercurrent of meaning and he was trying to gauge the depth of my knowledge. It was D'Arcy I had in mind, for D'Arcy had known something about Park and had been slain for what he knew, or because he might tell others what he knew. I was sure of that.

"It isn't only rustlers," I continued to Maclaren, "but others have schemes they can only bring to success through trouble here. There are those who wish this fight to continue so they may get rights and claims they could never secure if there was peace."

Morgan Park was glaring, fighting for control. He could see that unless he kept his temper and acted quickly his plans might be ruined. Something of what I'd said apparently touched Maclaren, for he was nodding.

"I'll have to think it over," Maclaren said. "This is no time to make decisions."

"By all means." Turning, I took Olga's arm. "Now if you'll excuse us?"

Morgan's face was a study in concentrated fury. He started forward, blood in his eye. Putting Olga hurriedly to one side, I was ready for him, but Canaval stepped between us.

"Hold it!" Canaval's command stopped Park in his tracks. "That's all, Park. We'll have no trouble here."

"What's the matter?" he sneered. "Sabre need a nurse-maid now?"

"No." The foreman was stiff. "He gave me his word, and I gave mine. As long as he is on this place, my word holds. If the boss wants him to go, he'll go."

In the silence that followed, Maclaren turned to me. "Sabre, I've no reason to like you, but you are my daughter's guest and you talk straight from the shoulder. Remain as long as you like."

Park started to speak, but realized he could do nothing. He turned his heavy head, staring at me from under heavy brows. That gaze was cold and deadly. "We can settle our differences elsewhere, Sabre."

Olga was worried when we got outside. "You shouldn't have come, Matt. There'll be trouble. Morgan is a bad enemy."

"He was my enemy, anyway. That he is a bad enemy, I know. I think another friend of yours found that out."

She looked up quickly, real fear in her eyes. "What do you mean?"

"Your friend, D'Arcy. He comes of a family that does not frighten easily. Did you ever have a note of acknowledgement from him?"

"No."

"Strange. I'd have said such a man would never neglect such an obvious courtesy."

We stood together then, looking out at the night and the desert, no words between us but needing no words, our hearts beating together, our blood moving together, feeling the newness of love discovered. The cottonwood leaves brushed their pale green hands together, and their muted whispering seemed in tune with our own thoughts. This was my woman. The one I would walk down the years with. The leaves said that and my blood said it, and I knew the same thoughts were in her, reluctant as she might be to admit it.

"This trouble will pass," I said softly, "as the night will pass, and, when it has gone, and the winds have blown the dust away, then I shall take you to Cottonwood Wash . . . to live." Her hand stayed in mine, and I continued. "We'll build something there to last down the years until this will all seem a bad dream, a nightmare dissipated by the morning sunlight."

"But could you ever settle down? Could you stay?"

"Of course. Men don't wander for the love only of wandering. They wander because they are in search of something. A place of one's own, a girl, a job accomplished. It is only you who has mattered since the day I rode into the streets of Hattan's Point and saw you there."

Turning toward her, I took her by the elbows and her breath caught, then came quickly and deeply, her lips parted slightly as she came into my arms, and I felt her warm body melt against mine, and her lips were warm and seeking, urgent, passionate. My fingers ran into her hair and along her scalp, and her kisses hurt my lips as mine must have hurt hers. All the fighting, all the waiting melted into nothingness then.

She pulled back suddenly, frightened yet excited, her breasts rising and falling as she fought for control. "This isn't good! We're . . . we're too violent. We've got to be more calm."

I laughed then, full of the zest of living and loving and seeing the glory of her there in the moonlight. I laughed and took her arms again. "You're not exactly a calm person."

"I?" A flush darkened her face. "Well, all right then. Neither of us is calm."

"Need we be?" My hands reached for her, and then I heard someone whistling, and irritably I looked up to hear feet grating on the gravel path.

It was Canaval. "Better ride," he said. "I wouldn't put it past Park to dry-gulch a man."

"Canaval!" Olga protested. "How can you say that?"

His slow eyes turned to her. "You think so, too, ma'am. You always was an uncommon smart girl. You've known him for what he was for a mighty long time." He turned back to me. "Mean what you said back there? About peace and all?"

"You bet I did. What can we gain by fighting?"

206

"You're right," Canaval agreed, "but there'll be blood-shed before it's over. Pinder won't quit. He hates Rud Maclaren and now he hates you. He won't back up or quit." Canaval turned to Olga. "Let me talk to Sabre alone, will you? There's something he should know."

"All right." She gave me her hand. "Be careful. And good night."

We watched her walk back up the path, and, when my eyes turned back to him, his were surprisingly soft. I could see his expression even in the moonlight. "Reminds me of her mother," he said quietly.

"You knew her?" I was surprised.

"She was my sister."

That was something I could never have guessed.

"She doesn't know," he explained. "Rud and I used to ride together. I was too fast with a gun and killed a man with too many relatives. I left and Rud married my sister. From time to time we wrote, and, when Rud was having trouble with rustlers, I came out to lend a hand. He persuaded me to stay."

He looked around at me. "One thing more. What did you mean about the Slades?"

So I told him in detail of my trip to Silver Reef, the killing of Lyell, and the conversation I'd overheard between Park and Booker. Where I had heard the conversation I did not tell him, and only said there was some deal between the two of them that depended upon results to be obtained by Morgan Park.

It was after midnight when I finally left the Bar M, turning off the main trail and cutting across country for the head of Gypsum Cañon.

Mulvaney was waiting for me. "Knowed the horse's walk," he explained. Nodding toward the hills, he added: "Too quiet out there."

The night was clear, wide, and peaceful. Later, during the night, I awakened with a start, the sound of a shot ringing in my ears. Mulvaney was sleeping soundly, so I did not disturb him. Afterward, all was quiet, so I dropped off to sleep once more.

In the morning I mentioned it to Mulvaney.

"Did you get up?" he asked.

"Yeah. Went out in the yard and listened, but heard nothing more. Could have been a hunter. Maybe one of the Benaras boys."

Two hours later I knew better. Riding past Maverick Spring, I saw the riderless horse grazing near a dark bundle that lay on the grass. The dark bundle was Rud Maclaren, and he was dead. He had been shot twice from behind, both shots through the head. He was sprawled on his face, both hands above his head, one knee drawn up. Both guns were in their holsters, and his belt gun was tied down. After one look I stood back and fired three shots as a signal to Mulvaney.

When he saw Maclaren, his face went white and he looked up. "You shouldn't have done it, boy. The country hated him but they respected him, too. They'll hang a man for this!"

"Don't be foolish!" I was irritated but appalled, too. "I didn't do this! Feel of him! It must have been that shot I heard last night."

"He's cold, all right. This'll blow the lid off, Matt. You'd best rig a story for them. And it had better be good!"

"No rigging. I'll tell the truth."

"They'll hang you, Matt. They'll never believe you didn't do it." He waved a hand around. "He's on your place. The two of you have been feudin'. They'll say you shot him in the back."

Standing over the body with the words of Mulvaney in my ears, I could see with piercing clarity the situation I was in.

What could he have been doing here? Why would he come to my ranch in the middle of the night?

I could see their accusing eyes when the death was reported, the shock to Olga, the reaction of the people, the accusations of Park. Somebody wanted Maclaren dead enough to shoot him in the back. Who?

VIII

Strangely the morning was cool with a hint of rain. Mulvaney, at my request, had gone to the Bar M to tell Canaval of the killing, and it was up to Canaval to tell Olga. I did not like to think of that. My luck held in one sense for Jolly Benaras came riding up the wash, and I asked him to ride to Hattan's Point to report to Key Chapin.

Covering the body with a tarp, I mounted and began to scout the area. How much time I had, I did not know, but it could not be much. Soon they would be arriving from Hattan's Point, and even sooner from the Bar M. One thing puzzled me. There had been but one shot fired, but there were two bullet holes in Maclaren's skull.

Carefully I examined the sand under the body and was struck by a curious thing. There was no blood! None on the sand, that is. There was plenty of blood on Rud himself, but all of it, strangely enough, seemed to come from one bullet hole. There was a confusion of tracks where his horse had moved about while he lay there on the ground, but at this point the wash was sandy, and no definite track could be distinguished. Then horses hoofs sounded, and I looked up to see five riders coming toward me. The nearest was Canaval, and, beside him, Olga. The others were all Bar M riders, and from one glance at their faces I knew there was no doubt in their minds and little reason for speculation that I had killed Rud Maclaren.

Canaval drew up, and his eyes pierced mine, cold, calculating, and shrewd. Olga threw herself from her horse and ran to the still form on the ground. She had refused to meet my eyes or to notice me.

"This looks bad, Canaval. When did he leave the ranch?"

He studied me carefully, as if he were seeing me for the first time. "I don't know exactly," he said. "No one heard him go. He must have pulled out sometime after two this morning."

"The shot I heard was close to four."

"One shot?"

"Only one . . . but he's been shot twice." Hesitating a little, I asked: "Who was with him when you last saw him?"

"He was alone. If it's Morgan Park you are thinkin' of, forget it. He left right after you did. When I last saw Rud, he was goin' to his room, feelin' mighty sleepy."

The Bar M riders were circling around. Their faces were cold and they started an icy chill coming up my spine. These men were utterly loyal, utterly ruthless when aroused. The night before they had given me the benefit of the doubt but now they saw no reason to think of any other solution but the obvious one.

Tom Fox, a lean, hard-bitten Bar M man, was staring at me. Coolly he took a rope from his pommel. "What we waitin' for, men?" he asked bitterly. "There's our man."

Turning, I said: "Fox, from what I hear you're a good man and a good hand. Don't jump to any hasty conclusions. I didn't kill Rud Maclaren and had no reason to. We made peace talk last night an' parted in good spirits."

Fox looked up at Canaval. "That right?"

Canaval hesitated, his expression unchanging. Then he spoke clearly. "It is . . . but Rud Maclaren changed his mind afterward."

"Changed his mind?" That I couldn't believe, yet at the

expression in Canaval's eyes, I knew he was speaking the truth. "Even so," I added, "how could I be expected to know that? When I left, all was friendly."

"You couldn't know it," Canaval agreed, "unless he got out of bed an' came to tell you. He might have done that, and I can think of no other reason for him to come here. He came to tell you . . . an' you killed him when he started away."

The hands growled and Fox shook out a loop. It was Olga who stopped them. "No! Wait until the others arrive. If he killed my father, I want him to die! But wait until the others come."

Reluctantly Fox drew in his rope and coiled it. Sweat broke out on my forehead. I could fight, and I would if it came to that, but these men only believed they were doing the right thing. They had no idea that I was innocent. My mouth was dry and my hands felt cold. I tried to catch Olga's eye but she ignored me. Canaval seemed to be studying something, but he did not speak a word.

The first one to arrive was Key Chapin, and behind him a dozen other men. He looked at me, a quick, worried glance, and then looked at Canaval. Without waiting for questions, the foreman quietly repeated what had happened, telling of the entire evening, facts that could not until then have been known to the men.

"There's one thing," I said suddenly, "that I want to call to your attention."

They looked at me, but there was not a friendly eye in the lot of them. Looking around the circle of their faces, I felt a cold sinking in my stomach, and a feeling came over me. *Matt Sabre*, I was telling myself, *this is the end. You've come to it at last, and you'll hang for another man's crime.*

Not one friendly face—and Mulvaney had not returned with the Bar M riders. There was no sign of Jolly Benaras.

"Chapin," I asked, "will you turn Maclaren over?"

The request puzzled them, and they looked from me to the covered body, then to Chapin. He swung down and walked across to the dead man. I heard Olga's breath catch, and then Chapin rolled Maclaren on his back.

He straightened up then, still puzzled. The others looked blankly at me.

"The reason you are so quick to accuse me is that he is here, on my ranch. Well, he was not killed here. There's no blood on the ground."

Startled, they all looked. Before any comment could be made, I continued: "One of the wounds bled badly, and the front of his shirt is dark with blood. The sand would be, too, if he'd been killed here. What I am saying is that he was killed elsewhere, then carried here!"

"But why?" Chapin protested.

Canaval said: "You mean to throw guilt onto you?"

"I sure do mean that. Also, that shot I heard fired was shot into him after he was dead."

Fox shook his head, and sneered: "How could you figure that?"

"A dead man does not bleed. Look at him. All the blood came from one wound."

Suddenly we heard more horsemen, and Mulvaney returned with his guns and the Benaras boys. Not one, but all of them.

Coolly they moved up to the edge of the circle.

"We'd be beholden," the elder Benaras said loudly, "if you'd all move back. We're friends to Sabre, an' we don't believe he done it. Now give him air an' listen."

They hesitated, not liking it. But their common sense told them that, if trouble started now, it would be a bloody mess. Carefully the nearest riders eased back. Whether Olga was listening, I had no idea. Yet it was she who I wanted most to convince.

"There are other men with axes to grind beside the Pinders and I," I said. "What had I to fear from Rud? Already I had shown I could take care of myself against all of them. Face to face, I was twice the man Rud was."

"You talk yourself up mighty well," Fox said.

"You had your chance in the cañon," I said brutally, "and, when I say I can hold this ranch, you know I'm not lying."

Horses came up the trail and the first faces I recognized were Bodie Miller and the redhead I'd whipped at the Two Bar. Bodie pushed his horse into the circle when he saw me. The devil was riding Bodie again, and I could see from Canaval's face that he knew it.

Right at the moment Bodie was remembering how I had dared him to gamble at pointblank range. "You, is it?" he said. "I'll kill you one day."

"Keep out of this, Bodie!" Canaval ordered sharply.

Miller's dislike was naked in his eyes. "Rud's dead now," he said. "Mebby you won't be the boss any more. Mebby she'll want a younger man for boss!"

The import of his words was like a blow across the face. Suddenly I wanted to kill him, suddenly I was going to. Canaval's voice was a cool breath of air through my fevered brain. "That will be for Miss Olga to decide." He turned to her. "Do you wish me to continue as foreman?"

"Naturally." Her voice was cold and even, and in that moment I was proud of her. "And your first job will be to fire Bodie Miller!"

Miller's face went white with fury, and his lips bared back from his teeth. Before he could speak, I interfered. "Don't say it, Bodie! Don't say it!" I stepped forward to face him across Maclaren's body.

The malignancy of his expression was unbelievable. "You an' me are goin' to meet," he said, staring at me.

"When you're ready, Bodie." Deliberately, not wanting the fight here, now, I turned my back on him.

Chapin and Canaval joined me while the men loaded the body into a buckboard. "We don't think you're guilty, Sabre. Have you any ideas?"

"Only that I believe he was killed elsewhere and carried here to cast blame on me. I don't believe it was Pinder. He would never shoot Maclaren in the back."

"You think Park did it?" Canaval demanded.

"Peace between myself and Maclaren would be the last thing he'd want," I said.

Bob Benaras was waiting for me. "You can use Jonathan an' Jolly," he said. "I ain't got work enough to keep 'em out of mischief."

He was not fooling me in the least. "Thanks. I can use them to spell Mulvaney on look-out, and there's plenty of work to do."

For two weeks we worked hard, and the inquest of Rud Maclaren turned up nothing new. There had been no will, so the ranch went to Olga. Yet nothing was settled. Some people believed I had killed Maclaren, most of them did not know, but the country was quiet.

Of Bodie Miller we heard much. He killed a man at Hattan's Point in a saloon quarrel, shot him before he could get his hand on a gun. Bodie and Red were riding with a lot of riff-raff from Hite. The Bar M was missing cattle and Bodie laughed when he heard it. He pistol-whipped a man in Silver Reef, and wounded a man while driving off the posse that came after him.

I worried more about Morgan Park. I had to discover just

what his plan was. My only chance was to follow Park every hour of the day and night. I must know where he went, what he was doing, with whom he was talking. One night I waited on a hill above Hattan's Point watching the house where he lived when in town.

When he came out of the house, I could feel the hackles rising on the back of my neck. There was something about him that would always stir me to fury, and it did now. Stifling it, I watched him go to Mother O'Hara's, watched him mount up, and ride out of town on the Bar M road. Yet scarcely a dozen miles from town he drew up and scanned his back trail. Safely under cover, I watched him. Apparently satisfied with what he did not see, he turned right along the ridge, keeping under cover. He now took a course that led him into the wildest and most remote corner of the Bar M, that neck of land north of my own and extending far west. His trail led him out upon Dark Cañon Plateau. Knowing little of this area, I closed the distance between us until I saw him making camp.

Before daylight he was moving again. The sun rose and the day became hot, with a film of heat haze obscuring all the horizons. He seemed headed toward the northwest where the long line of the Sweet Alice Hills ended the visible world. This country was a maze of cañons. To the south it fell away in an almost sheer precipice for hundreds of feet to the bottom of Dark Cañon. There were trails off the plateau, but I knew none of them.

The view was breathtaking, overlooking miles of columned and whorled sandstone, towering escarpments, minarets, and upended ledges. This had once been inhabited country for there were ruins of cliff dwellings about, and Indian writings.

The trail divided at the east end of the plateau and the flat rock gave no indication of which Park had taken. It looked as though I had lost him. Taking a chance, I went down a steep slide into Poison Cañon and worked back in the direction he must have taken, but the only tracks were of rodents and one of a bighorn sheep. Hearing a sound of singing, I dismounted. Rifle in hand, I worked my way through the rocks and brush.

"No use to shave," the man at the fire said. "We're stuck here. No chance' to get to Hattan's Point now."

"Yeah?" The shaver scoffed. "You see that big feller? Him an' Slade are talking medicine. We'll move out soon. I don't want to get caught with no beard when I go to town."

"Who'll care how you look? An' maybe the fewer who know how you look, the better."

"After this show busts open," the shaver replied, "it ain't goin' to matter who knows me. We'll have that town sewed up tighter'n a drum."

"Mebby." The cook straightened and rubbed his back. "Again, mebby not. I wish it was rustlin' cows. Takin' towns can be mighty mean."

"It ain't the town, just a couple o' ranches. Only three, four men on the Two Bar, an' about the same on the Bar M. Slade will have the toughest job done afore we start."

"That big feller looks man enough to do it by himself. But if he can pay, his money will look good to me."

"He better watch his step. That Sabre ain't no chicken with a pair o' Colts. He downed Rollie Pinder, an' I figure it was him done for Lyell over to the Reef."

"It'll be somethin' when he an' Bodie git together. Both faster'n greased lightnin'."

"Sabre won't be around. Pinder figures on raidin' that spread today. Sam wouldn't help him because he'd promised Park. Pinder'll hit 'em about sundown, an' that'll be the end of Sabre."

Waiting no longer, I hurried back to my horse. If Pinder was to attack the Two Bar, Park would have to wait. Glancing at the sun, fear rose in my throat. It would be nip and tuck if I was to get back. Another idea came to me. I would rely on Mulvaney and the Benaras boys to protect the Two Bar. I would counterattack and hit the CP!

When I reached the CP, it lay deserted and still but for the cook, baldheaded and big-bellied. He rushed from the door but I was on him too fast, and he dropped his rifle under the threat of my six-gun. Tying him up, I dropped him in a feed bin and went to the house. Finding a can of wagon grease, I smeared it thickly over the floor in front of both doors and more of it on the steps. Leaving the door partly open, I dumped red pepper into a pan and balanced it above the door where the slightest push would send it cascading over whoever entered, filling the air with fine grains.

Opening the corral, I turned the horses loose and started them down the valley. Digging out all the coffee on the place, I packed it to take away, knowing how a cowhand dearly loves his coffee. It was my idea to make their lives as miserable as possible to get them thoroughly fed up with the fight. Pinder would not abandon the fight, but his hands might get sick of the discomfort.

Gathering a few sticks, I added them to the fire already laid, but under them I put a half dozen shotgun shells. In the tool shed were six sticks of powder and some fuse left from blasting rocks.

Digging out a crack at one corner of the fireplace, I put two sticks of dynamite into the crack, then ran the fuse within two inches of the fire and covered it with ashes. The shotgun shells would explode and scatter the fire, igniting, I hoped, the fuse.

A slow hour passed after I returned to a hide-out in the

brush. What was happening at the Two Bar? In any kind of fight one has to have confidence in those fighting with him, and I had it in the men I'd left behind me. If one of them was killed, I vowed never to stop until all this crowd were finished.

Sweat trickled down my face. It was hot under the brush. Once a rattler crawled by within six or seven feet of me. A pack rat stared at me, then moved on. Crows quarreled in the trees over my head. And then I saw the riders.

One look told me. Whatever had happened at the Two Bar, I knew these men were not victorious. There were nine in the group, and two were bandaged. One had his arm in a sling, one had his skull bound up. Another man was tied over a saddle, head and heels hanging. They rode down the hill and I lifted my rifle, waiting for them to get closer to the ranch. Then I fired three times as rapidly as I could squeeze off the shots.

One horse sprang into the air, spun halfway around, scattering the group, then fell, sending his rider sprawling. The others rushed for the shelter of the buildings, but just as they reached them, one man toppled from his horse, hit the dirt like a sack of old clothes, and rolled over in the dust. He staggered to his feet and rushed toward the barn, fell again, then got up and ran on.

Others made a break for the house, and the first one to hit those greasy steps was Jim Pinder. He hit them running, his feet flew out from under him, and he hit the step on his chin. With a yell, the others charged by him, and even at that distance I could hear the crash of their falling, their angry shouts, and then the roaring sneezes and gasping yells as the red pepper filled the air and bit into their nostrils.

Coolly I proceeded to shoot out the windows, to knock the hinges off the door, and, when Jim Pinder staggered to his feet and reached for his hat, I put a bullet through the hat. He jumped as if stung and grabbed for his pistol. He swung it up, and I fired again as he did. What happened to his shot I never knew, but he dropped the pistol with a yell and plunged for the door.

One man had ducked for the heavily planked water trough and now he fired at me. Invisible from my position, I knew that he was somewhere under the trough, and so I drilled the trough with two quick shots, draining the water down upon him. He jumped to escape, and I put bullets into the dust to the left and right of his position. Like it or not, he had to lie there while all the water ran over him. A few scattered shots stampeded their horses, and then I settled down to wait for time to bring the real fireworks.

A few shots came my way after a while, but all were high or low and none came close to me.

Taking my time, I loaded up for the second time, and then rolled a smoke. My buckskin was in a low place and had cover from the shots. There was no way they could escape from the house to approach me. One wounded man had fallen near the barn, and I let him get up and limp toward it. Every once in a while somebody would fall inside the house and in the clear air I could hear the sound and each time I couldn't help but grin.

There was smashing and banging inside the house, and I could imagine what was happening. They were looking for coffee and not finding it. A few minutes later a slow trickle of smoke came out the chimney. My head resting on the palm of one hand, I took a deep drag on my cigarette and waited happily for the explosions.

They came, and suddenly. There was the sharp bark of a shotgun shell exploding, then a series of bangs as the others went off. Two men rushed from the door and charged for the barn. Bullets into the dust hurried them to shelter, and I laid back and laughed heartily. I'd never felt so good in my life, picturing the faces of those tired, disgruntled men, besieged in the cabin, unable to make coffee, sliding on the greasy floor, sneezing from the red pepper, ducking shotgun shells from the fire.

Not five minutes had passed when the powder went off with terrific concussion. I had planted it better than I knew, for it not only cracked the fireplace but blew a hole in it from which smoke gulped, then trickled slowly.

Rising, I drifted back to my horse and headed for the ranch. Without doubt the CP outfit was beginning to learn what war meant, and, furthermore, I knew my methods were far more exasperating to the cowhands than out and out fight. Your true cowhand savors a good scrap, but he does not like discomfort or annoyance, and I knew that going without water, without good food, and without coffee would do more to end the fight than anything else. All the same, as I headed the gelding back toward the Two Bar, I knew that, if any of my own boys had been killed, I would retaliate in kind. There could be no other answer.

Mulvaney greeted me at the door. "Sure, Matt, you missed a good scrap! We give them lads the fight of their lives!"

Jolly and Jonathan looked up at me. Jolly grinning, the more serious Jonathan smiling faintly. Jolly showed me a bullet burn on his arm, the only scratch any of them had suffered.

They had been watching, taking turn about, determined they would not be caught asleep while I was gone. The result was that they sighted the CP riders when they were still miles from the headquarters of the Two Bar. The Benaras boys began it with a skirmishers' battle, firing from rocks and brush in a continual running fight. A half dozen times they drove the CP riders to shelter, killing two horses and wounding a man.

They had retreated steadily until in a position to be covered by Mulvaney, who was ready with all the spare arms loaded. From the bunkhouse they stood off the attack. They had so many loaded weapons that there was no break in their fire until the CP retreated.

"Somebody didn't want to fight," Jolly explained. "We seen 'em argufyin' an' then finally somebody else joined in, an' they backed out on Pinder. He was almighty sore, believe you me."

Amid much laughter I told them about my own attack on the CP.

Mulvaney ended it suddenly. "Hey!" he turned swiftly. "I forgot to tell yer. That catamount of a Bodie Miller done shot Canaval!"

"Is he dead?"

"Not the last we heard, but he's hurt mighty bad. He took four bullets before he went down."

"Miller?"

"Never got a scratch. That kid's plumb poison, I tell you. Poison."

IX

For a minute I considered that, and liked none of it. Canaval had been a man with whom I could reason. More than that, with Canaval at hand there had always been protection for Olga.

There was no time to be wasted now. Telling Mulvaney of what I had seen in the cañon, I turned my buckskin toward the Bar M. I wanted first of all to talk with Olga, and second to see Canaval. If the man was alive, I had to talk to him. The gun star of Bodie Miller was rising now, and I knew how he would react. This new shooting would only serve to convince him of his speed. The confidence he had lacked on our first meeting he would now have.

He would not wait long to kill again, and he would seek out some known gunfighter, for his reputation could only grow now by killing the good ones, and Canaval had been one of the fastest around. And who would that mean? Jim Pinder, Morgan Park, or myself. And knowing how he felt about me, I had an idea who he would be seeking out.

Key Chapin was standing on the wide verandah of the Bar M house when I rode into the yard. Fox was loitering nearby and he started toward me. "You ain't wanted here, Sabre," he told me brusquely. "Get off the place."

"Don't be a fool, man. I've come on business."

He shook his head stubbornly. "Don't make no diff'rence. Start movin' an' don't reach for a gun. You're covered from the bunkhouse an' the barn."

"Fox," I persisted, "I've no row with you, and you're the

last man in the world I'd like to kill, but I don't like being pushed, and you're pushin' me. I've got Bodie Miller an' Morgan Park to take care of, as well as Jim Pinder. So get this straight. If you want to die, grab iron. Don't ride me, Fox, because I won't take it."

My buckskin started, and Fox, his face a study in conflicting emotion, hesitated. Then a cool voice interposed. "Fox! Step back! Let the gentleman come up."

It was Olga Maclaren.

Fox hesitated, then stepped back, and I drew up the buckskin for a minute. Fox looked up at me, and our eyes met. "I'm glad of that, Fox," I said. "I'd hate to have killed a man as good as you. They don't come often."

The sincerity in my voice must have reached him, for when I happened to glance back, he was staring after me, his face puzzled. As I dismounted, Chapin walked over toward the house.

Olga stood on the steps, awaiting me. There was no welcome in her eyes. Her face was cool, composed. "There was something you wanted?"

"Is that my only welcome?"

"What reason have you to expect anything more?"

That made me shrug. "None," I said, "none at all. How's Canaval?"

"Resting."

"Is he better? Is he conscious?"

"Yes to both questions. Can he see anybody? No."

Then I heard him speak. "Sabre? Is that you? Come in!"

Olga hesitated, and for a minute I believed she was going to defy the request, then with a shrug of indifference she led Chapin and me into the wounded man's room.

The foreman's appearance shocked me. He was drawn and thin, his eyes huge and hollow in the deathly pallor of his face. His hand gripped mine and he stared up at me. "Glad you're here, Sabre," he said \abruptly. "Watch that little demon. Oh, he's a fast man. He's blinding. He had a bullet into me before my gun cleared. He's a freak, Sabre."

"Sure," I agreed, "but that isn't what I came about. I came to tell you again. I had nothing to do with killing Rud Maclaren."

He nodded slightly. "I'm sure of it." I could feel Olga behind me. "I found . . . tracks. Not yours. Horse tracks, and tracks of a man carrying a heavy burden. Small feet."

Chapin interrupted suddenly. "Sabre, I've a message for you. Picked it up in Silver Reef yesterday." He handed me a telegram, still sealed. Ripping it open, I saw there what I had expected.

MY BROTHER UNHEARD OF IN MANY MONTHS. MORGAN PARK ANSWERS DESCRIPTION OF PARK CANTWELL, WANTED FOR MURDER AND EMBEZZLEMENT OF REGIMENTAL FUNDS. COMING WEST.

> **LEO D'ARCY**
> **COL. 12TH CAVALRY**

Without comment, I handed the message back to Chapin, who read it aloud. Olga grew pale, but she said nothing.

"Know anything about the case?" Canaval asked Chapin.

The editor nodded. "Yes, I do. It was quite an exciting case at the time. Park Cantwell was a captain in the cavalry. He embezzled some twenty thousand dollars, then murdered his commanding officer when faced with it. He got away, was recaptured, and then broke jail and killed two men in the process. He was last heard of in Mexico."

"Not much chance of a mistake, is there?"

"None," Chapin said, "or very slight. Not many men are so big, and he is a striking character. Out West here he probably believed he would not be discovered. Most of his time he spent on that lonely ranch of his, and he rarely was around town until lately. Apparently, if this is true, he hoped to realize enough money out of this deal of his with Jake Booker to retire in Mexico or elsewhere. Probably in this remote corner of the West, he believed he might never be recognized."

"And now?" Olga asked. "What will happen?"

Chapin shrugged. "I'll take this message to Sheriff Will Tharp, and then we'll wait for D'Arcy to arrive."

"There's not much else we can do," I agreed.

"What is it Park and Booker want?" Chapin wondered. "I don't grasp their motive."

"Who does?" I shrugged.

Olga had not looked at me. Several times I tried to catch her eyes, but she avoided my glance. Her face was quiet, composed, and she was, as always, perfectly poised. Not by so much as a flicker of an eyelash did she betray her feelings toward me, but I found no comfort in that. Whether or not she believed I had killed her father, she obviously wanted no part of me.

Discouraged, I turned toward the door.

"Where to now?" Canaval asked.

"Why"—I turned—"I'm heading for town to see Morgan Park. No man ever beat me with his fists yet and walked away scotfree. I'll have the hide off that brute, and now is as good a time as any."

"Leave him alone. Sabre!" Canaval tried to sit up. "I've seen him kill a man with his fists!"

"He won't kill me."

"What is this?" Olga turned around, her eyes blazing. "A

cheap childish desire for revenge? Or are you talking just to make noise? It seems all I've heard you do since you came here is to talk. You've no right to go in there and start trouble. You've no right to fight Morgan Park simply because he beat you. Leave him alone."

"Protecting him?" My voice was not pleasant. Did she, I wondered, actually love the man? The idea did not appeal to me, and the more it stayed in my mind the more angry I became.

"No!" she flared. "I am not protecting him! From what I saw of you after that first fight, I don't believe it is he who needs the protection."

She could have said nothing more likely to bring all my own temper to the surface. So when she spoke, I listened, my face stiffening. Then without another word I turned and walked from the room. I went down the steps to my horse, and into the saddle.

The buckskin leaned into the wind and kept the fast pace I set for him. Despite my fury, I kept my eyes open and on the hills. Right then, I would have welcomed a fight and any kind of a fight. I was mad all the way through, burning with it.

And perhaps it was lucky that right then I should round a bend of the trail and come into the midst of Jack Slade and his men. They had not heard me until I rounded the bend, and they were heading the same way I was, toward town. The sudden sound of horse's hoofs turned their heads, and Slade dove for his gun.

He was too late. Mad clear through, the instant I saw them I slammed the spurs into my startled buckskin. The horse gave a lunge, driving between the last two riders and striking Slade's horse with his shoulder. At the same instant, I lashed out with the barrel of my Colt and laid it above the ear of the nearest rider. He went off his horse as if struck by lightning, and I swung around, blasting a shot from my belt that knocked the gun from the hand of another rider. Slade was fighting his maddened horse, and I leaned over and hit it a crack with my hat. The horse gave a tremendous leap and started to run like a scared rabbit with Slade fighting to stay in the saddle. He had lost one stirrup when my horse lunged into his and had not recovered it. The last I saw of him was his running horse and a cloud of dust. It all happened in a split second, and one man had a smashed hand, one was knocked out, and Slade was fighting his horse.

The fourth man had been maneuvering for a shot at me, but among the plunging horses he was afraid of hitting his own friends. Wheeling my horse, I fired as he did and both of us missed. He tried to steady his horse and swung. Buck did not like it and was fighting to get away. I let him go, taking a backward shot at the man in the saddle, a shot that must have clipped his ear for he ducked like a bee-stung farmer, and then Buck was laying them down on the trail to town.

Feeding shells into my gun, I let him run. I felt better for the action and was ready for anything. The town loomed up, and I rode in and swung down in front of Mother O'Hara's. Buck's side looked bad, for the spurs had bit deep, and I'm a man who rarely touches a spur to a horse. After greasing the wounds and talking Buck into friendship again, I went inside.

There was nobody around, but Katie O'Hara came out of her kitchen. One look at me and she could see I was spoiling for trouble. "Morgan Park in town?"

She did not hesitate. "He is that. A moment ago I heard he was in the saloon."

Morgan Park was there, all right. He was sitting at a table with Jake Booker, and they both looked up when I entered. I didn't waste any time. I walked up to them.

"Booker," I said, "I've heard you're a no-account shyster,

a sheep-stealin', small-town shyster, at that. But you're doing business with a thief and a murderer, and the man I'm going to whip." With that I grabbed the table and hurled it out of the way, and then I slapped Morgan Park across the mouth with my hat.

Morgan Park came off his chair with a roar. He lunged and came up fast, and I smashed him in the teeth with a left. His lips flattened and blood showered from his mouth, and then I threw a right that caught him flush on the chin—and I threw it hard!

He blinked, but he never stopped coming, and he rushed me, swinging with both of those huge, iron-like fists. One of them rang bells on my skull and the other dug for my mid-section with a blow I partially blocked with an elbow, then I turned with his arm over my shoulder, and I threw him bodily across the floor against the bar rail. He came up fast, and I nailed him with another left. Then he caught me with both hands, and sparks danced among the stars in my skull. That old smoky taste came up inside of me, and the taste of blood in my mouth, and I walked in smashing with both hands! Something busted on his face, and his brow was cut to the bone and the blood was running all over him.

There was a crowd around, and they were yelling, but I heard no sound. I walked in, bobbing and weaving to miss as many of those jarring, brutal blows as possible, but they kept landing and battering me. He knocked me back into the bar, and then grabbed a bottle. He took a terrific cut at my skull, and I ducked, smashing him in the ribs. He staggered and sprawled out of balance from the force of his missed swing, and I rushed him and took a flying leap at his shoulders. I landed astride and jammed both spurs into his thighs and he let out a roar of agony.

I went over his head, lighting on all fours, and he sprang

atop my back. I flattened out on the floor with the feeling that he had me. He was yelling like a madman, and he grabbed my hair and began to beat my head against the floor. How I did it I'll never know, but I bowed my back under his weight and forced myself to my hands and knees. He ripped at me with his own spurs, and then I got his leg, and threw him off.

Coming up together, we circled, more wary now. His shirt was in ribbons, and he was covered with blood. I'd never seen Morgan stripped before. He had a chest and shoulders like a Hercules. He circled, and then came into me, snarling. I nailed that snarl into his teeth with both fists, and we stood there swinging them freely with both hands, rocking with the power of those punches and smelling of sweat, blood, and fury.

He backed up, and I went into him. Suddenly he caught my upper arms and, dropping, put a foot in my stomach and threw me over his head! For a fleeting instant I was flying through the air, and then I lit on a poker table and grabbed the sides with both hands. It went over on top of me, and that was all that saved me as he rushed in to finish me with the boots. I shoved the table at him and came up off the floor, and he hit me again, and I went right back down. He dropped a big palm on my head and shoved me at the floor. I sprawled out and he kicked me in the side. It missed my ribs and glanced off my gun belt, and I rolled over and grabbed his boot, twisting hard.

It threw him off balance and he hit the floor, which gave me a chance to get on my feet. I got him just as he was halfway up with a right that knocked him through the door and out onto the porch. I hit the porch in a jump, and he tackled me around the knees. We both were down then, and I slapped him with a cupped hand over his ear and knew from the way he let go that I'd busted an eardrum for him. I dropped him again with a solid right to the chin, and stood back, gasping and pain-wracked, fighting for breath. He got up more slowly, and I nailed him, left and right in the mouth, and he went down heavily.

Sprawled out, he lay there on the edge of the walk, one hand trailing in the dust, and I stared down at him. He was finished, through! Turning on my heels, I walked back inside, and, brushing off those who crowded around me, I headed for the bar. I took the glass of whiskey that was shoved at me and poured it in my hands and mopped the cuts on the lower part of my face with it. Then I took a quick gulp from the glass that was again put before me, and turned.

Morgan Park was standing three feet away from me, a bloody, battered giant with cold, ugly fury blazing from his eyes. "Give me a drink!" he bellowed.

He picked up the glass and tossed it off. "Another!" he yelled, while I stared at him. He picked that up, lifted it to his lips, then threw it in my eyes!

I must have blinked, for instead of getting the shot glass full, I got only part of it, but enough to blind me. And then he stepped close. As I fought for sight, I caught a glimpse of his boot toes, wide spread, and I was amazed that such a big man had such small feet. Then he hit me. It felt like a blow from an axe, and it knocked me into the bar. He faced around, taking his time, and he smashed one into my body, and I went down, gasping for breath. He kicked at me with the toe of one of those deadly boots that could have put an eye out, but the kick glanced off the side of my head.

It was my turn to be down and out. Then somebody drenched me with a bucket of water, and I looked up. Key Chapin was standing over me, but it was not Key Chapin who had thrown the water. It was Olga.

Right then I was only amazed that she was there at all, and

then I got up shakily and somebody said—"There he is!"— and I saw Park, standing there with his hands on his hips, leering at me, and with the same mutual hatred we went for each other again.

How we did it I don't know. Both of us had taken beatings that would have killed a horse. All I knew was that time for me had stopped. Only one thing remained. I had to whip that man, whip him or kill him with my bare hands, and I was not stopping until I was sure I had done it.

"Stop it, you crazy fools! Stop it or I'll throw you both in jail!" Sheriff Will Tharp was standing in the door with a gun on me. His cold blue eyes were blazing.

Behind him were maybe twenty men, staring at us. One of them was Key Chapin. Another was Bodie Miller.

"Take him out of here, then," I said. "If he wants more of this, he can have it in the morning."

Park backed toward the door, then turned away. He looked punch drunk.

After that I sat up for an hour putting hot water on my face.

Then I went to the livery stable and crawled into the loft, taking a blanket with me. I had worn my guns and had my rifle along.

How long I slept I have no idea except that, when I awakened, bright sunlight was streaming through the cracks in the walls of the old stable, and the loft was like an oven with the heat. Sitting up, I touched my face. It was sore all right, but felt better. I worked my fingers to loosen them up, and then heard a movement and looked around. Morgan Park was on the ladder, staring at me. And I knew then that I was not looking at a sane man.

X

He stood there on the ladder in that hot old barn, staring at me with hatred and a fury that seemed no whit abated from the previous night.

"You back again?" I spoke quietly, yet lay poised for instant movement. I knew now the tremendous vitality that huge body held. "After the way I licked you last night?"

The veins distended in his brow and throat. "Whipped me?" His voice was hoarse with anger. "Why, you . . . !" He started over the end of the ladder, and I let him come. Right then I could have cooled him, knocked him off that ladder, but something within me wouldn't allow it. With a lesser man, one I could have whipped easily, I might have done it just to end the fighting, but not with Morgan Park. Right then I knew I had to whip him fairly, or I could never be quite comfortable again.

He straightened from the ladder, and I could see that he was a little stiff. Well, so was I. But my boxing with Mulvaney and the riding I had done had been keeping me in trim. My condition was better than his, almost enough to equalize his greater size and strength. He straightened and turned toward me. He did not rush, just stood there studying me with cool calculation, and I knew that he, too, had come here to make an end to this fight and to me.

Right then he was studying how best to whip me, and suddenly I perceived his advantage. In the loft, one side open to the barn, the rest of it stacked with hay, I was distinctly at a disadvantage. Here his weight and strength could be decisive. He moved toward me, backing me toward the hay. I feinted, but he did not strike. He merely moved on in, his head hunched behind a big shoulder, his fists before him, moving slightly. Then he lunged. My back came up against the slanting wall of hay and my feet slipped. Off balance, lying against the hay, I had no power in my blows. With cold brutality he began to swing, his eyes were exultant and wicked with sadistic delight. Lights exploded in my brain, and then another punch hit me, and another.

My head spinning, my mouth tasting of smoke, I let myself slide to a sitting position, then threw my weight sidewise against his knees. He staggered and, fearing the fall off the edge of the loft, fought for balance. Instantly I smashed him in the mouth. He went to his haunches, and I sprang past him, grabbed a rope that hung from the rafters and dropped to the hard-packed earth of the barn's floor.

He turned and glared at me, and I waited. A man appeared in the door, and I heard him yell: "They're at it again!" And then Morgan Park clambered down the ladder and turned to me.

Now it had to be ended. Moving in quickly, I jabbed a stiff left to his face. The punch landed on his lacerated mouth and started the blood. Circling carefully, I slipped a right, and countered with a right to the ribs. Then I hit him, fast and rolling my shoulders, with a left and right to the face. He came in, but I slipped another punch and uppercut hard to the wind. That slowed him down. He hit me with a glancing left and took two punches in return.

He looked sick now, and I moved in, smashing him on the chin with both hands. He backed up, bewildered, and I knocked his left aside and hit him on the chin. He went to his knees, and I stepped back and let him get up.

Behind me there was a crowd and I knew it. Waiting, I let him get up. He wiped off his hands, then lunged at me, head down and swinging. Side-stepping swiftly, I evaded the rush, and, when he tried it again, I dropped my palm to the top of his head and spun him. At the same instant I uppercut with a wicked right that straightened him up. He turned toward me, and then I pulled the trigger on a high hard one. It struck his chin with the solid thud of the butt end of an axe striking a log.

He fell—not over backwards, but face down. He lay there, still and quiet, unmoving. Out cold.

Sodden with weariness and fed up with fighting for once, I turned away from him and picked up my hat and rifle. Nobody said anything, staring at my battered face and torn clothing. Then they walked to him.

At the door I met Sheriff Tharp. He glared at me. "Didn't I tell you to stop fighting in this town, Sabre?"

"What am I going to do? Let him beat my head off? I came here to sleep without interruption and he followed me, found me this morning." Jerking my head toward the barn's interior, I told him: "You'll find him in there, Tharp."

He hesitated. "Better have some rest, Sabre. Then ride out of town for a few days. After all, I have to have peace. I'm arresting Park."

"Not for fighting?"

"For murder. This morning I received an official communication confirming your message."

Actually I was sorry for him. No man ever hates a man he has whipped in a hand-to-hand fight. All I wanted now was sleep, food, and gallons of cold spring water. Right then I felt as if it had been weeks since I'd had a decent drink.

Yet all the way to O'Hara's I kept remembering that bucket of water doused over me the night before. Had it really been Olga Maclaren there? Or had I been out of my head from the punches I'd taken?

When my face was washed off, I came into the restaurant, and the first person I saw was Key Chapin. He looked at my face and shook his head. "I'd never believe anything human could fight the way you two did!" he exclaimed. "And again this morning! I hear you whipped him good this time."

"Yeah." I was tired of it all. Somberly I ate breakfast, listening to the drone of voices in my ears.

"Booker's still in town." Chapin was speaking. "What's he after, I wonder?"

Right then I did not care, but, as I ate and drank coffee, my mind began to function once more. After all, this was my country. I belonged here. For the first time I really felt that I belonged some place.

"Am I crazy, or was Olga here last night?"

"She was here, all right. She saw part of your fight."

"Did she leave?"

"I think not. I believe she's staying over at Doc and Missus West's place. They're old friends of hers." Chapin knocked out his pipe. "As a matter of fact, you'd better go over there and have him look at those cuts. One of them at least needs some stitches."

"Tharp arrested Park."

"Yes, I know. Park is Cantwell, all right."

Out in the air I felt better. With food and some strong black coffee inside of me. I felt like a new man, and the mountain air was fresh and good to the taste. Turning, I started up the street, walking slowly. This was Hattan's Point. This was my town. Here, in this place, I would remain, I would ranch here, graze my cattle, rear my sons to manhood. Here I would take my place in the world and be something more than the careless, cheerful, trouble-hunting

236

rider. Here, in this place, I belonged.

Doc West lived in a small white cottage surrounded by rose bushes and shrouded in vines. Several tall poplars reached toward the sky and there was a small patch of lawn inside the white picket fence.

He answered the door at my rap, a tall, austere-looking man with gray hair and keen blue eyes. He smiled at me. "You're Matt Sabre? I was expecting you."

That made me grin. "With a face like this, you should expect me. I took a licking for a while."

"And gave one to Morgan Park. I have just come from the jail where I looked him over. He has three broken ribs and his jaw is broken."

"No!" I stared at him.

He nodded. "The ribs were broken last night sometime, I'd guess."

"There was no quit in him."

West nodded seriously. "There still isn't. He's a dangerous man, Sabre. A very dangerous man."

That I knew. Looking around, I saw nothing of Olga Maclaren. Hesitating to ask, I waited and let him work on me. When he was finished, I got to my feet and buckled on my guns.

"And now?" he asked.

"Back to the Two Bar. There's work to do there."

He nodded, but seemed to be hesitating about something. Then he asked: "What about the murder of Rud Maclaren? What's your view on that?"

Something occurred to me then that I had forgotten. "It was Morgan Park," I said. "Canaval found the footprint of a man nearby. The boots were very small. Morgan Park . . . and I noticed it for the first time during our fight . . . has very small feet despite his size."

"You may be right," he agreed hesitantly. "I've wondered."

"Who else could it have been? I know I didn't do it."

"I don't believe you did, but . . . ," he hesitated, then dropped the subject.

Slowly I walked out to the porch and stopped there, fitting my hat on my head. It had to be done gently for I had two good-size lumps just at my hairline. A movement made me turn, and Olga was standing in the doorway.

Her dark hair was piled on her head, the first time I had seen it that way, and she was wearing something green and summery that made her eyes an even deeper green. For a long moment neither of us spoke, and then she said: "Your face . . . does it hurt very much?"

"Not much. It mostly just looks bad, and I'll probably not be able to shave for a while. How's Canaval?"

"He's much better. I've put Fox to running the ranch."

"He's a good man." I twisted my hat in my hands. "When are you going back?"

"Tomorrow, I believe."

How lovely she was! At this moment I knew that I had never in all my life seen anything so lovely, or anyone so desirable, or anyone who meant so much to me. It was strange, all of it. But how did she feel toward me?

"You're staying on the Two Bar?"

"Yes, my house is coming along now, and the cattle are doing well. I've started something there, and I think I'll stay. This," I said quietly, "is my home, this is my country. This is where I belong."

She looked up, and, as our eyes met, I thought she was going to speak, but she said nothing. Then I stepped quickly to her and took her hands. "Olga. You can't really believe that I killed your father? You can't believe I ever would do such a thing?"

"No. I never really believed you'd killed him."

"Then . . . ?"

She said nothing, not meeting my eyes.

"I want you, Olga. You, more than anything. I want you on the Two Bar. You are the reason I have stayed here, and you are the reason I am going to remain."

"Don't. Don't talk like that. We can never be anything to each other."

"What are you saying? You can't mean that."

"I do mean it. You . . . you're violent. You're a killer. You've killed men here, and I think you live for fighting. I watched you in that fight with Morgan. You . . . you actually enjoyed it."

Thinking that over, I had to agree. "In a way, yes. After all, fighting has been a necessity too long in the life of men upon earth. It is not an easy thing to be rid of. Mentally I know that violence is always a bad means to an end. I know that all disputes should be settled without it. Nevertheless, deep inside me there is something that does like it. It is too old a feeling to die out quickly, and as long as there are men in the world like Morgan Park, the Pinders, and Bodie Miller, there must be men willing and able to fight them."

"But why does it have to be you?" She looked up at me quickly. "Don't fight any more, Matt. Stay on the Two Bar for a while. Don't come to town. I don't want you to meet Bodie Miller. You mustn't. You mustn't!"

Shrugging, I drew back a little. "Honey, there are some things a man must do, some things he has to do. If meeting Bodie Miller is one of them, I'll do it. Meeting a man who challenges you may seem very foolish to a woman's world, but a man cannot live only among women. He must live with men, and that means he must be judged by their standards, and, if I back down for Miller, then I'm through here."

"You can go away. You could go to California. You could go and straighten out some business for me there. Matt, you could. . . ."

"No. I'm staying here."

There were more words and hard words, but when I left her, I had not changed. Not that I underestimated Miller in any way. I had seen such men before. Billy the Kid had been like him. Bodie Miller was full of salt now. He was riding his luck with spurs. Remembering that sallow face with its hard, cruel eyes, I knew I could not live in the country around Hattan's Point without facing Miller.

Yet I saw nothing of Bodie Miller in Hattan's Point, and took the trail for the Two Bar, riding with caution. The chances were he was confident enough now to face me, especially after the smashing I'd taken. Moreover, the Slades were in the country and would be smarting over the beating I had given them.

The Two Bar looked better than anything I had seen in a long time. It was shadowed now with late evening, but the slow smoke lifted straight above the chimney, and I could see the horses in the corral. As I rode into the yard, a man materialized from the shadows. It was Jonathan Benaras, with his long rifle.

When I swung down from the saddle, he stared at my face, but said nothing. Knowing he would be curious, I explained simply. "Morgan Park and I had it out. It was quite a fight. He took a licking."

"If he looks worse'n you, he must be a sight."

"He does, believe me. Anybody been around?"

"Nary a soul. Jolly was down the wash this afternoon. Them cows are sure fattenin' up fast. You got you a mighty fine ranch here. Paw was over. He said, if you needed another hand, you could have Zeb for the askin'."

"Thanks. Your father's all man."

Jonathan nodded. "I reckon. We aim to be neighbors to folks who'll neighbor with us. We won't have no truck with them as walks it high an' mighty. Paw took to you right off. Said you come an faced him like a man an' laid your cards on the table."

Mulvaney grinned when I walked through the door, and then indicated the food on the table. "Set up. You're just in time."

It was good, sitting there in my own home, seeing the light reflecting from the dishes and feeling the warmth and pleasantness of it. But the girl I wanted to share these things with was not here to make it something more than just a house.

"You are silent tonight," Mulvaney said shrewdly. "Is it the girl, or is it the fight?"

I grinned and my face hurt with the grinning. "I was thinking of the girl, but not of Park."

"I was wondering about the fight," Mulvaney said. "I wish I'd been there to see it."

I told them about it, and, as I talked, I began to wonder what Park would do now, for he would not rest easy in jail, and there was no telling what trick Jake Booker might be up to. And what was it they wanted? Until I knew that, I knew nothing,

The place to look was where the Bar M and the Two Bar joined. And tomorrow I would do my looking, and would do it carefully.

On this ride Mulvaney joined me, and I welcomed the company as well as the Irishman's shrewd brain. We rode east, toward the vast wilderness that lay there, east toward the country where I had followed Morgan Park toward his rendezvous with Jack Slade. East, toward the maze of cañons, desert, and lonely lands beyond the river.

"See any tracks up that way before?" Mulvaney asked suddenly.

"Some," I admitted, "but I was following the fresh trail. We'll have a look around."

"Think it will be that silver you found out about in Booker's office?"

"Could be. We'll head for Dark Cañon Plateau and work north from there. I think that's the country."

"I'd feel better," Mulvaney admitted after a pause, "if we knew what had become of that Slade outfit. They'll be feelin' none too kindly after the whippin' you gave 'em."

I agreed. Studying the narrowing point, I knew we would soon strike a trail that led back to the northwest, a trail that would take us into the depths of Fable Cañon. Nearing that trail, I suddenly saw something that looked like a horse track. A bit later we found the trail of a single horse, freshly shod and heading northeast—a trail no more than a few hours old.

"Could be one o' the Slade outfit," Mulvaney speculated dubiously. "Park's in jail, an' nobody else would come over here."

We fell in behind, and I could see these tracks must have been made during the night. At one place a hoof had slipped and the earth had not yet dried out. Obviously, then, the horse had passed after the sun went down.

We rode with increasing care, and we were gaining. When the cañon branched, we found a water hole where the rider had filled his canteen and prepared a meal. "He's no woodsman, Mulvaney. Much of the wood he used was not good burning wood and some of it green. Also, his fire was in a place where the slightest breeze would swirl smoke in his face."

"He didn't unsaddle," Mulvaney said, "which means he was in a hurry."

This was not one of Slade's outlaws, for always on the dodge nobody knew better than they how to live in the wilds. Furthermore, they knew these cañons. This might be a stranger drifting into the country looking for a hide-out. But it was somewhere in this maze that we would find what it was that drew the interest of Morgan Park.

Scouting around, I suddenly looked up. "Mulvaney! He's whipped us! There's no trail out!"

"Sure 'n' he didn't take wings to get out of here," Mulvaney growled. "We've gone blind, that's what we've done."

Returning to the spring, we let the horses drink while I did some serious thinking. The rock walls offered no route of escape. The trail had been plain to this point, and then vanished. No tracks. He had watered his horse, prepared a meal—and afterward left no tracks. "It's uncanny," I said. "It looks like we've a ghost on our hands."

Mulvaney rubbed his grizzled jaw and chuckled. "Who would be better to cope with a ghost than a couple of Irishmen?"

"Make some coffee, you bog-trotter," I told him. "Maybe then we'll think better."

"It's a cinch he didn't fly," I said later, over coffee, "and not even a snake could get up these cliffs. So he rode in, and, if he left, he rode out."

"But he left no tracks, Matt. He could have brushed them out, but we saw no signs of brushing. Where does that leave us?"

"Maybe"—the idea came suddenly—"he tied something on his feet?"

"Let's look up the cañons. He'd be most careful right here, but if he is wearin' somethin' on his feet, the farther he goes, the more tired he'll be . . . or his horse will be."

"You take one cañon, and I'll take the other. We'll meet back here in an hour."

Walking, leading my buckskin, I scanned the ground. At no place was the sand hard-packed, and there were tracks of deer, lion, and an occasional bighorn. Then I found a place where wild horses had fed, and there something attracted me. Those horses had been frightened.

From quiet feeding they had taken off suddenly, and no bear or lion would frighten them so. They would leave, but not so swiftly. Only one thing could make mild horses fly so quickly—man.

The tracks were comparatively fresh, and instinct told me this was the right way. The wild horses had continued to run. Where their tracks covered the bottom of the cañon, and where the unknown rider must follow them, I should find a clue. And I did, almost at once.

Something foreign to the rock and manzanita caught my eye. Picking it free of a manzanita branch, I straightened up. It was sheep's wool.

Swearing softly, I swung into the saddle and turned back. The rider had brought sheepskins with him, tied some over his horse's hoofs and some over his own boots, and so left no defined tracks. Mulvaney was waiting for me. "Find anything?"

He listened with interest, and then nodded. "It was a good idea he had. Well, we'll get him now."

The trail led northeast and finally to a high, windswept plateau unbroken by anything but a few towering rocks or low-growing sagebrush. We sat our horses, squinting against the distance, looking over the plateau and then out over the vast maze of cañons, a red, corrugated distance of land almost untrod by men. "If he's out there," Mulvaney said, "we may never find him. You could lose an army in that."

"We'll find him. My hunch is that it won't be far." I nodded at the distance. "He had no pack horse, only a canteen to carry water, and, even if he's uncommonly shrewd, he's not experienced in the wilds."

Mulvaney had been studying the country. "I prospected through here, boy." He indicated a line of low hills to the east. "Those are the Sweet Alice Hills. There are ruins ahead of us, and away yonder is Beef Basin."

"We'll go slow. My guess is we're not far behind him."

As if in acknowledgement of my comment, a rifle shot rang out sharply in the clear air! We heard no bullet, but only the shot, and then another, closer, sharper!

"He's not shootin' at us," Mulvaney said, staring with shielded eyes. "Where is he?"

"Let's move!" I called. "I don't like this spot!"

Recklessly we plunged down the steep trail into the cañon. Down, down, down. Racing around elbow turns of the switchback trail, eager only to get off the skyline and into shelter. If the unknown rider had not fired at us, whom had he fired at? Who was the rider? Why was he shooting?

XI

Tired as my buckskin was, he seemed to grasp the need for getting under cover, and he rounded curves in that trail that made my hair stand on end. At the bottom we drew up in a thick cluster of trees and brush, listening. Even our horses felt the tension, for their ears were up, their eyes alert.

All was still. Some distance away a stone rattled. Sweat trickled behind my ear, and I smelled the hot aroma of dust and baked leaves. My palms grew sweaty and I dried them, but there was no sound. Careful to let my saddle creak as little as possible, I swung down, Winchester in hand. With a motion to wait, I moved away.

From the edge of the trees I could see no more than thirty yards in one direction, and no more than twenty in the other. Rock walls towered above and the cañon lay, hot and still, under the midday sun. From somewhere came the sound of trickling water, but there was no other sound or movement. My neck felt hot and sticky, my shirt clung to my shoulders. Shifting the rifle in my hands, I studied the rock walls with misgiving. Drying my hands on my jeans, I took a chance and moved out of my cover, moving to a narrow, six-inch band of shade against the far wall. Easing myself to the bend of the rock, I peered around.

Sixty yards away stood a saddled horse, head hanging. My eyes searched and saw nothing, and then, just visible beyond a white, water-worn boulder, I saw a boot and part of a leg. Cautiously I advanced, wary for any trick, ready to shoot instantly. There was no sound but an occasional chuckle of water over rocks. Then suddenly I could see the dead man.

His skull was bloody, and he had been shot over the eye with a rifle and at fairly close range. He had probably never known what hit him. There was vague familiarity to him and his skull bore a swelling. This had been one of Slade's men who I had slugged on the trail to Hattan's Point.

The bullet had struck over the eye and ranged downward, which meant he had been shot from ambush, from a hiding place high on the cañon wall. Lining up the position, I located a tuft of green that might be a ledge.

Mulvaney was approaching me. "He wasn't the man we followed," he advised. "This one was comin' from the other way."

"He's one of the Slade crowd. Dry-gulched."

"Whoever he is," Mulvaney assured me, "we can't take chances. The fellow who killed this man shot for keeps."

We started on, but no longer were the tracks disguised. The man we followed was going more slowly now. Suddenly I spotted a boot print. "Mulvaney," I whispered hoarsely. "That's the track of the man who killed Rud Maclaren."

"But Morgan Park is in the hoosegow," Mulvaney protested.

"Unless he's broken out. But I'd swear that was the track found near Maclaren's body. The one Canaval found."

My buckskin's head came up and his nostrils dilated. Grabbing his nose, I stifled the neigh, then stared up the cañon. Less than 100 yards away a dun horse was picketed near a patch of bunchgrass. Hiding our horses in a box cañon, we scaled the wall for a look around. From the top of the badly fractured mesa we could see all the surrounding country. Under the southern edge of the mesa was a cluster of ancient ruins, beyond them some deep cañons. With my glasses shielded from sun reflection by my hat, I watched a man emerge from a crack in the earth, carrying a heavy sack. Placing it on the ground, he removed his coat and with a pick and bar began working at a slab of rock.

"What's he doin'?" Mulvaney demanded, squinting his eyes.

"Pryin' a slab of rock," I told him, and, even as I spoke, the rock slid, rumbled with other débris, then settled in front of the crack. After a careful inspection the man concealed his tools, picked up his sack and rifle, and started back. Studying him, I could see he wore black jeans, very dusty now, and a small hat. His face was not visible. He bore no resemblance to anyone I had seen before.

He disappeared near the base of the mountain and for a long time we heard nothing.

"He's gone," I said.

"We'd best be mighty careful," Mulvaney warned uneasily. "That's no man to be foolin' with, I'm thinkin'."

A shot shattered the clear, white radiance of the afternoon. One shot, and then another.

We stared at each other, amazed and puzzled. There was no other sound, no further shots. Then uneasily we began our descent of the mesa, sitting ducks if he was waiting for us. To the south and west the land shimmered with heat, looking like a vast and unbelievable city, long fallen to ruin. We slid into the cañon where we'd left the horses, and then the shots were explained.

Both horses were on the ground, sprawled in pools of their own blood. Our canteens had been emptied and smashed with stones. We were thirty miles from the nearest ranch, and the way lay through some of the most rugged country on earth.

"There's water in the cañons," Mulvaney said at last, "but

no way to carry it. You think he knew who we were?"

"If he lives in this country, he knows that buckskin of mine," I said bitterly. "He was the best horse I ever owned."

To have hunted for us and found us, the unknown man would have had to take a chance on being killed himself, but by this means he left us small hope of getting out alive.

"We'll have a look where he worked," I said. "No use leaving without knowing about that."

It took us all of an hour to get there, and night was near before we had dug enough behind the slab of rock to get at the secret. Mulvaney cut into the bank with his pick. Ripping out a chunk and grabbing it, he thrust it under my eyes, his own glowing with enthusiasm. "Silver," he said hoarsely. "Look at it! If the vein is like that for any distance, this is the biggest strike I ever saw! Richer than Silver Reef!"

The ore glittered in his hand. There was what had killed Rud Maclaren and all the others. "It's rich," I said, "but I'd settle for the Two Bar."

Mulvaney agreed. "But still," he said, "the silver is a handsome sight."

"Pocket it, then," I said dryly, "for it's a long walk we have."

"But a walk we can do!" He grinned at me. "Shall we start now?"

"Tonight," I said, "when the walking will be cool."

We let the shadows grow long around us while we walked and watched the thick blackness choke the cañons and deepen in the shadows of trees. We walked on steadily, with little talk, up Ruin Cañon and over a saddle of the Sweet Alice Hills, and down to the spring on the far side of the hills.

There we rested, and we drank several times. From the stars I could see that it had taken us better than two hours of walking to make less than five miles. But now the trail would be easier along Dark Cañon Plateau—and then I remembered Slade's camp. What if they were back there again? Holed up in the same place?

It was a thought, and to go down the cañon toward them was actually none out of the way. Although the walking might be rougher at times, we would have the stream beside us, a thing to be considered. Mulvaney agreed and we descended into the cañon.

Dark it was there, and quiet except for the rustle of water over stones, and there was a cool dampness that was good to our throats and skins after the heat. We walked on, taking our time, for we'd no records to break. And then we heard singing before we saw the reflection of the fire.

We walked on, moving more carefully, for the cañon walls caught and magnified every sound.

Three men were about the fire and one of them was Jack Slade. Two were talking while one man sang as he cleaned his rifle. We reached the edge of the firelight before they saw us, and I had my Winchester on them, and Mulvaney that cannon-like four-shot pistol of his. "Grab the sky, Slade!" I barked the order at him, and his hand dropped, then froze.

"Who is it?" he demanded hoarsely, straining his eyes at us. Our faces being shielded by the brims of our hats, he could not see enough of them. I stepped nearer so the firelight reached under my hat brim.

"It's Matt Sabre," I said, "and I'm not wanting to kill you or anybody. We want two horses. You can lend them to us, or we'll take them. Our horses were shot by the same man that killed your partner."

Slade jerked, his eyes showing incredulity. "Killed? Lott killed?"

"That's right. Intentionally or otherwise he met up with the *hombre* we were following. He drilled your man right over

250

the eyes. We followed on, and he found where we left our horses and shot them both to leave us afoot."

"Damn a man that'll kill a horse," Slade said. "Who was he?"

"Don't know," I admitted. "Only he leaves a track like Morgan Park. At least, he's got a small foot."

"But Park's in jail," Mulvaney added.

"Not now he isn't," Slade said. "Morgan Park broke jail within an hour after darkness last night. He pulled one of those iron bars right out of that old wall, stole a horse, and got away. He's on the loose and after somebody's scalp."

Park free! But the man we had followed had not been as big as Park was. I did not tell them that. "How about the horses?" I asked.

"You can have them, Sabre," Slade said grudgingly. "I'm clearing out. I've no stomach for this sort of thing."

"Are they spares?"

Slade nodded. "We've a half dozen extras. In our business it pays to keep fresh horses." He grinned. "No hard feelin's, Sabre?"

"Not me," I said. "Only don't you boys get any wild ideas about jumpin' me. My trigger finger is right jittery."

Slade shrugged wryly. "With two guns on us? Not likely. I don't know whether your partner can shoot or not but with a cannon that big he doesn't need to. What kind of a gun is that, anyway?"

"She's my own make," Mulvaney said cheerfully, "but the slug kills just as dead."

"Give this *hombre* an old stove pipe and he'd make a cannon," I told them. "He's a genius with tools."

While Mulvaney got the horses, I stood over the camp. "Any other news in town?" I asked Slade.

"Plenty," he admitted. "Some Army officer came into

town claimin' Park killed his brother. Seems a right salty gent. And"—his eyes flickered to mine—"Bodie Miller is talkin' it big around town. He says you're his meat."

"He's a heavy eater, that boy," I said carelessly. "He may tackle something one of these days that will give him indigestion."

Jack Slade shrugged and watched Mulvaney lead up the horses. As we mounted, I glanced back at him. "We'll leave these horses at the corral of the livery stable in town, if you like."

Slade's eyes twinkled a little. "Better not. First time you get a chance take 'em to a corral you'll find in the woods back of Armstrong's. Towns don't set well with me, nor me with them."

The horses were fresh and ready to go, and we let them run. Daylight found us riding up the street of Hattan's Point, a town that was silent and waiting. The loft was full of hay and both of us headed for it. Two hours later I was wide awake. Splashing water on my face, I headed for O'Hara's. The first person I saw as we came through the door was Key Chapin. Olga Maclaren was with him.

Chapin looked up as we entered. "Sorry, Sabre," he said. "I've just heard."

"Heard what?" I was puzzled.

"That you're losing the Two Bar."

"Are you crazy? What are you talking about?"

"You mean you haven't heard? Jake Booker showed up the other day and filed a deed to the Two Bar. He purchased the rights to it from Ball's nephew, the legitimate heir. He also has laid claim to the Bar M, maintaining that it was never actually owned by Rud Maclaren, but belonged to his brother-in-law, now dead. Booker has found some relative of the brother-in-law's and bought his right to the property."

"Well of all the . . . that's too flimsy, Chapin. He can't hope to get away with that! What's on his mind?"

Chapin shrugged. "If he goes to court, he can make it tough. You have witnesses to the fact that Ball gave you the ranch, but whether that will stand in court, I don't know. Especially with a shrewd operator like Booker fighting it. As to Maclaren, it turns out he did leave the ranch to his brother-in-law during a time some years ago when he was suffering from a gunshot wound, and apparently never made another will. What's important right now is that Jake is going to court to get both you and Olga off the ranches and he plans to freeze all sales, bank accounts, and other money or stock until the case is settled."

"In other words, he doesn't want us to have the money to fight him."

Chapin shrugged. "I don't know what his idea is, but I'll tell you one thing. He stands in well with the judge, who is just about as crooked as he is, and they'll use your reputation against you. Don't think Booker hasn't considered all the angles, and don't think he doesn't know how flimsy his case may be. He'll bolster it every way possible, and he knows every trick in the book."

I sat down. This had come so suddenly that it took the wind out of my sails. "Has this news gone to the Bar M yet? Has it got out to Canaval?"

Chapin shrugged. "Why should it? He was only the foreman. Olga has been told and you can imagine how she feels."

My eyes went to hers, and she looked away. Katie O'Hara came in, and I gave her my order for breakfast and tried the coffee she had brought with her. It tasted good.

Sitting there, my mind began to work swiftly. There was still a chance, if I figured things right. Jake Booker was no fool. He had not paid out money for those claims unless he believed he could make them stand in court. He knew about how much money I had, and knew that Olga Maclaren, with the ranch bank accounts frozen, would be broke. Neither of us could afford to hire an attorney, and so far as that went there was no attorney within miles able to cope with Booker. What had started as a range war had degenerated into a range steal by a shyster lawyer, and he had arguments that could not be answered with a gun.

"How was Canaval when you left?"

"Better," Olga said, still refusing to meet my eyes.

"What about Morgan Park? I heard he escaped."

"Tharp's out after him now. That Colonel D'Arcy went with him and the posse. There had been a horse left for Park. Who was responsible for that, we don't know, but it may have been one of his own men."

"Where did Tharp go?"

"Toward the ranch, I think. There was no trail they could find."

"They should have gone east, toward Dark Cañon. That's where he'll be."

Chapin looked at me curiously, intently. "Why there?"

"That's where he'll go," I replied definitely. "Take my word for it."

They talked a little between them, but I ate in silence, always conscious of the girl across the table, aware of her every move.

Finishing my meal, I got up and reached for my hat. Olga looked up quickly. "Don't go out there. Bodie Miller is in town."

"Thanks." Our eyes met and held. Were they saying something to me? Or was I reading into their depths the meaning I wanted them to hold? "Thanks," I repeated. "I'd prefer not to meet him now. This is no time for personal grudges."

It was a horse I wanted, a better horse than the one borrowed from Slade, and which might have been stolen. This, I reflected dryly, would be a poor time to be hung as a horse thief. There was no gate at the corral on this side, so I climbed over, crossing the corral. At the corner I stopped in my tracks. A horse was tied to the corral, a horse stripped but recently of a saddle, a dun horse that showed evidence of hard riding. And in the damp earth near the trough was a boot print. Kneeling, I examined the hocks of the tied horse. From one of them I picked a shred of wool, then another. Spinning around, I raced for the restaurant. "Katie!" I demanded. "Who owns that horse? Did you see the rider?"

"If you're thinkin' o' Park, that horse couldn't carry him far. An' he would not stay in the town. Not him."

"Did you see anyone else?"

"Nobody . . . wait a minute! I did so. 'Twas Jake Booker. Not that I saw him with the horse, but a bit before daylight he came around the corner from that way and asked if I'd coffee ready."

Booker! He had small feet. He was in with Park. He wanted Maclaren dead. He had killed Slade's man and shot our horses. Booker had some explaining to do.

Mulvaney was crawling from the loft where I'd slept but was all attention at once. He listened, then ran to the stable office. Waiting only until he was on a horse and racing from town, I started back to O'Hara's. My mind was made up.

The time had come for a showdown, and this time we would all be in it, and Jake Booker would not be forgotten.

Key Chapin looked up when I came up. "Key," I said quickly, "this is the pay-off. Find out for me where Booker is. Get somebody to keep an eye on him. He's not to leave town if he tries. Keep him under observation all the time until

Mulvaney gets back from the ranch." Turning to Olga, I asked her: "How about Canaval? Can he ride yet? Could he stand a buckboard trip?"

She hesitated. "He couldn't ride, but he might stand it in the buckboard."

"Then get him into town, and have the boys come with him. Fox especially. I like that man Fox, and Canaval may need protection. Bring him in, and bring him here."

"What is it? What have you learned?" Chapin demanded.

"About everything I need to know," I replied. "We're going to save the Bar M for Olga, and perhaps we'll save my ranch, too. In any event, we'll have the man who killed Rud Maclaren!"

"What?" Olga's face was pale. "Matt, do you mean that?"

"I do. I only hope that Tharp gets back with Morgan Park, but I doubt if we'll see him again." Turning to Key, who was at the door. "Another thing. We might as well settle it all. Send a rider to the CP and have Jim Pinder in here. Get him here fast. We'll have our showdown the first thing in the morning."

Twice I walked up the street and back. Nowhere was there any sign of Bodie Miller, or of Red, his riding partner. The town still had that sense of expectancy that I had noticed upon coming into town. And they were right—for a lot of things were going to happen and happen fast.

Key met me in the saloon. He walked toward me quickly, his face alive with interest. "What have you got in mind, Matt? What are you planning?"

"Several things. In the first place, there has been enough fighting and trouble. We're going to end it right here. We're going to close up this whole range fight. There aren't going to be any halfway measures. How well do you know Tharp?"

"Very well, why?"

"Will he throw his weight with us? It would mean a lot if he would."

"You can bank on him. He's a solid man, Matt. Very solid."

"All right, in the morning then. In the morning we'll settle everything."

There was a slight movement at the door and I looked up. My pulse almost stopped with the shock of it.

Bodie Miller stood there, his hands on his hips, his lips smiling. "Why, sure!" he said. "If that's what you want. The morning is as good a time as any."

XII

The sun came up, clear and hot. Already at daybreak the sky was without a cloud, and the distant mountains seemed to shimmer in a haze of their own making. The desert lost itself in heat waves before the day had scarce begun, and there was a stillness lying upon both desert and town, a sort of poised awareness without sound.

When I emerged upon the street, I was alone. Like a town of ghosts, the street was empty, silent except for the echo of my steps on the boardwalk. Then, as if their sound had broken the spell, the saloon door opened and the bartender emerged and began to sweep off the walk. He glanced quickly around at me, bobbed his head, and then with an uneasy look around finished his sweeping hurriedly and ducked back inside. A man carrying two wooden buckets emerged from an alley and looked cautiously about. Assured there was no one in sight, he started across the street, glancing apprehensively first in one direction, then the other.

Sitting down in one of the polished chairs before the saloon, I tipped back my hat and stared at the mountains. In a few minutes or a few hours, I might be dead.

It was not a good morning on which to die—but what morning is? Yet in a few minutes or hours another man and myself would probably meet out there in that street, and we would exchange shots, and one or both of us would die.

A rider came into the street. Mulvaney. He left his horse at the stable and clumped over to me. He was carrying enough guns to fight a war.

"Comin'," Mulvaney said, "the whole kit an' kaboodle of 'em. Be here within the hour. Jolly's already in town. Jonathan went after the others."

Nodding, I watched a woman looking down the street from the second floor. Suddenly she turned and left the window as if she had seen something or been called.

"Eat yet?"

"Not yet."

"Seen Olga? Or Chapin?"

"No."

"If Red cuts into this scrap," Mulvaney said, "he's mine."

"You can have him."

A door slammed somewhere, and then the man with the two wooden buckets hurried fearfully across the street, slopping water at every step. "All right," I said, "we'll go eat."

There was no sign of Bodie Miller, or of Jim Pinder. Sheriff Tharp was still out hunting Morgan Park. Unless he got back soon, I'd have to run my show alone.

Mother O'Hara had a white tablecloth over the oilcloth, and her best dishes were out. She brought me coffee and said severely: "You should be ashamed. That girl laid awake half the night, thinkin' of nothin' but you!"

"About me?" I was incredulous.

"Yes, about you! Worried fair sick, she is! About you an' that Bodie Miller!"

The door opened and Olga walked in. Her eyes were very green today, and her hair drawn back to a loose knot at the back of her neck, but curled slightly into two waves on her forehead. She avoided my glance, and it was well she did, or I'd have come right out of my chair.

Then men entered the restaurant—Chapin, looking unusually severe, Colonel D'Arcy, and last of all, Jake Booker.

259

D'Arcy caught my eye and a slow smile started on his lips. "Sabre! Well, I'm damned! The last time I saw Sabre he was in China!"

He took my hand and we grinned at each other. He was much older than I, but we talked the same language. His hair was gray at the temples. "They say you've had trouble with Cantwell."

"And more to come if the sheriff doesn't get him. Park is mixed up in a shady deal with Jake Booker, the man across the table from me."

"I?" Booker smiled but his eyes were deadly. "You're mistaken, Mister Sabre. It is true that Mister Park asked me to represent him in some trouble he was having, but we've no other connection. None at all."

Jim Pinder stalked in at that moment, but, knowing that Mulvaney and Jolly were watching, I ignored him.

"From the conversation I overheard in Silver Reef," I said to Booker, "I gathered you had obtained a buyer for some mining property he expected to have."

Fury flickered across his face. He had no idea how much I knew.

"It might interest you to know, Booker, that the fighting in this area is over. Pinder is here and we're having a peace meeting. Pinder is making a deal with us and with the Bar M. The fun's over."

"I ain't said nothin' about no deal," Pinder declared harshly. "I come in because I figured you was ready to sell."

"I might buy, Pinder, but I wouldn't sell. Furthermore, I'm with Chapin and Tharp in organizing this peace move. You can join or stay out, but if you don't join, you'll have to haul supplies from Silver Reef. This town will be closed to you. Each of us who has been in this fight is to put up a bond to keep the peace, effective at daybreak tomorrow.

260

You can join or leave the country."

"After you killed my brother?" Pinder demanded. "You ask for peace?"

"You started the trouble in the livery stable, figuring you were tough enough to hire me or run me out of the country. You weren't big enough or fast enough then, and you aren't now. Nobody doubts your nerve. You've too much for your own good, and so have the lot of us, but it gets us nothing but killing and more killing. You can make money on the CP, or you can try to buck the country. As for Rollie, he laid for me and he got what he asked for. You're a hard man, Pinder, but you're no fool, and I've an idea you're square. Isn't it true Rollie started out to get me?"

Pinder hesitated, rubbing his angular jaw. "It is," he said finally, "but that don't make no. . . ."

"It makes a lot of difference," I replied shortly. "Now look, Pinder. You've lost more than you've cost us. You need money. You can't ship cattle. You sign up or you'll never ship any. Everybody here knows you've nerve enough to face me, but everybody knows you'd die. All you'd prove would be that you're crazy. You know I'm the faster man."

He stared stubbornly at the table. Finally he said: "I'll think it over. It'll take some time."

"It'll take you just two minutes," I said, laying it on the line.

He stared hard at me, his knuckles whitening on the arms of the chair. Suddenly, reluctantly he grinned. Sinking back into his chair, he shrugged. "You ride a man hard, Sabre. All right, peace it is."

"Thanks, Pinder." I thrust out my hand. He hesitated, then took it.

Katie O'Hara filled his cup.

"Look," he said, "I've got to make a drive. The only way

there's water is across your place."

"What's wrong with that? Drive 'em across, and whatever water your herd needs is yours. Just so it doesn't take you more than a week to get 'em across."

Pinder smiled bleakly, but with humor. "Aw, you know it won't take more'n a day." He subsided into his chair and started on the coffee.

Jake Booker had been taking it all in, looking from one to the other of us with his sharp little eyes.

Canaval opened the door and stepped in, looking pale and drawn, followed by Tom Fox. "Miss Olga could have signed for me," he said. "She's the owner."

"You sign, too," I insisted. "We want to cover every eventuality."

Booker was smiling. He rubbed his lips with his thin, dry fingers. "All nonsense," he said briskly. "Both the Bar M and the Two Bar belong to me. I've filed the papers. You've twenty-four hours to get off and stay off."

"Booker," I said, "has assumed we are fools. He believed, if he could get a flimsy claim, he could get us into court and beat us. Well, this case will never go to court."

Booker's eyes were beady. "Are you threatening me?"

Sheriff Will Tharp came into the room. His eyes rested on Jake but he said nothing.

"We aren't threatening," I said. "On what does your claim to the Bar M stand?"

"Bill of sale," he replied promptly. "The ranch was actually left to Jay Collins, the gunfighter. He was Maclaren's brother-in-law. His will left all his property to a nephew, and I bought it, including the Bar M and all appurtenances thereto."

Canaval gave me a brief nod. "Sorry, Jake. You've lost your money. Jay Collins is not dead."

The lawyer jumped as if slapped. "Not dead? I saw his grave!"

"Booker"—I smiled—"look down the table at Jay Collins." I pointed to Canaval.

Booker broke into a fever of protest, but I was looking at Olga Maclaren. She was staring at Canaval and he was smiling.

"Sure, honey," he said. "That's why I knew so much about your mother. She was the only person in the world I ever really loved . . . until I knew my niece."

Booker was worried now, really worried. In a matter of minutes half his plan had come to nothing. He was shrewd enough to know we would not bluff, and that we had proof of what we said.

"As for the Two Bar," I added, "don't worry about it. I've my witnesses that the estate was given me. Not that it will matter to you."

"What's that? What'd you mean?" Booker stared at me.

"Because you were too greedy. You'll never rob another man, Booker. For murder, you'll hang."

He protested, but now he was cornered and frightened.

"You killed Rud Maclaren," I told him, "and, if that's not enough, you killed one of Slade's men from ambush. We can trail your horse to the scene of the crime, and, if you think a Western jury won't take the word of an Indian tracker, you're wrong."

"He killed Maclaren?" Canaval asked incredulously.

"He got him out of the house on some trumped up excuse. To show him the silver, or to show him something I was planning . . . it doesn't matter what excuse was used. He shot him, then loaded him on a horse and brought him to my place. He shot him again, hoping to draw me to the vicinity as he wanted my tracks around the body."

"Lies!" Booker was recovering his assurance. "Sabre had trouble with Maclaren, not I. We knew each other only by sight. The idea that I killed him is preposterous." He got to his feet. "In any event, what have the ranches to do with the silver claim of which you speak?"

"Morgan Park found the claim while trailing a man he meant to murder, Arnold D'Arcy who knew him as Cantwell. Arnold had stumbled upon the old mine. Park murdered him only to find there was a catch in the deal. D'Arcy had already filed on the claim and had done assessment work on it. Legally there was no way Park could gain possession, and no one legally could work the mine until D'Arcy's claim lapsed. Above all, Park wanted to avoid any public connection with the name of D'Arcy. He couldn't sell the claim, because it wasn't his, but if he could get control of the Bar M and the Two Bar, across which anyone working the claim must go, he could sell them at a fabulous price to an unscrupulous buyer. The new owner of the ranches could work the claim quietly, and by owning the ranches he could deny access to the vicinity so it would never be discovered what claims were being worked. When D'Arcy's assessment work lapsed, the claims could be filed upon by the new owners."

"Booker was to find a buyer?" asked Tharp.

"Yes. Park wanted money, not a mine or a ranch. Booker, I believe, planned to be that buyer himself. He wanted possession of the Bar M, so he decided to murder Rud Maclaren."

"You've no case against me that would stand in court!" Booker sneered. "You can prove nothing! What witnesses do you have?"

We had none, of course. Our evidence was a footprint. All the rest of what I'd said was guesswork. Tharp couldn't arrest the man on such slim grounds. We needed a confession.

Tom Fox leaned over the table, his eyes cold. "Some of us are satisfied. We don't need witnesses an' we don't need to hear no more. Some of us are almighty sure you killed Rud Maclaren. Got any arguments that will answer a six-gun? Or a rope?"

Booker's face thinned down and he crouched back against his chair. "You can't do that! The law! Tharp will protect me!"

Sighting a way clear, I smiled. "That might be, Booker. Confess and Tharp will protect you. He'll save you for the law to handle. But if you leave here a free man, you'll be on your own."

"An' I'll come after you," Fox said.

"Confess, Booker." I suggested, "and you'll be safe."

"Aw! Turn him loose!" Fox protested angrily. "No need to have trouble, a trial an' all. Turn him loose! We all know he's a crook an' we all know he killed Rud Maclaren! Turn him loose!"

Booker's eyes were haunted with fear. There was no acting in Tom Fox and he knew it. The rest of us might bluff, but not Fox. The Bar M hand wanted to kill him, and, given an opportunity, he would.

Right then I knew we were going to win. Jake Booker was a plotter and a conniver, not a courageous man. His mean little eyes darted from Fox to the sheriff. His mouth twitched and his face was wet with sweat. Tom Fox, his hand on his gun, moved relentlessly closer to Booker.

"All right, then!" he screamed. "I did it! I killed Maclaren. Now, Sheriff, save me from this man!"

I relaxed at last, as Tharp put the handcuffs on Booker. As they were leaving, I said: "What about Park? What happened to him?"

Tharp cleared his throat. "Morgan Park is dead. He was

killed last night on the Woodenshoe."

We all looked at him, waiting. "That Apache of Pinder's killed him," Tharp explained. "Park ran for it after he busted out of jail. He killed his horse crossin' the flats an' he run into the Injun with a fresh horse. He wanted to swap, the 'Pache wouldn't go for the deal, so Park tried to dry-gulch him. He should have knowed better. The Injun killed him an' lit out."

"You're positive?" D'Arcy demanded.

Tharp nodded. "Yeah, he died hard, Park did."

The door opened and Jonathan Benaras was standing there. "Been scoutin' around," he said. "Bodie Miller's done took out. He hit the saddle about a half hour back an' headed north out of town."

Bodie Miller gone! It was impossible. Yet, he had done it. Miller was gone! I got to my feet. "Good," I said quietly, "I was afraid there would be trouble."

Pinder got to his feet. "Don't you trust that Miller," he said grudgingly. "He's a snake in the grass. You watch out."

So there it was. Pinder was no longer an enemy. The fight had been ended and I could go back to the Two Bar. I should feel relieved, and yet I did not. Probably it was because I had built myself up for Bodie Miller and nothing had come of it. I was so ready, and then it all petered out to nothing at all.

Olga had the Bar M, and her uncle to run it for her, and nobody would be making any trouble for Canaval. There was nothing for me to do but to go back home.

My horse was standing at the rail and I walked out to him and lifted the stirrup leather to tighten the cinch. But I did not hurry. Olga was standing there in front of the restaurant, and the one thing I wanted most was to talk to her. When I looked up, she was standing there alone.

"You're going back to the Two Bar?" Her voice was hesitant.

"Where else? After all, it's my home now."

"Have . . . have you done much to the house yet?"

"Some." I tightened the cinch, then unfastened the bridle reins. "Even a killer has to have a home." It was rough, and I meant it that way.

She flushed. "You're not holding that against me?"

"What else can I do? You said what you thought, didn't you?"

She stood there, looking at me, uncertain of what to say, and I let her stand there.

She watched me put my foot in the stirrup and swing into the saddle. She looked as if she wanted to say something, but she did not. Yet, when I looked down at her, she was more like a little girl who had been spanked than anything else I could think of.

Suddenly I was doing the talking. "Ever start that trousseau I mentioned?"

She looked up quickly. "Yes," she admitted, "but . . . but I'm afraid I didn't get very far with it. You see, there was. . . ."

"Forget it." I was brusque. "We'll do without it. I was going to ride out of here and let you stay, but I'll be double damned if I will. I told you I was going to marry you, and I am. Now, listen, trousseau or not, you be ready by tomorrow noon, understand?"

"Yes. All right. I mean . . . I will."

Suddenly we were both laughing like fools and I was off that horse and kissing her, and all the town of Hattan's Point could see us. It was right there in front of the café, and I could see people coming from the saloons and standing along the boardwalks, all grinning.

Then I let go of her and stepped back, and said: "Tomorrow noon. I'll meet you here." And with that I wheeled my horse and lit out for the ranch.

Ever feel so good it looks as if the whole world is your big apple? That was the way I felt. I had all I ever wanted. Grass, water, cattle, and with a home and wife of my own. The trail back to the Two Bar swung around a huge mesa and opened out on a wide desert flat, and far beyond it I could see the suggestion of the stones and pinnacles of badlands beyond Dry Mesa. A rabbit burst from the brush and sprinted off across the sage, and then the road dipped down into a hollow. There, in the middle of the road, was Bodie Miller.

He was standing with his hands on his hips laughing and there was a devil in his eyes. Off to one side of the road was Red, holding their horses and grinning, too.

"Too bad!" Bodie said. "Too bad to cut down the big man just when he's ridin' highest, but I'll enjoy it."

This horse I rode was skittish and unacquainted with me. I'd no idea how he'd stand for shooting, and I wanted on the ground. Suddenly I slapped spurs to that gelding, and, when the startled animal lunged toward the gunman, I went off the other side. Hitting the ground running, I spun on one heel and saw Bodie's hands blur as they dove for their guns, and then I felt my own gun buck in my hand. Our bullets crossed each other, but mine was a fraction the fastest despite that instant of hesitation when I made sure it would count.

His slug ripped a furrow across my shoulder that stung like a thousand needles, but my own bullet caught him in the chest and he staggered back, his eyes wide and agonized. Then I started forward and suddenly the devil was up in me. I was mad, mad as I had never been before. I opened up with both guns. "What's the matter?" I was yelling. "Don't you like it, gun slick? You asked for it, now come and get it! Fast, are you? Why you cheap, two-bit gunman, I'll . . . !"

But he was finished. He stood there, a slighter man than I was, with blood turning his shirt front crimson, and with his

268

mouth ripped by another bullet. He was white as death, even his lips were gray, and against that whiteness was the splash of blood. In his eyes now there was another look. The killing lust was gone, and in its place was an awful terror, for Bodie Miller had killed, and enjoyed it with a kind of sadistic bitterness that was in him—but now he knew he was being killed and the horror of death was surging through him.

"Now you know how they felt, Bodie," I said bitterly. "It's an ugly thing to die with a slug in you because some punk wants to prove he's tough. And you aren't tough, Bodie, just mean."

He stared at me, but he didn't say anything. He was gone, and I could see it. Something kept him upright, standing in that white hot sun, staring at me, the last face he would ever look upon.

"You asked for it, Bodie, but I'm sorry for it. Why didn't you stay to punching cows?"

Bodie backed up another step, and his gun slid from his fingers. He tried to speak, and then his knees buckled, and he went down. Standing over him, I looked at Red.

"I'm ridin'," Red said huskily. "Just give me a chance." He swung into the saddle, then looked down at Bodie. "He wasn't so tough, was he?"

"Nobody is," I told him. "Nobody's tough with a slug in his belly."

He rode off, and I stood there in the trail with Bodie dead at my feet. Slowly I holstered my guns, then led my horse off the trail to the shade where Bodie's horse still stood.

Lying there in the dusty trail, Bodie Miller no longer looked mean or even tough, he looked like a kid that had tackled a job that was too big for him.

There was a small gully off the trail. It looked like a grave, and I used it that way. Rolling him into it, I shoved the banks

269

in on top of him, and then piled on some stones. Then I made a cross for him and wrote his name on it, and the words: **HE PLAYED OUT HIS HAND**. Then I hung his guns on the cross and his hat.

It was not much of an end for a man, not any way you looked at it, but I wanted no more reputation as a killer—mine had already grown too big.

Maybe Red would tell the story, and maybe in time somebody would see the grave, but if Red's story was told, it would be somewhere far away and long after, and that suited me.

A stinging in my own shoulder reminded me of my own wound, but when I opened my shirt and checked my shoulder, I found it a mere scratch.

Ahead of me the serrated ridges of the wild lands were stark and lonely along the sky, and the sun behind me was picking out the very tips of the peaks to touch them with gold. Somehow the afternoon was gone, and now I was riding home to my own ranch, and tomorrow was my wedding day.

About the Editor

Jon Tuska is the editor of several anthologies of Western stories, including *The Western Story: A Chronological Treasury* (University of Nebraska Press, 1995), and with Vicki Piekarski *The Morrow Anthology of Great Western Short Stories* (Morrow, 1997) and *The First Five Star Western Corral* (Five Star Westerns, 2000). He has been editing a series of short novel collections, *Stories of the Golden West*, of which this is the seventh volume.